HELL
HOUSE

T0021800

BY RICHARD MATHESON

The Beardless Warriors
Bid Time Return
Earthbound
Fury on Sunday
Hell House
I Am Legend
Journal of the Gun Years
Now You See It . . .
The Path
Ride the Nightmare
7 Steps to Midnight
The Shrinking Man
Someone Is Bleeding
Somewhere in Time
A Stir of Echoes
What Dreams May Come
Other Kingdoms
By the Gun
Shadow on the Sun
Abu and the 7 Marvels
Offbeat: Uncollected Stories
The Best of Richard Matheson

RICHARD MATHESON

NIGHTFIRE
TOR PUBLISHING GROUP
NEW YORK

This is a work of fiction. All of the characters, organizations, and events portrayed in this novel are either products of the author's imagination or are used fictitiously.

HELL HOUSE

A Nightfire Book
Published by Tom Doherty Associates / Tor Publishing Group
120 Broadway
New York, NY 10271

www.tornightfire.com

The Library of Congress has cataloged the Viking Press edition as follows:

Names: Matheson, Richard, 1926–2013, author.
Title: Hell House / Richard Matheson.
Description: New York, Viking Press [1971]
Identifiers: LCCN 77149273 (print) | ISBN 9780670365852 (hardcover)
Subjects: LCSH: Haunted houses—Fiction. | LCGFT: Ghost stories. |
Horror tales.
Classification: LCC PZ4.M429 He PS3563.A8355 (print) |
DDC 813/.5/4
LC record available at https://lccn.loc.gov/77149273

ISBN 978-1-250-88352-0 (second trade paperback)
ISBN 978-1-4299-1364-5 (ebook)

Our books may be purchased in bulk for promotional, educational, or business use. Please contact your local bookseller or the Macmillan Corporate and Premium Sales Department at 1-800-221-7945, extension 5442, or by email at MacmillanSpecialMarkets@macmillan.com.

First published in the United States by The Viking Press, Inc.

First Nightfire Edition: 2023

Printed in the United States of America

0 9 8 7 6 5 4 3

With love, for my daughters
Bettina and Alison,
who have haunted my life so sweetly

HELL
HOUSE

DECEMBER 18, 1970

3:17 P.M.

It had been raining hard since five o'clock that morning. Brontean weather, Dr. Barrett thought. He repressed a smile. He felt rather like a character in some latter-day Gothic romance. The driving rain, the cold, the two-hour ride from Manhattan in one of Deutsch's long black leather-upholstered limousines. The interminable wait in this corridor while disconcerted-looking men and women hurried in and out of Deutsch's bedroom, glancing at him occasionally.

He drew his watch from its vest pocket and raised the lid. He'd been here more than an hour now. What did Deutsch want of him? Something to do with parapsychology, most likely. The old man's chain of newspapers and magazines were forever printing articles on the subject. "Return from the Grave"; "The Girl Who Wouldn't Die"—always sensational, rarely factual.

Wincing at the effort, Dr. Barrett lifted his right leg over his left. He was a tall, slightly overweight man in his middle fifties, his thinning blond hair unchanged in color, though his trimmed beard showed traces of white. He sat erect on the straight-back chair, staring at the door to Deutsch's bedroom.

Edith must be getting restless downstairs. He was sorry she'd come. Still, he'd had no way of knowing it would take this long.

The door to Deutsch's bedroom opened, and his male secretary, Hanley, came out. "Doctor," he said.

Barrett reached for his cane and, standing, limped across the hallway, stopping in front of the shorter man. He waited while the secretary leaned in through the doorway and announced, "Doctor Barrett, sir." Then he stepped past Hanley, entering the room. The secretary closed the door behind him.

The darkly paneled bedroom was immense. Sanctum of the monarch, Barrett thought as he moved across the rug. Stopping by the massive bed, he looked at the old man sitting in it. Rolf Rudolph Deutsch was eighty-seven, bald, and skeletal, his dark eyes peering out from bony cavities. Barrett smiled. "Good afternoon." Intriguing that this wasted creature ruled an empire, he was thinking.

"You're crippled." Deutsch's voice was rasping. "No one told me that."

"I beg your pardon?" Barrett had stiffened.

"Never mind." Deutsch cut him off. "It's not that vital, I suppose. My people have recommended you. They say you're one of the five best in your field." He drew in laboring breath. "Your fee will be one hundred thousand dollars."

Barrett started.

"Your assignment is to establish the facts."

"Regarding what?" asked Barrett.

Deutsch seemed hesitant about replying, as though he felt it was beneath him. Finally he said, "Survival."

"You want me—?"

"—to tell me if it's factual or not."

Barrett's heart sank. That amount of money would make

all the difference in the world to him. Still, how could he in conscience accept it on such grounds?

"It isn't lies I want," Deutsch told him. "I'll buy the answer, either way. So long as it's definitive."

Barrett felt a roil of despair. "How can I convince you, either way?" He was compelled to say it.

"By giving me *facts*," Deutsch answered irritably.

"Where am I to find them? I'm a physicist. In the twenty years I've studied parapsychology, I've yet to—"

"If they exist," Deutsch interrupted, "you'll find them in the only place on earth I know of where survival has yet to be refuted. The Belasco house in Maine."

"Hell House?"

Something glittered in the old man's eyes.

"Hell House," he said.

Barrett felt a tingling of excitement. "I thought Belasco's heirs had it sealed off after what happened—"

"That was thirty years ago." Deutsch cut him off again. "They need the money now; I've bought the place. Can you be there by Monday?"

Barrett hesitated, then, seeing Deutsch begin to frown, nodded once. "Yes." He couldn't let this chance go by.

"There'll be two others with you," Deutsch said.

"May I ask who—?"

"Florence Tanner and Benjamin Franklin Fischer."

Barrett tried not to show the disappointment he felt. An over-emotive Spiritualist medium, and the lone survivor of the 1940 debacle? He wondered if he dared object. He had his own group of sensitives and didn't see how Florence Tanner or Fischer could be of any help to him. Fischer had shown incredible abilities as a boy, but after his breakdown had obviously lost his gift, been caught in fraud a number of times, finally disappearing from the field entirely. He listened, half-attentive, as Deutsch told him that Florence Tanner would fly north with him, while Fischer would meet them in Maine.

The old man noted his expression. "Don't worry, you'll be in charge," he said; "Tanner's only going because my people tell me she's a first-class medium—"

"But a mental medium," said Barrett.

"—and I want that line of approach employed, as well as yours," Deutsch went on, as though Barrett hadn't spoken. "Fischer's presence is obvious."

Barrett nodded. There was no way out of it, he saw. He'd have to bring up one of his own people after the project was under way. "As to costs—" he started.

The old man waved him off. "Take that up with Hanley. You have unlimited funds."

"And time?"

"That you don't have," Deutsch replied. "I want the answer in a week."

Barrett looked appalled.

"Take it or leave it!" the old man snapped, sudden, naked rage in his expression. Barrett knew he had to accede or lose the opportunity—and there *was* a chance if he could get his machine constructed in time.

He nodded once. "A week," he said.

3:50 P.M.

Anything else?" asked Hanley.

Barrett reviewed the items in his mind again. A list of all phenomena observed in the Belasco house. Restoration of its electrical system. Installation of telephone service. The swimming pool and steam room made available to him. Barrett had ignored the small man's frown at the fourth item. A daily swim and steam bath were mandatory for him.

"One more item," he said. He tried to sound casual but felt that his excitement showed. "I need a machine. I have the blueprints for it at my apartment."

"How soon will you need it?" Hanley asked.

"As soon as possible."

"Is it large?"

Twelve years, Barrett thought. "Quite large," he said.

"That's it?"

"All I can think of at the moment. I haven't mentioned living facilities, of course."

"Enough rooms have been renovated for your use. A couple from Caribou Falls will prepare and deliver your meals." Hanley seemed about to smile. "They've refused to sleep in the house."

Barrett stood. "It's just as well. They'd only be in the way."

Hanley walked him toward the library door. Before they reached it, it was opened sharply by a stout man, who glared at Barrett. Although he was forty years younger and a hundred pounds heavier, William Reinhardt Deutsch bore an unmistakable resemblance to his father.

He shut the door. "I'm warning you right now," he said, "I'm going to block this thing."

Barrett stared at him.

"The truth," Deutsch said. "This is a waste of time, isn't it? Put it in writing, and I'll make you out a check for a thousand dollars right now."

Barrett tightened. "I'm afraid—"

"There's no such thing as the supernatural, is there?" Deutsch's neck was reddening.

"Correct," said Barrett. Deutsch began to smile in triumph. "The word is '*supernormal.*' Nature cannot be transcen—"

"What the hell's the difference?" interrupted Deutsch. "It's superstition, all of it!"

"I'm sorry, but it isn't." Barrett started past him. "Now, if you'll excuse me."

Deutsch caught his arm. "Now, *look,* you better drop this thing. I'll see you never get that money—"

Barrett pulled his arm free. "Do what you will," he said. "I'll proceed until I hear otherwise from your father."

He closed the door and started down the corridor. In light of present knowledge, his mind addressed Deutsch, anyone who chooses to refer to psychic phenomena as superstition simply isn't aware of what's going on in the world. The documentation is immense—

Barrett stopped and leaned against the wall. His leg was starting to ache again. For the first time, he allowed himself to recognize what a strain on his condition it might be to spend a week in the Belasco house.

What if it was really as bad as the two accounts claimed it was?

4:37 P.M.

The Rolls-Royce sped along the highway toward Manhattan.

"That's an awful lot of money." Edith still sounded incredulous.

"Not to him," said Barrett. "Especially when you consider that what he's paying for is an assurance of immortality."

"But he must know that you don't believe—"

"I'm sure he does," Barrett interrupted. He didn't want to consider the possibility that Deutsch hadn't been told.

"He's not the sort of man who goes into anything without being totally informed."

"But a hundred thousand dollars."

Barrett smiled. "I can scarcely believe it myself," he said. "If I were like my mother, I'd undoubtedly consider this a miracle from God. The two things I've failed to accomplish both supplied at once—an opportunity to prove my theory, and provision for our later years. Really, I could ask no more."

Edith returned his smile. "I'm happy for you, Lionel," she said.

"Thank you, my dear." He patted her hand.

"Monday afternoon, though." Edith looked concerned. "That doesn't give us too much time."

Barrett said, "I'm wondering if I shouldn't go alone on this one."

She stared at him.

"Well, not alone, of course," he said. "There are the two others."

"What about your meals?"

"They'll be provided. All I'll have to do is work."

"I've always helped you, though," she said.

"I know. It's just that—"

"What?"

He hesitated. "I'd rather you weren't along this time, that's all."

"*Why*, Lionel?" She looked uneasy when he didn't answer. "Is it me?"

"Of course not." Barrett's smile was quick, distracted. "It's the house."

"Isn't it just another so-called haunted house?" she asked, using his phrase.

"I'm afraid it isn't," he admitted. "It's the Mount Everest of haunted houses, you might say. There were two attempts to investigate it, one in 1931, the other in 1940. Both were disasters. Eight people involved in those attempts were killed, committed suicide, or went insane. Only one survived, and I have no idea how sound he is—Benjamin Fischer, one of the two who'll be with me.

"It's not that I fear the ultimate effect of the house," he continued, trying to ameliorate his words. "I have confidence in what I know. It's simply that the details of the investigation may be"—he shrugged—"a little nasty."

"And yet you want me to let you go there alone?"

"My dear—"

"What if something happens to you?"

"Nothing will."

"What if it does? With me in New York, and you in Maine?"

"Edith, nothing's going to happen."

"Then there's no reason I can't go." She tried to smile. "I'm not afraid, Lionel."

"I know you're not."

"I won't get in your way."

Barrett sighed.

"I know I don't understand much of what you're doing, but there are always things I can do to help. Pack and unload your equipment, for instance. Help you set up your experiments. Type the rest of your manuscript; you said you wanted to have it ready by the first of the year. And I want to be with you when you prove your theory."

Barrett nodded. "Let me think about it."

"I won't be in your way," she promised. "And I know there are any number of things I can do to help."

He nodded again, trying to think. It was obvious she didn't want to stay behind. He could appreciate that. Except for his three weeks in London in 1962, they'd never been separated since their marriage. Would it really hurt that much to take her? Certainly, she'd experienced enough psychic phenomena by now to be accustomed to it.

Still, that house was such an unknown factor. It hadn't been called Hell House without reason. There was a power there strong enough to physically and/or mentally demolish eight people, three of whom had been scientists like himself.

Even believing that he knew exactly what that power was, dare he expose Edith to it?

DECEMBER 20, 1970

10:39 P.M.

Florence Tanner crossed the yard which separated her small house from the church and walked along the alley to the street. She stood on the sidewalk and gazed at her church. It was only a converted store, but it had been everything to her these past six years. She looked at the sign in the painted window: TEMPLE OF SPIRITUAL HARMONY. She smiled. It was indeed. Those six years had been the most spiritually harmonious of her life.

She walked to the door, unlocked it, and went inside. The warmth felt good. Shivering, she turned on the wall lamp in the vestibule. Her eye was caught by the bulletin board:

Sunday Services—11:00 a.m., 8:00 p.m.

Healing and Prophecy—Tuesdays, 7:45 p.m.

Lectures and Spirit Greetings—Wednesdays, 7:45 p.m.

Messages and Revelations—Thursdays, 7:45 p.m.

Holy Communion—1st Sunday of Month

She turned and gazed at her photograph tacked to the wall, the printed words above it: *The Reverend Florence Tanner.*

For several moments she was pleased to be reminded of her beauty. Forty-three, she still retained it unimpaired, her long red hair untouched by grayness, her tall, Junoesque figure almost as trim as it had been in her twenties. She smiled in self-depreciation then. Vanity of vanities, she thought.

She went into the church, walked along the carpeted aisle, and stepped onto the platform, taking a familiar pose behind the lectern. She looked at the rows of chairs, the hymnals set on every third one. She visualized her congregation sitting before her. "My dears," she murmured.

She had told them at the morning and evening services. Told them of the need for her to be away from them for the next week. Told them of the answer to their prayers—the means to build a true church on their own property. Asked them to pray for her while she was gone.

Florence clasped her hands on the lectern and closed her eyes. Her lips moved slightly as she prayed for the strength to cleanse the Belasco house. It had such a dreadful history of death and suicide and madness. It was a house most horribly defiled. She prayed to end its curse.

The prayer completed, Florence lifted her head and gazed at her church. She loved it deeply. Still, to be able to build a real church for her congregation was truly a gift from heaven. And at Christmastime . . . She smiled, eyes glistening with tears.

God was good.

11:17 P.M.

Edith finished brushing her teeth and gazed at her reflection in the mirror—at her short-cut auburn hair, her strong, almost masculine features. Her expression was a worried one. Disturbed by the sight of it, she switched off the bathroom light and returned to the bedroom.

Lionel was asleep. She sat on her bed and looked at him, listening to the sound of his heavy breathing. Poor dear, she thought. There had been so much to do. By ten o'clock he'd been exhausted, and she'd made him go to bed.

Edith lay on her side and continued looking at him. She'd never seen him so concerned before. He'd made her promise that she'd never leave his side once they'd entered the Belasco house. Could it be that bad? She'd been to haunted houses with Lionel and never been frightened. He was always so calm, so confident; it was impossible to be afraid when he was near.

Yet, he was disturbed enough about the Belasco house to make an issue of her staying by his side at all times. Edith shivered. Would her presence harm him? Would looking after her use up so much of his limited energy that his work would suffer? She didn't want that. She knew how much his work meant to him.

Still, she had to go. She'd face anything rather than be alone. She'd never told Lionel how close she'd come to a mental breakdown during those three weeks he'd been gone in 1962. It would only have distressed him, and he'd needed all his concentration for the work he was doing. So she'd lied and sounded cheerful on the telephone the three times he'd called—and, alone, she'd wept and shaken, taken tranquilizers, hadn't slept or eaten, lost thirteen pounds, fought off compulsions to end it all. Met him at the airport finally, pale and smiling, told him that she'd had the flu.

Edith closed her eyes and drew her legs up. She couldn't face that again. The worst haunted house in the world threatened her less than being alone.

11:41 P.M.

He couldn't sleep. Fischer opened his eyes and looked around the cabin of Deutsch's private plane. Strange to be sitting in an armchair in an airplane, he thought. Strange to be sitting in an airplane at all. He'd never flown in his life.

Fischer reached for the coffeepot and poured himself another cupful. He rubbed a hand across his eyes and picked up one of the magazines lying on the coffee table in front of him. It was one of Deutsch's. What else? he thought.

After a while his eyes went out of focus, and the words on the page began to blur together. Going back, he thought. The only one of nine people still walking around, and he was going back for more.

They'd found him lying on the front porch of the house that morning in September 1940, naked, curled up like a fetus, shivering and staring into space. When they'd put him on a stretcher, he'd begun to scream and vomit blood, his muscles knotting, rocklike. He'd lain in a coma three months in the Caribou Falls Hospital. When he'd opened his eyes, he'd looked like a haggard man of thirty, a month short of his sixteenth birthday. Now he was forty-five, a lean, gray-haired man with dark eyes, his expression one of hard, suspicious readiness.

Fischer straightened in the chair. Never mind; it's time, he thought. He wasn't fifteen anymore, wasn't naïve or gullible, wasn't the credulous prey he'd been in 1940. Things would be different this time.

He'd never dreamed in his wildest fancies that he'd be given a second chance at the house. After his mother had died, he'd traveled to the West Coast. Probably, he later realized, to get as far away as possible from Maine. He'd committed clumsy fraud in Los Angeles and San Francisco, deliberately alienating Spiritualists and scientists alike in order to be free of them. He'd existed barely for thirty years, washing dishes, doing farmwork, selling door to door, janitoring, anything to earn money without using his mind.

Yet, somehow, he'd protected his ability and nurtured it. It was still there, maybe not as spectacular as it had been when he was fifteen, but very much intact—and backed now by the thoughtful caution of a man rather than the suicidal arrogance of a teenager. He was ready to shake loose the dormant psychic muscles, exercise and strengthen them, use them once more. Against that pesthole up in Maine.

Against Hell House.

DECEMBER 21, 1970

11:19 A.M.

The two black Cadillacs moved along the road, which twisted through dense forest. In the lead car was Deutsch's representative. Dr. Barrett, Edith, Florence Tanner, and Fischer rode in the second, chauffeur-driven limousine, Fischer sitting on the pull-down seat, facing the other three.

Florence put her hand on Edith's. "I hope you didn't think me unfriendly before," she said. "It was only that I felt concern for you, going into that house."

"I understand," said Edith. She drew her hand away.

"I'd appreciate it, Miss Tanner," Barrett told her, "if you wouldn't alarm my wife prematurely."

"I had no intention of doing that, Doctor. Still—" Florence hesitated, then went on. "You *have* prepared Mrs. Barrett, I trust."

"My wife has been advised that there will be occurrences."

Fischer grunted. "One way of putting it," he said. It was the first time he'd spoken in an hour.

Barrett turned to him. "She has also been advised," he

said, "that these occurrences will not, in any way, signify the presence of the dead."

Fischer nodded, taking out a pack of cigarettes. "All right if I smoke?" he asked. His gaze flicked across their faces. Seeing no objection, he lit one.

Florence was about to say something more to Barrett, then changed her mind. "Odd that a project such as this should be financed by a man like Deutsch," she said. "I would never have thought him genuinely interested in these matters."

"He's an old man," Barrett said. "He's thinking about dying, and wants to believe it isn't the end."

"It isn't, of course."

Barrett smiled.

"You look familiar," Edith said to Florence. "Why is that?"

"I used to be an actress years ago. Television mostly, an occasional film. My acting name was Florence Michaels."

Edith nodded.

Florence looked at Barrett, then at Fischer. "Well, this *is* exciting," she said. "To work with two such giants. How can that house not fall before us?"

"Why is it called Hell House?" Edith asked.

"Because its owner, Emeric Belasco, created a private hell there," Barrett told her.

"Is he supposed to be the one who haunts the house?"

"Among many," Florence said. "The phenomena are too complex to be the work of one surviving spirit. It's obviously a case of multiple haunting."

"Let's just say there's something there," said Barrett.

Florence smiled. "Agreed."

"Will you get rid of it with your machine?" asked Edith.

Florence and Fischer looked at Barrett. "I'll explain it presently," he said.

They all looked toward the windows as the car angled

downward. "We're almost there," Barrett said. He looked at Edith. "The house is in the Matawaskie Valley."

All of them gazed at the hill-ringed valley lying ahead, its floor obscured by fog. Fischer stubbed his cigarette in the ashtray, blowing out smoke. Looking forward again, he winced. "We're going in."

The car was suddenly immersed in greenish mist. Its speed was decreased by the driver, and they saw him leaning forward, peering through the windshield. After several moments he switched on the fog lights and wipers.

"How could anyone want to build a house in such a place?" asked Florence.

"This was sunshine to Belasco," Fischer said.

They all stared through the windows at the curling fog. It was as though they rode inside a submarine, slowly navigating downward through a sea of curdled milk. At various moments, trees or bushes or boulder formations would appear beside the car, then disappear. The only sound was the hum of the engine.

At last the car was braked. They all looked forward to see the other Cadillac in front of them. There was a faint sound as its door was closed. Then the figure of Deutsch's representative loomed from the mist. Barrett depressed a button, and the window by his side slid down. He grimaced at the fetid odor of the mist.

The man leaned over. "We're at the turnoff," he said. "Your chauffeur is going into Caribou Falls with us, so one of you will have to drive to the house—it's just a little way. The telephone has been connected, the electricity is on, and your rooms are ready." He glanced at the floor. "The food in that basket should see you through the afternoon. Supper will be delivered at six. Any questions?"

"Will we need a key for the front door?" Barrett asked.

"No, it's unlocked."

"Get one anyway," Fischer said.

Barrett looked at him, then back at the man. "Perhaps we'd better."

The man withdrew a ring of keys from his overcoat pocket and disconnected one of them, handing it to Barrett. "Anything else?"

"We'll phone if there is."

The man smiled briefly. "Good-bye, then," he said. He turned away.

"I trust he meant *au revoir*," said Edith.

Barrett smiled as he raised the window.

"I'll drive," Fischer said. He clambered over the seat and got in front. Starting the motor, he turned left onto the rutted blacktop road.

Edith drew in sudden breath. "I wish I knew what to expect."

Fischer answered without looking back. "Expect anything," he said.

11:47 A.M.

For the past five minutes Fischer had been inching the Cadillac along the narrow, fog-bound road. Now he braked and stopped the engine. "We're here." he said. He wrenched up the door handle and ducked outside, buttoning his Navy pea coat.

Edith turned as Lionel opened the door beside him. She waited as he struggled out, then edged across the seat after him. She shivered as she got out. "Cold," she said, "and that *smell*."

"Probably a swamp around here somewhere."

Florence joined them, and the four stood silent for a few moments, looking around.

"That way," Fischer said then. He was gazing across the hood of the car.

"Let's take a look," said Barrett. "We can get our luggage afterward." He turned to Fischer. "Would you lead?"

Fischer moved off.

They had gone only a few yards when they reached a narrow concrete bridge. As they walked across it, Edith looked over the edge. If there was water below, the mist obscured it from sight. She glanced back. Already the limousine was swallowed by fog.

"Don't fall in the tarn." Fischer's voice drifted back. Edith turned and saw a body of water ahead, a gravel path curving to its left. The surface of the water looked like clouded gelatin sprinkled with a thin debris of leaves and grass. A miasma of decay hovered above it, and the stones which lined its shore were green with slime.

"Now we know where the odor comes from," Barrett said. He shook his head. "Belasco *would* have a tarn."

"Bastard Bog," said Fischer.

"Why do you call it that?"

Fischer didn't answer. Finally he said, "I'll tell you later."

They walked in silence now, the only sound the crunching of gravel underneath their shoes. The cold was numbing, a clammy chill that seemed to dew itself around their bones. Edith drew up the collar of her coat and stayed close to Lionel, holding on to his arm and looking at the ground. Just behind them walked Florence Tanner.

When Lionel stopped at last, Edith looked up quickly.

It stood before them in the fog, a massive, looming specter of a house.

"Hideous," said Florence, sounding almost angry. Edith looked at her. "We haven't even gone inside, Miss Tanner," Barrett said.

"I don't have to go inside." Florence turned to Fischer,

who was staring at the house. As she looked at him, he shuddered. Reaching out, she put her hand in his. He gripped it so hard it made her wince.

Barrett and Edith gazed up at the shrouded edifice. In the mist, it resembled some ghostly escarpment blocking their path. Edith leaned forward suddenly. *"It has no windows,"* she said.

"He had them bricked up," Barrett said.

"Why?"

"I don't know. Perhaps—"

"We're wasting time," Fischer cut him off. He let go of Florence's hand and lurched forward.

They walked the final yards along the gravel path, then started up the wide porch steps. Edith saw that all the steps were cracked, fungus and frosted yellow grass sprouting from the fissures.

They stopped before the massive double doors.

"If they open by themselves, I'm going home," Edith said, trying to sound amused. Barrett gripped the handle on the door and depressed its thumb plate. The door held fast. He glanced at Fischer. "This happen to you?"

"More than once."

"Good we have the key, then." Barrett removed it from his overcoat pocket and slid it into the lock. It wouldn't turn. He wiggled the key back and forth, attempting to loosen the bolt.

Abruptly the key turned over, and the heavy door began to swing in. Edith twitched as Florence caught her breath. "What is it?" she asked. Florence shook her head. "No cause for alarm," Barrett said. Edith glanced at him in surprise.

"It's just reaction, Mrs. Barrett," Florence explained. "Your husband is quite right. It's nothing to be alarmed about."

Fischer had been reaching in to locate the light switch.

Now he found it, and they heard him flick it up and down without result. "So much for restored electrical service," he said.

"Obviously the generator is too old," Barrett said.

"Generator?" Edith looked surprised again. "There's no electrical service here?"

"There aren't enough houses in the valley to make it worth the effort," Barrett answered.

"How could they put in a telephone, then?"

"It's a field telephone," Barrett said. He looked into the house. "Well, Mr. Deutsch will have to provide us with a new generator, that's all."

"You think that's the answer, do you?" Fischer sounded dubious.

"Of course," said Barrett. "The breakdown of an antique generator can scarcely be classified as a psychic phenomenon."

"What are we going to do?" asked Edith. "Stay in Caribou Falls until the new generator is installed?"

"That might take days," said Barrett. "We'll use candles until it arrives."

"Candles," Edith said.

Barrett smiled at her expression. "Just for a day or so."

She nodded, her returned smile wan. Barrett looked inside the house. "The question now," he said, "is how do we find some candles? I assume there must be some inside—" He broke off, looking at the flashlight Fischer had taken out of his coat pocket. *"Ah,"* he said.

Fischer switched on the flashlight, pointed the beam inside, then, bracing himself, stepped across the threshold.

Barrett went in next. He stepped through the doorway, seemed to listen briefly. Turning then, he extended his hand to Edith. She entered the house, clutching at his hand. "That *smell,*" she said. "It's even worse than outside."

"It's a very old house with no aeration," Barrett said. "It

could also be the furnace, which hasn't been used in more than twenty-nine years." He turned to Florence. "Coming, Miss Tanner?" he asked.

She nodded, smiling faintly. "Yes." She took a deep breath, held herself erect, and stepped inside. She looked around. "The *atmosphere* in here—" She sounded queasy.

"An atmosphere of this world, not the next," said Barrett dryly.

Fischer played the flashlight beam around the dark immensity of the entry hall. The narrow cone of light jumped fitfully from place to place, freezing momentarily on hulking groups of furniture; huge, leaden-colored paintings; giant tapestries filmed with dust; a staircase, broad and curving, leading upward into blackness; a second-story corridor overlooking the entry hall; and far above, engulfed by shadows, a vast expanse of paneled ceiling.

"Be it ever so humble," Barrett said.

"It isn't humble at all," said Florence. "It reeks of arrogance."

Barrett sighed. "It reeks, at any rate." He looked to his right. "According to the floor plan, the kitchen should be that way."

Edith walked beside him as they started across the entry hall, the sound of their footsteps loud on the hardwood floor.

Florence looked around. "It knows we're here," she said.

"Miss Tanner—" Barrett frowned. "Please don't think I'm trying to restrict you—"

"Sorry." Florence said. "I'll try to keep my observations to myself."

They reached a corridor and walked along it, Fischer in the lead, Barrett and Edith behind him, Florence last. At the end of the corridor stood a pair of metal-faced swinging doors. Fischer pushed one of them open and stepped into the kitchen, holding the door ajar for the others. When all of them had gone inside, he let the door swing back and turned.

"Good Lord." Edith's eyes moved with the flashlight beam as Fischer shifted it around the room.

The kitchen was twenty-five by fifty feet, its perimeter rimmed by steel counters and dark-paneled cupboards, a long, double-basin sink, a gigantic stove with three ovens, and a massive walk-in refrigerator. In the center of the room, like a giant's steel-topped casket, stood a huge steam table.

"He must have entertained a good deal," Edith said.

Fischer pointed the flashlight at the large electric wall clock above the stove. Its hands were stopped at 7:31. A.M. or P.M., and on what day? Barrett wondered as he limped along the wall to his right, pulling open drawers. Edith and Florence stood together, watching him. Barrett pulled open one of the cupboard doors and grunted as Fischer shone the light over. "Genuine spirits," he said, looking at the shelves of dust-filmed bottles. "Perhaps we'll raise some after supper."

Fischer pulled a sheet of yellow-edged cardboard from one of the drawers and pointed the flashlight at it.

"What's that?" Barrett asked.

"One of their menus, dated March 27, 1928. Shrimp bisque. Sweetbreads in gravy. Stewed capon. Bread sauce in gravy. Creamed cauliflower. For dessert, *amandes en crème:* crushed almonds in whipped egg whites and heavy cream."

Barrett chuckled. "His guests must have all had heartburn."

"The food wasn't aimed at their hearts," said Fischer, taking a box of candles from the drawer.

12:19 P.M.

They started back across the entry hall, each carrying a candle in a holder. As they moved, the flickering illumination made their shadows billow on the walls and ceiling.

"This must be the great hall over here," said Barrett.

They moved beneath an archway six feet deep and stopped, Edith and Florence gasping almost simultaneously. Barrett whistled softly as he raised his candle for a maximum of light.

The great hall measured ninety-five by forty-seven feet, its walls two stories high, paneled in walnut to a height of eight feet, rough-hewn blocks of stone above. Across from where they stood was a mammoth fireplace, its mantel constructed of antique carved stone.

The furnishings were all antique except for scattered chairs and sofas upholstered in the fashion of the twenties. Marble statues stood on pedestals in various locations. In the northwest corner was an ebony concert grand piano, and in the center of the hall stood a circular table, more than twenty feet across, with sixteen high-backed chairs around it and a large chandelier suspended over it. Good place to set up my equipment, Barrett thought; the hall had obviously been cleaned. He lowered his candle. "Let's push on," he said.

They left the great hall, moved across the entry hall, beneath the overhanging staircase, and turned right into another corridor. Several yards along its length, they reached a pair of swinging walnut doors set to their left. Barrett pushed one in and peered inside. "The theater," he said.

They went inside, reacting to the musty smell. The theater was designed to seat a hundred people, its walls covered with an antique red brocade, its sloping, three-aisled floor with thick red carpeting. On the stage, gilded Renaissance columns flanked the screen, and spaced along the walls were silver candelabra wired for electricity. The seats were custom-made, upholstered with wine-red velvet.

"Just how wealthy *was* Belasco?" Edith asked.

"I believe he left in excess of seven million dollars when he died," Barrett answered.

"Died?" said Fischer. He held open one of the doors.

"If there's anything you care to tell us . . ." Barrett said as he stepped into the corridor.

"What's to tell? The house tried to kill me; it almost succeeded."

Barrett looked as though he meant to speak. Then he changed his mind and peered down the corridor. "I think that staircase leads down to the pool and steam room," he said. "No point in going there until the electricity's on." He limped across the corridor and opened a heavy wooden door.

"What is it?" Edith asked.

"Looks like a chapel."

"A *chapel?*" Florence looked appalled. As she neared the door, she started making sounds of apprehension in her throat. Edith glanced at her uneasily.

"Miss Tanner?" Barrett said.

She didn't answer. Almost to the door, she held back.

"Better not," said Fischer.

Florence shook her head. "I must." She began to enter.

With a faint, involuntary cry, she shrank back. Edith started. "What *is* it?" Florence was unable to reply. She sucked in breath and shook her head with tiny movements. Barrett put his hand on Edith's arm. She looked at him and saw his lips frame the words, "It's all right."

"I can't go in," Florence said, as though apologizing. "Not now, anyway." She swallowed. "The atmosphere is more than I can bear."

"We'll only be a moment," Barrett told her.

Florence nodded, turning away.

As she went inside the chapel, Edith braced herself, expecting a shock of some kind. Feeling nothing, she turned to Lionel in confusion, started to speak, then waited until they were apart from Fischer. "Why couldn't she come in?" she whispered then.

"Her system is attuned to psychic energy," Barrett explained. "Obviously it's very strong in here."

"Why here?"

"Contrast, perhaps. A church in hell; that sort of thing."

Edith nodded, glancing back at Fischer. "Why doesn't it bother him?" she asked.

"Perhaps he knows how to protect himself better than she does."

Edith nodded again, stopping as Lionel did to look around the low-ceilinged chapel. There were wooden pews for fifty people. In front was an altar; above it, glinting in the candlelight, a life-size, flesh-colored figure of Jesus on the cross.

"It *looks* like a chapel," she started to say, breaking off in shock as she saw that the figure of Jesus was naked, an enormous phallus jutting upward from between the legs. She made a sound of revulsion, staring at the obscene crucifix. The air seemed suddenly thick, coagulating in her throat.

Now she noticed that the walls were covered with pornographic murals. Her eye was caught by one on her right, depicting a mass orgy involving half-clothed nuns and priests. The faces on the figures were demented—leering, slavering, darkly flushed, distorted by maniacal lust.

"Profanation of the sacred," Barrett said. "A venerable sickness."

"He *was* sick," Edith murmured.

"Yes, he was." Barrett took her arm. As he escorted her along the aisle, Edith saw that Fischer had already left.

They found him in the corridor.

"She's gone," he said.

Edith stared at him. "How can she—?" She broke off, looking around.

"I'm sure it's nothing," Barrett said.

"*Are* you?" Fischer sounded angry.

"I'm sure she's all right," said Barrett firmly. "Miss Tanner!" he called. "Come along, my dear." He started down the corridor. "Miss Tanner!" Fischer followed him without making a sound.

"Lionel, why would she—?"

"Let's not jump to conclusions," Barrett said. He called again. "Miss Tanner! Can you hear me?"

As they reached the entry hall, Edith pointed. There was candlelight inside the great hall.

"Miss Tanner!" Barrett called.

"Yes!"

Barrett smiled at Edith, then glanced over at Fischer. Fischer's expression had not relaxed.

She was standing on the far side of the hall. Their footsteps clicked in broken rhythm on the floor as they crossed to her. "You shouldn't have done that, Miss Tanner," Barrett said. "You caused us undue alarm."

"I'm sorry," Florence said, but it was only a token apology. "I heard a voice in here."

Edith shuddered.

Florence gestured toward the piece of furniture she was standing beside, a phonograph installed inside a walnut Spanish cabinet. Reaching down to its turntable, she lifted off a record and showed it to them. "It was this."

Edith didn't understand. "How could it play without electricity?"

"You forget they used to wind up phonographs." Barrett set his candle holder on top of the cabinet and took the record from Florence. "Homemade," he said.

"Belasco."

Barrett looked at her, intrigued. "His voice?" She nodded, and he turned to put it back on the turntable. Florence looked at Fischer, who was standing several yards away, staring at the phonograph.

Barrett wound the crank tight, ran a fingertip across the end of the steel needle, and set it on the record edge. There was a crackling noise through the speaker, then a voice.

"Welcome to my house," said Emeric Belasco. "I'm delighted you could come."

Edith crossed her arms and shivered.

"I am certain you will find your stay here most illuminating." Belasco's voice was soft and mellow, yet terrifying—the voice of a carefully disciplined madman. "It is regrettable I cannot be with you," it said, "but I had to leave before your arrival."

Bastard, Fischer thought.

"Do not let my physical absence disturb you, however. Think of me as your unseen host and believe that, during your stay here, I shall be with you in spirit."

Edith's teeth were set on edge. *That voice.*

"All your needs have been provided for," Belasco's voice continued. "Nothing has been overlooked. Go where you will, and do what you will—these are the cardinal precepts of my home. Feel free to function as you choose. There are no responsibilities, no rules. 'Each to his own device' shall be the only standard here. May you find the answer that you seek. It is here, I promise you." There was a pause. "And now . . . *auf Wiedersehen.*"

The needle made a scratching noise on the record. Barrett

raised the needle arm and switched off the phonograph. The great hall was immensely still.

"Auf Wiedersehen" said Florence. *"Until we meet again."* "Lionel—?"

"The record wasn't meant for us," he said.

"But—"

"It was cut a good half-century ago," said Barrett. "Look at it." He held it up. "It's merely a coincidence that what he said seems applicable to us."

"What made the phonograph go on by itself, then?" Florence asked.

"That is a separate problem," Barrett said. "I'm only discussing the record now." He looked at Fischer. "Did it play by itself in 1940? The accounts say nothing of it."

Fischer shook his head.

"Do you know anything about the record?"

It appeared that Fischer wasn't going to answer. Then he said, "Guests would arrive, to find him gone. That record would be played for them." He paused. "It was a game he played. While the guests were here, Belasco spied on them from hiding."

Barrett nodded.

"Then, again, maybe he was invisible," Fischer continued. "He claimed the power. Said that he could will the attention of a group of people to some particular object, and move among them unobserved."

"I doubt that," Barrett said.

"Do you?" Fischer's smile was strange as he looked at the phonograph. "We all had our attention on that a few moments ago," he said. "How do you know he didn't walk right by us while we were listening?"

12:46 P.M.

They were moving up the staircase when an icy breeze passed over them, causing their candle flames to flicker. Edith's flame went out. "What was that?" she whispered.

"A breeze," said Barrett instantly. He declined his candle to relight hers. "We'll discuss it later."

Edith swallowed, glancing at Florence. Barrett took her by the arm, and they started up the stairs again. "There'll be many things like that during the week," he said. "You'll get used to them."

Edith said no more. As she and Lionel ascended the stairs, Florence and Fischer exchanged a look.

They reached the second floor and, turning to the right, started along the balcony corridor. On their right, the heavy balustrade continued. To their left, set periodically along a paneled wall, were bedroom doors. Barrett approached the first of these and opened it. He looked inside, then turned to Florence. "Would you like this one?" he asked.

She stepped into the doorway. After several moments, she turned back to them. "Not too bad," she said. She smiled at Edith. "You'll rest more comfortably here."

Barrett was about to comment, then relented. "Fine," he said. He gestured toward the room.

He followed Edith inside and shut the door. Edith watched as he limped around the bedroom. To her left were a pair of carved walnut Renaissance beds, between them a small table with a lamp and a French-style telephone on it. A fireplace was centered on the opposite wall, in front of it a heavy walnut rocking chair. The teakwood floor was almost covered by a twenty-by-thirty-foot blue Persian rug, in the middle of which stood an octagonal-topped table with a matching chair upholstered in red leather.

Barrett glanced into the bathroom, then returned to her. "About that breeze," he said. "I didn't want to get involved in a discussion with Miss Tanner. That's why I glossed over it."

"It really happened, didn't it?"

"Of course," he answered, smiling. "A manifestation of simple kinetics: unguided, unintelligent. No matter what Miss Tanner thinks. I should have mentioned that before we left."

"Mentioned what?"

"That you'll need to inure yourself to what she'll be saying in the next week. She's a Spiritualist, as you know. Survival of and communication with the so-called disincarnate is the foundation of her belief; an erroneous foundation, as I intend to prove. In the meantime, though"—he smiled—"be prepared to hear her views expressed. I can't very well ask that she remain mute."

To her right, their heads against the wall, were a pair of beds with elaborately carved headboards, between them a huge chest of drawers. Above the chest, suspended from the ceiling, was a large Italian silver lamp.

Directly across from her, by the paneled window shutters, was a Spanish table with a matching chair. On top of the table was a Chinese lamp and a French-style telephone. Florence crossed the room and picked up the receiver. It was dead. Did I expect it to be working? she thought, amused. At any rate, it had doubtless been used only for calls made within the house.

She turned and looked around the room. There was something in it. What, though? A personality? A residue of emotion? Florence closed her eyes and waited. Something in the air; no doubt of it. She felt it shift and throb, advancing on her, then retreating like some unseen, timorous beast.

After several minutes she opened her eyes. It will come, she thought. She crossed to the bathroom, squinting slightly as its white tile walls glittered with reflected candlelight. Setting the holder on the sink, she turned the hot-water faucet. For a moment, nothing happened. Then, with a gurgling rattle, a gout of darkly rusted water splattered into the basin. Florence waited until the water cleared before she held her hand beneath it. She hissed at its coldness. I hope the water heater isn't broken too, she thought. Bending over, she started patting water onto her face.

I should have gone into the chapel, she thought. I shouldn't have backed off from the very first challenge. She winced, remembering the violent nausea she'd felt as she was about to enter. An awful place, she thought. She'd have to work her way up to it, that was all. If she forced it now, she might lose consciousness. I'll get in there soon enough, she promised herself. God will grant the power when it's time.

His room was smaller than the other two. There was only one bed with a canopy top. Fischer sat at the foot of it, staring at the intricate pattern on the rug. He could feel the house around him like some vast, invisible being. It knows I'm here, he thought; Belasco knows, they all know that I'm here: their single failure. They were watching him, waiting to see what he'd do.

He wasn't going to do anything prematurely, that was certain. He wasn't going to do a thing until he got the feel of the place.

2:21 P.M.

Fischer came into the great hall carrying his flashlight. He had changed into a black turtleneck sweater, black corduroy trousers, and a pair of scuffed white tennis shoes. His steps were soundless as he moved toward the huge round table where Barrett, seated, and Edith, standing, were opening wooden boxes and unloading equipment. In the fireplace, a fire was burning.

Edith started as Fischer emerged from the shadows. "Need help?" he asked.

"No, it's going fine," said Barrett, smiling. "Thank you for the offer, though."

Fischer sat in one of the chairs. His eyes remained on Barrett as the tall, bearded man removed an instrument from protective excelsior, wiped it carefully with a cloth, and set it on the table. Fussy about his equipment, Fischer thought. He pulled a pack of cigarettes from his pocket and lit one, watching the gamboling deformity of Edith's shadow on the wall as she picked up another wooden box and carried it to the table.

"Still teach physics?" he asked.

"Limitedly, because of health." Barrett hesitated, then continued. "I had polio when I was twelve; my right leg is partially paralyzed."

Fischer gazed at him in silence. Barrett took another instrument from its box and wiped it off. He set the instrument on the table and looked at Fischer. "It won't affect our project in any way," he said.

Fischer nodded.

"You referred to the tarn before as Bastard Bog," Barrett said, returning to his work. "Why was that?"

"Some of Belasco's female guests got pregnant while they were here."

"And they actually—?" Barrett broke off, glancing up.

"Thirteen times."

"That's hideous," said Edith.

Fischer blew out smoke. "A lot of hideous things happened here," he said.

Barrett ran his eyes across the instruments already on the table: astatic galvanometer, mirror galvanometer, quadrant electrometer, Crookes balance, camera, gauze cage, smoke absorber, manometer, weighing platform, tape recorder. Still to be unpacked were the contact clock, electroscope, lights (standard and infrared), maximum and minimum thermometer, hygroscope, sthenometer, phosphorescent sulfide screen, electric stove, the box of vessels and tubes, the molding materials, and the cabinet equipment. And the most important instrument of all, Barrett thought with satisfaction.

He was unpacking the rack of red, yellow, and white lights when Fischer asked, "How are you going to use those when there's no electricity?"

"There will be by tomorrow," Barrett said. "I telephoned Caribou Falls; the phone is near the front door, incidentally. They'll install a new generator in the morning."

"And you think it will work?"

Barrett repressed a smile. "It will work."

Fischer said no more. Across the hall, a burning log popped, making Edith twitch as she walked to one of the larger wooden boxes.

"Not that one, it's too heavy," Barrett told her.

"I'll do it." Rising from his chair, Fischer walked to Edith and, stooping, lifted the box. "What is it, an anvil?" he asked as he set it on the table.

Barrett was aware of Fischer's curious gaze as he pried up the boards on top of the box. "Would you—?" he asked. Fischer lifted out the bulky metal instrument and set it on the table. It was cube-shaped, painted dark blue, an uncomplicated dial in front of it numbered 0-900, the thin red needle pointed at zero. Across the top of the instrument was stenciled, in black letters: BARRETT—EMR.

"EMR?" asked Fischer.

"I'll explain it later," said Barrett.

"This your machine?"

Barrett shook his head. "That's being constructed."

They all turned toward the archway at the sound of heels. Florence was approaching, carrying a candle in its holder. She had changed to a heavy green, long-sleeved sweater, thick tweed skirt, and low-heeled shoes. "Hello," she said cheerfully.

As she came up to them, her gaze ran across the array of devices on the table, and she smiled. She turned to Fischer. "Like to take a walk with me?" she asked.

"Why not?"

After they were gone, Edith saw a typed list on the table and picked it up. It was headed, "Observed Psychic Phenomena at the Belasco House":

> Apparitions; Apports; Asports; Automatic drawing; Automatic painting; Automatic speaking ; Automatic writing; Autoscopy; Bilocation; Biological phenomena; Book tests; Breezes; Catalepsy; Chemical phenomena; Chemicographs; Clairaudience; Clairsentience; Clairvoyance; Communication; Control; Crystal gazing; Dematerialization; Direct drawing; Direct painting; Direct voice; Direct writing; Divination; Dreams; Dream communications; Dream prophecies; Ectoplasm; Eidolons; Electrical phenomena; Elongation; Emanations; Exteriorization of motricity; Exteriorization of sensation; Extras; Extratemporal perception; Eyeless sight; Facsimile writing; Flower clairsentience; Ghosts; Glossolalia; Hyperamnesia; Hyperesthesia; Ideomorphs; Ideoplasm; Impersonation; Imprints; Independent voice; Interpenetration of matter; Knot tying; Levitation; Luminous phenomena; Magnetic phenomena; Materialization; Matter

through matter; Metagraphology; Monition; Motor automatism; Newspaper tests; Obsession; Paraffin molds; Parakinesis; Paramnesia; Paresthesia; Percussion; Phantasmata; Poltergeist phenomena; Possession; Precognition; Presentiment; Prevision; Pseudopods; Psychic photography; Psychic rods; Psychic sounds; Psychic touches; Psychic winds; Psychokinesis; Psychometry; Radiesthesia; Radiographs; Raps; Retrocognition; Scriptograph; Sensory automatism; Skin writing; Skotography; Slate writing; Smells; Somnambulism; Stigmata; Telekinesis; Teleplasm; Telescopic vision; Telesthesia; Transcendental music; Transfiguration; Transportation; Typtology; Voices; Water sprinkling; Xenoglossy.

Edith put the list down numbly. My God, she thought. What kind of week was it going to be?

2:53 P.M.

The garage had been built to accommodate seven automobiles. Now it was empty. As they entered, Fischer thumbed off his flashlight, enough daylight filtering through the grimy door windows for them to see. He looked at the greenish mist which pressed against the panes of glass. "Maybe we should keep the car in here," he said.

Florence didn't answer. She was walking across the oil-spotted floor, turning her head from side to side. She paused by a shelf and touched a dirty, rust-flecked hammer.

"What did you say?" she asked.

"Maybe we should keep the car in here."

Florence shook her head. "If a generator can be tampered with, so can a car."

Fischer watched the medium move around the garage. As

she passed close by, he caught a scent of the cologne she wore. "Why did you give up acting?" he asked.

Florence glanced at him with a fleeting smile. "It's a long story, Ben. When we've settled down a bit, I'll tell it to you. Right now, I'd better get the feeling of the place." She stopped in a patch of light and closed her eyes.

Fischer stared at her. In the dim illumination, the medium's ivory skin and lustrous red hair gave her the appearance of a Dresden doll.

After a while she returned to Fischer. "Nothing here," she said. "You agree?"

"Whatever you say."

Fischer switched on his flashlight as they ascended the steps to the corridor. "Which way now?" she asked.

"I don't know the place that well. I was here only three days."

"We'll just explore, then," Florence said. "No need—" She broke off suddenly and stopped, head twisted to the right, as though she heard a noise behind them. "Yes," she murmured. "*Yes*. Sorrow. Pain." She frowned and shook her head. "No, no." At length she sighed and looked at Fischer. "You felt it," she said.

Fischer didn't answer. Florence smiled and looked away. "Well, let's see what else we can find," she said.

"Have you read Doctor Barrett's article in which he compares sensitives to Geiger counters?" she asked as they walked along the corridor.

"No."

"It's not a bad comparison. We *are* like Geiger counters in a way. Expose us to psychic emanations, and we tick. Of course, the difference is that we are judge as well as instrument, not only picking up impressions, but evaluating them as well."

"Uh-huh," said Fischer. Florence glanced at him.

They started down the flight of stairs across from the chapel, Fischer pointing the flashlight beam at their feet. "I wonder if we're going to need the full week," Florence said.

"A full year wouldn't be too long."

Florence tried to make her sound of disagreement mild. "I've seen the most abstruse of psychic problems solved overnight. We mustn't—" She stopped, hand clamping on the banister rail. *"This goddamn sewer,"* she muttered in a savage voice. She jolted in dismay and shook her head. "Oh, dear. Such fury. Such destructive venom." She drew in trembling breath. "A very hostile man," she said. "No wonder. Who can blame him, imprisoned in this house?" She glanced at Fischer.

Reaching the lower corridor, they moved to a pair of swinging metal doors with porthole windows in them. Fischer pushed at one of the doors and held it open for Florence. As they went inside, their footsteps sounded sharply on a tile floor and reverberated off the ceiling.

The pool was Olympic size. Fischer shone his flashlight into the murky green depths of it. He walked to the end of the pool and knelt at its corner. Pulling up the sleeve of his sweater, he put his hand in the water. "Not too cold," he said, surprised. He felt around. "And water's coming in. The pool must work on a separate generator."

Florence gazed across the glinting pool. The ripples made by Fischer were gliding across its surface. "Something in here," she said. She did not look to Fischer for verification.

"Steam room's down the other end." Fischer returned to her side.

"Let's look at it."

The ringing echoes of their footsteps as they walked along the edge of the pool made it sound as though someone were following them. Florence glanced across her shoulder. "Yes," she murmured, unaware that she had spoken.

Fischer pulled open the heavy metal door and held it ajar, playing the flashlight beam inside. The steam room was twelve feet square, its walls, floor, and ceiling tiled in white. Built-in wooden benches lined the walls, and spiraling across the floor like some petrified serpent was a length of faded green hose connected to a water outlet.

Florence grimaced. "Perverted," she said. "In there—" She swallowed as though to rid her throat of sour bile. "In *there*," she said. "But what?"

Fischer let the door swing shut, the thumping closure of it echoing loudly. Florence glanced at him; then, as he turned away, she fell into step beside him. "Doctor Barrett is certainly well equipped, isn't he?" she said, trying to lighten his mood. "It's strange to think he really believes that science alone can end the power of this house."

"What will?"

"Love," she answered. She squeezed his arm. "We know that, don't we?"

Fischer held open the swinging door for her, and they went back into the corridor. "What's over there?" Florence crossed the hallway and opened a wooden door. Fischer pointed the flashlight beam inside. It was a wine cellar, all its shelves and racks empty. Florence winced. "I see this room completely filled with bottles." She turned away. "Let's not go in."

They went back up the staircase and started along the first-floor corridor. As they passed the chapel door, Florence shuddered. "That place is the worst of all," she said. "Even though I haven't seen the entire house, somehow I have the feeling . . ." Her voice faded as she spoke. She cleared her throat. "I'll get in there," she said.

They turned into an adjoining corridor. Twenty yards along its right wall was an archway. "What have we here?"

Florence walked beneath the archway and caught her breath. *"This house,"* she said.

The ballroom was immense, its lofty, brocaded walls adorned with red velvet draperies. Three enormous chandeliers hung, spaced, along the paneled ceiling. The floor was oak, elaborately parqueted. At the far end of the room was an alcove for musicians.

"A theater, yes, but this?" said Florence. "Can a ballroom be an evil place?"

"The evil came later," Fischer said.

Florence shook her head. "Contradictions." She looked at Fischer. "You're right, it's going to take a while. I feel as if I'm standing in the center of a labyrinth of such immeasurable intricacy that the prospect of emerging is—" She caught herself. "We *will* emerge, however."

Overhead, there was a tinkling noise. Fischer jerked up his arm, pointing the flashlight at the parabola of heavy hanging crystal above them. Its pendants refracted the light, splaying colors of the spectrum across the ceiling. The chandelier was motionless.

"The challenge is met," whispered Florence.

"Don't be too quick to accept it," Fischer warned.

Florence looked at him abruptly. "You're blocking it off," she said.

"What?"

"You're blocking it off. That's why you didn't feel those things."

Fischer's smile was cold. "I didn't feel them because they weren't there. I was a Spiritualist too, remember. I know how you people find things in every corner when you want to."

"Ben, that isn't true." Florence looked hurt. "Those things *were* there. You would have felt them just as I did if you weren't obstructing—"

"I'm not obstructing anything," he cut her off. "I'm just

not sticking my head on the block a second time. When I came here in 1940, I was just like you—no, worse, much worse. I really thought I was something. God's gift to psychical research."

"You were the most powerful physical medium this country has ever known, Ben."

"Still am, Florence. Just a little bit more careful now, that's all. I suggest the same approach for you. You're walking around this house like an open nerve. When you really *do* hit something, it'll tear your insides out. This place isn't called Hell House for nothing, you know. It intends to kill every one of us, so you'd damn well better learn to protect yourself until you're ready. Or you'll just be one more victim on the list."

They looked at each other in silence for a long time. Finally she touched his hand. " 'But he who buried his talent—' " she began

"Oh, shit." Turning on his heel, he stalked away from her.

6:42 P.M.

The dining hall was sixty feet in length, and as high as it was wide—twenty-seven feet in both directions. There were two entrances to it—one an archway from the great hall, the other a swinging door leading to the kitchen.

Its ceiling was divided into a series of elaborately carved panels, its floor polished travertine. Its walls were paneled to a height of twelve feet, stone-blocked above. In the center of the west wall was a giant fireplace, its Gothic mantel reaching to the ceiling. Spaced at intervals above the length of the forty-foot table in the center of the hall hung four immense sanctuary lamps, wired for electricity. Thirty chairs stood around the table, all of them constructed of antique walnut with wine-red velvet upholstery.

The four were sitting at one end of the table, Barrett at its head. The unseen couple from Caribou Falls had left the supper at six-fifteen.

"If no one objects, I'd like to try a sitting tonight," Florence said.

Barrett's hand froze momentarily before continuing to spoon himself a second portion of broccoli. "I have no objection," he said.

Florence glanced at Edith, who shook her head. She looked at Fischer. "Fine," he said, reaching for the coffeepot.

Florence nodded. "After supper, then." Her plate was empty; she'd been drinking only water since they'd sat down.

"Would *you* care to sit in the morning, Mr. Fischer?" Barrett asked.

Fischer shook his head. "Not yet."

Barrett nodded. There; it's done, he thought. He'd asked and been refused. Since his part in the project required the services of a physical medium, Deutsch couldn't object to his sending for one of his own people. *Excellent,* he thought. He'd get it settled in the morning.

"Well," he said, "I must say that the house has scarcely lived up to its reputation so far."

Fischer looked up from the scraps of food on his plate. "It hasn't taken our measure yet," he said. His lips flexed briefly in a humorless smile.

"I think we'd be mistaken to consider the house as the haunting force," Florence said. "Quite evidently, the trouble is created by surviving personalities—whoever they may be. The only one we can be sure of is Belasco."

"You contacted him today, did you?" Barrett asked. His tone was mild, but Florence sensed the goading in it. "No," she said. "But Mr. Fischer did when he was here in 1940. And Belasco's presence *has* been documented."

"Reported," Barrett said.

Florence hesitated. Finally she said, "I think it might be well for us to lay our cards on the table, Doctor Barrett. I take it you are still convinced that no such things as ghosts exist."

"If, by that, you mean surviving personalities," said Barrett, "you are quite correct."

"Despite the fact that they've been observed throughout the ages?" Florence asked. "Have been seen by more than one person at a time? Been seen by animals? Been photographed? Have imparted information that was later verified? Have touched people? Moved objects? Been weighed?"

"These are facts in evidence of a phenomenon, Miss Tanner, not proof of ghosts."

Florence smiled wearily. "I don't know how to answer that," she said.

Barrett returned her smile, gesturing with his hands as though to say: We don't agree, so why not let it go at that?

"You don't accept survival, then," Florence persisted.

"It's a charming notion," Barrett said. "I have no objection to it, so long as I am not expected to give credence to the concept of communicating with the so-called survivors."

Florence regarded him sadly. "You can say that, having heard the sobs of joy at séances?"

"I've heard similar sobs in mental institutions."

"Mental institutions?"

Barrett sighed. "No offense intended. But the evidence is clear that belief in communication with the dead has led more people to madness than to peace of mind."

"That isn't true," said Florence. "If it were, all attempts at spirit communication would have ended long ago. They haven't, though; they've lasted through the centuries." She looked intently at Barrett, as though trying to understand his point of view. "You call it a charming notion, Doctor. Surely

it's more than that. What about the religions that accept the idea of life after death? Didn't Saint Paul say: 'If the dead rise not from the grave, then is our religion vain'?"

Barrett didn't respond.

"But you don't agree," she said.

"I don't agree."

"Have you any alternative to offer, though?"

"Yes." Barrett returned her gaze with challenge. "An alternative far more interesting, albeit far more complex and demanding; namely, *the subliminal self*, that vast, concealed expanse of the human personality which, iceberglike, inheres beneath the so-called threshold of consciousness. That is where the fascination lies, Miss Tanner. Not in the speculative realms of afterlife, but *here, today; the challenge of ourselves*. The undiscovered mysteries of the human spectrum, the infrared capacities of our bodies, the ultraviolet capacities of our minds. This is the alternative I offer: *the extended faculties of the human system not as yet established*. The faculties by which, I am convinced, all psychic phenomena are produced."

Florence remained silent for a few moments before she smiled. "We'll see," she said.

Barrett nodded once. "Indeed we shall."

Edith looked around the dining hall. "When was this house built?" she asked.

Barrett looked at Fischer. "Do you know?"

"Nineteen-nineteen," Fischer answered.

"From several things you said today, I have the impression that you know quite a bit about Belasco," Barrett said. "Would you care to tell us what you know? It might not be amiss to"—he repressed a smile—"know our adversary."

Amused? thought Fischer. You won't be when Belasco

and the others get to work. "What do you want to know?" he asked.

"Whatever you can tell us," Barrett said. "A general account of his life might be helpful."

Fischer poured himself another cupful of coffee, then set the pot back on the table, wrapped his hands around the cup, and began to speak.

"He was born in 1879, the illegitimate son of Myron Sandler, an American munitions maker, and Noelle Belasco, an English actress."

"Why did he take his mother's name?" Barrett asked.

"Sandler was married," Fischer said. He paused, went on. "His childhood is a blank except for isolated incidents. At five he hanged a cat to see if it would revive for the second of its nine lives. When it didn't, he became infuriated and chopped the cat to pieces, flinging the parts from his bedroom window. After that, his mother called him Evil Emeric."

"He was raised in England, I presume," Barrett interjected.

Fischer nodded. "The next verified incident was a sexual assault on his younger sister," he said.

Barrett frowned. "Is it all to be like this?"

"He didn't live an exemplary life, Doctor," Fischer said, a caustic edge to his voice.

Barrett hesitated. "Very well." he said. He looked at Edith. "You object, my dear?" Edith shook her head. He glanced at Florence. "Miss Tanner?"

"Not if it will help us understand," she said. Barrett gestured toward Fischer, bidding him continue.

"The assault put his sister in the hospital for two months," Fischer said. "I won't go into details. Belasco was sent to a private school—he was ten and a half at the time. There, he was abused for a number of years, mostly by one of the homosexual teachers. Belasco later invited the man to visit his house for a week; at the end of that time, the retired teacher went home and hanged himself."

"What did Belasco look like?" Barrett asked, attempting to guide the course of Fischer's account.

Fischer stared into his memory. After a while, he began to quote: " 'His teeth are those of a carnivore. When he bares them in a smile, it gives one the impression of an animal snarling. His face is white, for he despises the sun, eschews the out-of-doors. He has astonishingly green eyes, which seem to possess an inner light of their own. His forehead is broad, his hair and short-trimmed beard jet black. Despite his handsomeness, his is a frightening visage, the face of some demon who has taken on a human aspect' "

"Whose description is that?" asked Barrett.

"His second wife's. She committed suicide here in 1927."

"You know that description word for word," said Florence. "You must have read it many times."

Fischer's smile was somber. "As the Doctor said," he answered, "know thine adversary."

"Was he tall or short?" asked Barrett.

"Tall, six-foot-five. 'The Roaring Giant,' he was called."

Barrett nodded. "Education?"

"New York. London. Berlin. Paris. Vienna. No specific course of study. Logic, ethics, religion, philosophy."

"Just enough with which to rationalize his actions, I imagine," Barrett said. "He inherited his money from his father, did he?"

"Mostly. His mother left him several thousand pounds, but his father left him ten and a half million dollars—his share of the proceeds from the sales of rifles and machine guns."

"That could have given him a sense of guilt," said Florence.

"Belasco never felt a twinge of guilt in his life."

"Which only serves to verify his mental aberration," Barrett said.

"His mind may have been aberrant, but it was brilliant, too," Fischer went on. "He could master any subject he chose to study. He spoke and read a dozen languages. He was versed in natural and metaphysical philosophy. He'd studied all the religions, cabalist and Rosicrucian doctrines, ancient mysteries. His mind was a storehouse of information, a powerhouse of energy." He paused. *"A charnelhouse of fancies."*

"Did he ever love a single person in his life?" asked Florence.

"He didn't believe in love," Fischer answered. "He believed in will. 'That rare *vis viva* of the self, that magnetism, that most secret and prevailing delectation of the mind: influence.' Unquote. Emeric Belasco, 1913."

"What did he mean by 'influence'?" asked Barrett.

"The power of the mind to dominate," Fischer said. "The control of one human being by another. He obviously had the kind of hypnotic personality men like Cagliostro and Rasputin had. Quote: 'No one ever went too close to him, lest his terrible presence overpower and engulf them.' His second wife, again."

"Did Belasco have any children?" Florence asked.

"A son, they say. No one's really sure, though."

"You said the house was built in 1919," Barrett said. "Did the corruption start immediately?"

"No, it was innocent at first. *Haut monde* dinner parties. Lavish dances in the ballroom. Soirées. People traveling from all over the country and world to spend a weekend here. Belasco was a perfect host—sophisticated, charming.

"Then—" He raised his right hand, thumb and index finger almost touching. "In 1920: *'un peu,'* as he referred to it. A *soupçon* of debasement. The introduction, bit by bit, of open sensuality—first in talk, then in action. Gossip. Court intrigues. Aristocratic machinations. Flowing wine and bedroom-hopping. All of it induced by Belasco and his *influences*.

"What he did, in this phase, was create a parallel to eighteenth-century European high society. It would take too long to describe in detail how he did it. It was subtle, though, engineered with great finesse."

"I presume that the result of this was primarily sexual license," Barrett said.

Fischer nodded. "Belasco formed a club he called Les Aphrodites. Every night—later, two and three times a day—they'd hold a meeting; what Belasco called his Sinposium. Having all partaken of drugs and aphrodisiacs, they'd sit around that table in the great hall talking about sex until everyone was what Belasco referred to as 'lubricous.' Then an orgy would commence.

"Still, it wasn't exclusively sex. The principle of excess was applied to every phase of life here. Dining became gluttony, drinking turned to drunkenness. Drug addiction mounted. And, as the physical spectrum of his guests was perverted, so, too, was their mental."

"How?" asked Barrett.

"Visualize twenty to thirty people set loose upon each other mentally—encouraged to do whatever they wanted to one another; no limits set but those of imagination. As their minds began to open up—or close in, if you like—so did every aspect of their lives together. People stayed here months, then years. The house became their way of life. A way of life that grew a little more insane each day. Isolated from the contrast of normal society, the society in this house became the norm. Total self-indulgence became the norm. Debauchery became the norm. Brutality and carnage soon became the norm."

"How could all this . . . bacchanalia take place without repercussions?" Barrett asked. "Surely someone must have—what's the expression?—blown the whistle on Belasco?"

"The house is isolated; really isolated. There were no outside telephones. But, just as important, no one dared to implicate Belasco; they were too afraid of him. Once in a while, private detectives might do a little probing. They never found a thing. Everyone was on their best behavior while the investigation was taking place. There was never any evidence. Or, if there was, Belasco bought it."

"And, during all this time, people kept coming to the house?" Barrett asked, incredulous.

"In droves," said Fischer. "After a while, Belasco got so tired of having only eager sinners in his house, he started to travel around the world enlisting young, creative people for a visit to his 'artistic retreat'—to write or compose, paint or meditate. Once he got them here, of course—" He gestured. "*Influences.*"

"The most vile of evils," Florence said, "corruption of the innocent." She looked at Fischer almost pleadingly. "Had the man no trace of decency at all?"

"None," said Fischer. "One of his favorite hobbies was destroying women. Being so tall and imposing, so magnetic, he could make them fall in love with him at will. Then, when they were in the deepest throes of adoration, he'd dump them. He did it to his own sister—the same one he'd assaulted. She was his mistress for a year. After he rejected her, she became a drug addict and the leading lady of his Little Theater Company. She died here of an overdose of heroin in 1923."

"Did Belasco take drugs?" asked Barrett.

"In the beginning. Later on, he started to withdraw from all involvement with his guests. He had it in mind to make a study of evil, and he decided that he couldn't do that if he was an active participant. So he began to remove himself, concentrating his energies on the mass corruption of his people.

"About 1926, he started his final thrust. He increased his efforts at encouraging guests to conceive of every cruelty, perversion, and horror they could. He conducted contests to see who could come up with the ghastliest ideas. He started what he termed 'Days of Defilement,' twenty-four-hour periods of frenzied, nonstop depravities. He attempted a literal enactment of de Sade's *120 Days of Sodom*. He began to import monstrosities from all over the world to mingle with his guests—hunchbacks, dwarfs, hermaphrodites, grotesques of every sort."

Florence closed her eyes and bowed her head, pressing tightly clasped hands against her forehead.

"About that time," continued Fischer, "everything began to go. There were no servants to maintain the house; they were indistinguishable from the guests by then. Laundry service failed, and everyone was forced to wash their own clothes—which they refused to do, of course. There being no cooks, everyone had to prepare their own meals with whatever was at hand—which was less and less, because the pick-ups of food and liquor had dwindled so much, with no acting servants.

"An influenza epidemic hit the house in 1927. Believing the reports of several of his doctor guests that the Matawaskie Valley fog was injurious to health, Belasco had the windows sealed. About that time, the main generator, no longer being maintained, started functioning erratically, and everyone was forced to use candles most of the time. The furnace went out in the winter of 1928, and no one bothered to relight it. The house became as cold as a refrigerator. Pneumonia killed off thirteen guests.

"None of the others cared. By then they were so far gone

that all they were concerned with was their 'daily diet of debaucheries,' as Belasco put it. They were at the bottom by 1928, delving into mutilation, murder, necrophilia, cannibalism."

The three sat motionless and silent, Florence with her head inclined, Barrett and Edith staring at Fischer as he kept on speaking, quietly, virtually without expression, as though he were recounting something very ordinary.

"In June of 1929, Belasco held a version of the Roman circus in his theater," he said. "The highlight was the eating of a virgin by a starving leopard. In July of the same year, a group of drug-addicted doctors started to experiment on animals and humans, testing pain thresholds, exchanging organs, creating monstrosities.

"By then everyone but Belasco was at an animal level, rarely bathing, wearing torn, soiled clothes, eating and drinking anything they could get their hands on, killing each other for food or water, liquor, drugs, sex, blood, even for the taste of human flesh, which many of them had acquired by then.

"And, every day, Belasco walked among them, cold, withdrawn, unmoved. Belasco, a latter-day Satan observing his rabble. Always dressed in black. A giant, terrifying figure, looking at the hell incarnate he'd created."

"How did it end?" asked Barrett.

"If it had ended, would we be here?"

"It will end now," Florence said.

Barrett persisted. "What happened to Belasco?"

"No one knows," said Fischer. "When relatives of some of his guests had the house broken into in November of 1929, everyone inside was dead—twenty-seven of them.

"Belasco was not among them."

8:46 P.M.

Florence came walking back across the great hall. For the past ten minutes, she'd been sitting in a corner, "preparing herself," she'd told them. Now she was ready. "As ready as one can be in this kind of climate. Excessive dampness is always a handicap." She smiled. "Shall we take our places?"

The four sat at the huge round table, Fischer across from Florence, Barrett several chairs away from her, Edith next to him.

"It's occurred to me," Florence said as she settled herself, "that the evil in this house is so intensely concentrated that it might be a constant lure to earthbound spirits everywhere. In other words, the house might be acting like a giant magnet for degraded souls. This could explain its complicated texture."

What is one supposed to say to that? Barrett thought. He glanced at Edith, forced to repress a smile at her expression as she gazed at Florence. "You're certain this equipment isn't going to bother you?" he said.

"Not at all. As a matter of fact, it might not be amiss for you to switch on your tape recorder when Red Cloud starts to speak. He might say something valuable."

Barrett nodded noncommittally.

"It works on battery as well, doesn't it?"

Barrett nodded again.

"Good." Florence smiled. "The rest of the instruments, of course, are of no use to me." She looked at Edith. "Your husband has explained to you, I'm sure, that I'm not a physical medium. Mine is solely a mental contact with those in spirit. I admit them only in the form of thought." She glanced around. "Will you put out your candles now?"

Edith tensed as Lionel wet two fingers and crimped out

the wick of his candle, Fischer blew his out. Only hers remained, a tiny, pulsing aura of light in the vastness of the hall; the fire had gone out an hour earlier. Edith was unable to make herself extinguish it. Barrett reached out and did it for her.

Blackness seemed to crash across her like a tidal wave, taking her breath. She groped for Lionel's hand, the moment reminding her of a visit she had made once to the Carlsbad Caverns. In one of the caverns, the guide had turned out the lights, and the darkness had been so intense that she had felt it pressing at her eyes.

"O Spirit of Love and Tenderness," Florence began. "We gather here tonight to discover a more perfect understanding of the laws which govern our being."

Barrett felt how cold Edith's hand was and smiled in sympathy. He knew what she was going through; he'd been through the same thing dozens of times in the early days of his work. True, she'd been to séances with him before, but never in a place with such an awesome size and history.

"Give us, O Divine Teacher, avenues of communication with those beyond, particularly those who walk this house in restless torment."

Fischer pulled in a long, erratic breath. He recalled his first sitting here in 1940—in this hall, at this very table. Objects had been hurled about; Dr. Graham had been knocked unconscious by one of them. A greenish, glowing mist had filled the air. Fischer's throat felt parched. I shouldn't be sitting in on this, he thought.

"May the work of bridging the chasm of death be, by us, so faithfully accomplished that pain may be transformed into joy, sorrow into peace. All this we ask in the name of our infinite Father. Amen."

It was silent for a while. Then Edith's legs retracted as Florence began to sing in a soft, melodious voice: " 'The world hath felt a quickening breath from heaven's eternal shore. And souls, triumphant over death, return to earth once more.' " Something about the sound of her muted singing in the darkness made Edith's flesh crawl.

When the hymn had ended. Florence started to breathe in deeply, making passes in front of her face. After several minutes, she began to rub both hands over her arms and shoulders, down across her breasts, and over her stomach and thighs. The strokings were almost sensual as she massaged herself, lips parted, eyes half-closed, an expression of torpid abandonment on her face. Her breathing became slower and louder. Soon it was a hoarsely sibilant, wheezing sound. By then, her hands lay flaccid in her lap, her arms and legs twitching slightly. Bit by bit, her head leaned back until it touched the chair. She drew in an extended, quavering breath, then was still.

The great hall was without a sound. Barrett stared at the place where Florence sat, though nothing was visible to him. Edith had closed her eyes, preferring an individual darkness to that of the room. Fischer sat tensely in his chair, waiting.

Florence's chair made a creaking noise. "Me Red Cloud," she said in a sonorous voice. Her face, in the darkness, was stone-like, her expression imperious. "Me Red Cloud," she repeated.

Barrett sighed. "Good evening."

Florence grunted, nodding. "Me come from afar. Bring greeting to you from realm of Eternal Peace. Red Cloud happy see you. Always happy see earthlings gather in circle of belief. We with you always, watch and ward. Death not end of road. Death but door to world without end. This we know."

"Could you—?" Barrett started.

"Earthling souls in prison," Florence interrupted. "Bound in dungeons of flesh."

"Yes," said Barrett. "Could you—?"

"Death the pardon, the release. Leave behind what poet call 'muddy vesture of decay.' Find freedom—light—eternal joy."

"Yes, but do you think—?"

Edith bit her lower lip to keep from laughing as Florence interrupted again. "Tanner woman say put on machine, get voice on ribbon. Not know what she mean. You do that?"

Barrett grunted. "Very well." Reaching across the table, he felt around for the tape recorder, switched it on, and pushed the microphone toward Florence. "Now, if you'd—"

"Red Cloud Tanner woman guide. Guide second medium on this side. Talk with Tanner woman. Bring other spirits to her."

Florence looked around abruptly, teeth bared, eyebrows pressing down, a growl of disapproval rumbling in her throat "Bad house. Place of sickness. Evil here. Bad medicine." She shook her head and growled again. "*Bad* medicine."

She twisted around the other way, grunting in surprise, as though someone had come up behind her and attracted her attention. "Man here. Ugly man. Like caveman. Long hair. Dirt on face. Scratches, sores. Yellow teeth. Man bent over, twisted. No clothes. Like animal. Breathing hard. In pain. Very sick. Say: 'Give me peace. Let free.' "

Edith clutched at Lionel's hand, afraid to open her eyes lest she see the figure Florence had described.

Florence shook her head, then slowly raised her arm and pointed toward the entry hall. "Go. Leave house." She stared into the darkness, turned back with a grunt. "No good. Here too long. Not listen. Not understand." She tapped her head with an index finger. "Too much sick inside."

She made a sound as though something interesting had been imparted to her. "Limits," she said. "Nations. Terms. Not know what that mean. Extremes and limits. Terminations and extremities." She shook her head. "Not know."

She jerked around as though someone had grabbed her rudely by the shoulder. "No. Go away." She grunted. "Young man here. Say must talk—must talk." She made a grumbling noise and then was still.

All three twitched as Florence cried out, "I don't know you people!" She looked around the table, her expression one of rabid agitation. "Why are you here? It does no good. Nothing ever changes. *Nothing!* Get out of here, or I'll hurt you! I can't help myself! God damn you filthy sons of bitches!"

Edith pressed back hard against her chair. The voice was totally unlike Florence's—hysterical, unbalanced, threatening. "Can't you see I'm helpless! I don't want to hurt you, but I *must!*" Florence's head shifted forward, eyes hooding, lips drawn back from clenching teeth. "I warn you," she told them in a guttural voice. "*Get out of this house before I kill you all.*"

Edith cried out as a series of loud, staccato rappings sounded on the table. "What's that?" she asked. Her voice was lost beneath the chain of savage blows. It sounded as though a berserk man were pounding a hammer on the tabletop as hard and fast as he could. Barrett started to reach for his instruments, then remembered that there was no electricity. Damn! he thought.

Abruptly, the rappings ceased. Edith looked toward Florence as the medium started making groaning noises. She could still hear the blows ringing in her ears. Her body felt numb, as though the vibrations had deadened her flesh.

She started as Lionel pulled his hand free. She heard a rustling of his clothes, then started again as a small red light appeared where he was sitting. He had taken the pencil flashlight from his pocket and was pointing it at Florence. In the dim illumination, Edith could see the medium's head lolling back against the chair, eyes shut, mouth hanging open.

She stiffened, suddenly aware of a mounting coldness underneath the table. Shuddering, she crossed her arms. Fischer clenched his teeth together, willing himself not to jump from his chair.

Barrett tugged at the microphone wire, the scraping of the microphone across the table making Edith shudder. Picking it up, he noted quickly, "Temperature decline. Strictly tactile. Instrument reading impossible. Physical phenomena commenced with series of severe percussions." He pointed the flashlight at Florence again. "Miss Tanner reacting erratically. Trance state retained, but variable. Possible confusion at onset of unexpected physical phenomena. Absence of cabinet a probable factor. Handing subject tube of uranium-salt solution."

Edith watched the red light flicking around the tabletop. She saw Lionel's dark hand pick up the tube. The coldness beneath the table was making her legs and ankles ache. Still, she felt a little better, the unruffled tone of Lionel's voice having had a quieting effect on her. She watched as he pressed the tube into Florence's hands.

Florence sat up quickly, opening her eyes.

Barrett frowned in disappointment. "Subject out of trance." He switched off the tape recorder and struck a match. Florence averted her face while he relit the candles.

Fischer stood and moved around the table to a pitcher of water. As he poured some into a glass, the lip of the pitcher rattled on the glass edge. Barrett glanced at him. Fischer handed the glass to Florence, who drank its contents in a single swallow. "There." She smiled at Fischer. "Thank you." She set the glass down, shivering. "What happened?"

When Barrett told her, she stared at him in confusion. "I don't understand. I'm not a physical medium."

"You were just now. The embryo of one, at any rate."

Florence looked disturbed. "That doesn't make sense. Why should I suddenly become a physical medium after all these years?"

"I have no idea."

Florence gazed at him. Finally she nodded with reluctance. "Yes; this house." She looked around. At last she sighed. "God's will, not mine," she said. "If my part in the cleansing is to alter my mediumship, so be it. All that matters is the end." She didn't look at Fischer as she spoke. The weight's been lifted from his shoulders to be put on mine, she thought.

"We can work together now if you're amenable," said Barrett.

"Yes, of course."

"I'll telephone Deutsch's man and have him see to the construction of a cabinet tomorrow morning." Barrett wasn't convinced that what had happened indicated a physical mediumship in Florence extensive enough for his needs. There was certainly no immediate harm in seeing if she had the capability, however. If she did it would be more expeditious to work with her than be forced to wait for Deutsch's permission to bring up one of his own people.

Seeing her expression still reflect uneasy doubt, he asked, "You really want this?"

"*Yes, yes.*" Her smile was disconcerted. "It's just that . . . well, it's difficult for me to understand. All these years, a mental medium." She shook her head. "Now this." She made a sound of wry amusement. "The Lord moves in mysterious ways indeed."

"So does this house," said Fischer.

Florence looked at him in surprise. "You think the house had something to do with me—?"

"Just watch your step," he cut her off. "The Lord may not have too much influence in Hell House."

9:49 P.M.

Science is more than a body of facts. It is, first and foremost, a method of investigation, and there is no acceptable reason why parapsychological phenomena should not be investigated by this method, for, as much as physics and chemistry, parapsychology is a science of the natural.

This, then, is the intellectual barrier through which man must inevitably break. No longer can parapsychology be classified as a philosophical concept. It is a biological reality, and science cannot permanently avoid this fact. Already it has wasted too much time skirting the borders of this irrefutable realm. Now it must enter, to study and learn. Morselli expressed it thus: "The time has come to break with this exaggerated, negative attitude, this constant casting of the shadow of doubt with its smile of sarcasm."

It is a sorry condemnation of our times that these words were published sixty years ago—because the negative attitude of which Morselli wrote still persists. Indeed—

"Lionel?"

Barrett looked up from his manuscript.

"Can I help?"

"No, I'll be finished in a few moments." He looked at her propped against a bank of pillows. She was wearing blue ski pajamas, and with her short hair and slight figure she looked, somehow, like a child. Barrett smiled at her. "Oh, it can wait," he said, deciding with the words.

He put the manuscript back in its box, looking briefly at the title page: "Borders of the Human Faculty, by Lionel Barrett, B.S., M.A., Ph.D." The sight of it gratified him. Really, everything was going wonderfully. The chance to prove his theory, ample funds for retirement, and the book almost completed. Perhaps he'd add an epilogue about the week here; maybe even do a thin, appending volume. Smiling, he extinguished the candle on the octagonal table, stood, and crossed the room. He had a momentary vision of himself as some baronial lord crossing a palace chamber to converse with his lady. The vision amused him, and he chuckled.

"What?" she asked.

He told her, and she smiled. "It is a fantastic house, isn't it? A museum of treasures. If it weren't haunted—" Lionel's expression made her stop.

Barrett sat down on her bed and put aside his cane. "Were you frightened before?" he asked. "You were very quiet after the sitting."

"It was a bit unnerving. Especially the coldness; I can never get used to that."

"You know what it is," he said. "The medium's system drawing heat from the air to convert it into energy."

"What about those things she said?"

Barrett shrugged. "Impossible to analyze. It might take years to trace down each remark and determine its source. We only have a week. The physical effects are where the answer lies."

He broke off as she looked across his shoulder with a gasp. Twisting around, he saw that the rocking chair had begun to move.

"What is it?" Edith whispered.

Barrett stood and limped across the room. He stood beside the chair and watched it rocking back and forth. "It's likely the breeze," he told her.

"It moves as though someone were sitting in it." Edith had unconsciously pressed back against the pillows.

"No one's sitting in it, that I guarantee you," Barrett said. "Rocking chairs are easy to set in motion. That's why the phenomenon is so frequent in haunted houses. The least application of pressure suffices."

"But—"

"—what applies the pressure?" Barrett finished for her. "Residual energy." Edith tensed as he reached out and stopped the chair. "See?" His hand had withdrawn, and the chair remained motionless. "It's dissipated now." He pushed the chair. It rocked a few times, then was still again. "All gone," he said.

He returned to her bed and sat beside her. "I'm not very good parapsychologist material, I'm afraid," she said.

Barrett smiled and patted her hand.

"Why does this residual energy suddenly make a chair rock?" she asked.

"No specific reason I've been able to discover. Although our presence in the room undoubtedly has something to do with it. It's a kind of random mechanics which follows the line of least resistance—sounds and movements which occurred most often in the past, establishing a pattern of dynamics: breezes, door slams, rappings, footsteps, rocking chairs."

She nodded, then touched the tip of his nose. "You have to sleep," she said.

Barrett kissed her on the cheek, then stood and moved to the other bed. "Shall I leave the candle on?" he asked.

"Would you mind?"

"No. We'll use a night light while we're here. No harm in it."

They settled down, and Edith looked up at the shell design carved in the walnut ceiling panels. "Lionel?" she asked.

"Yes?"

"Are you sure there are no such things as ghosts?"

Barrett chuckled. "Nary a one."

10:21 P.M.

The hot stream of water sprayed off Florence's upper chest and rivuleted down between her breasts. She stood in the shower stall, head back, eyes shut, feeling the ribbons of water lace across her stomach and down her thighs and legs.

She was thinking about the tape recording of her sitting. Only one thing in it seemed of import: that crazed and trembling voice which had told them to get out of the house or be killed. There was something there. It was amorphous, just beginning, but most compelling. *Can't you see I'm helpless?* she heard the pitiful voice in her mind. *I don't want to hurt you, but I must!*

It could be part of the answer.

She twisted off the faucets and, pushing open the shower door, stepped out onto the bathmat. Hissing at the cold, she grabbed a bath towel from its rack and rubbed herself briskly. Dry, she pulled the heavy flannel gown across her head and thrust her arms into its full-length sleeves. She brushed her teeth, then moved across the bedroom with the candle, set it down, and got into the bed closest to the bathroom door. She thrashed her legs to warm the sheets, then stretched out, pulling the bedclothes to her chin. After a while, her shivering stopped. She wet two fingers and, reaching out, crimped the candle flame between them.

The house was massively silent. I wonder what Ben is doing, she thought. She clucked in distress. Poor, deluded man. She brushed aside the thought. That was for tomorrow. Now she had to think about her part in the project. That voice. Whose had it been? Beneath its threatening had been such despair, such harrowed anguish.

Florence turned her head. The door to the corridor had just been opened. She looked across the darkness of the room. The door closed quietly.

Footsteps started toward her.

"Yes?" she said.

The footsteps kept approaching, muffled on the rug. Florence started reaching for the candle, then withdrew her hand, knowing it was not one of the other three. "All right," she murmured.

The footsteps halted. Florence listened carefully. There was a sound of breathing at the foot of the bed. "Who's there?" she asked.

Only the sound of breathing. Florence peered into the darkness, but it was impenetrable. She closed her eyes. Her tone was even, undismayed. "Who is it, please?"

The breathing continued.

"You wish to speak to me?"

Breathing.

"Are you the one who warned us to get out?"

The sound of breathing quickened. "*Yes,*" she said. "It *is* you, isn't it?"

The breathing grew more labored. It was that of a young man. She could almost visualize him standing at the foot of the bed, his posture tense, his face tormented.

"You must speak or give me some sign," she said. She waited. There was no reply. "I wait for you with God's love. Let me help you find the peace I know you hunger for."

Was that a sob? She tightened. "Yes, I hear, I understand. Tell me who you are, and I can help you."

Suddenly the room was still. Florence cupped her hands behind her ears and listened intently.

The sound of breathing had stopped.

With a sigh of disappointment, she reached to the left until her fingers found the matchbook on the chest of drawers. Striking one, she lit her candle and looked around. There was still something in the room.

"Shall I put out the candle?" she asked.

Silence.

"Very well." She smiled. "You know where I am. Anytime you want—"

She broke off, gasping, as the bedspread leaped into the air and sailed across the foot of the bed, then stopped and settled downward flutteringly.

A figure stood beneath it.

Florence regained her breath. "Yes, I can see you now," she said. She estimated height. "How tall you are." She shivered as Fischer's words flashed across her mind. *"The Roaring Giant," he was called.* She stared at the figure. She could see its broad chest rise and fall, as though with breath.

"No," she said abruptly. It was not Belasco. She began to rise, easing the bedclothes from her body, gazing at the figure. She let her legs slide off the mattress, stood. The head of the figure turned, as though to watch her while she drifted toward it. "You're not Belasco, are you? Such pain would not be in Belasco. And I feel your anguish. Tell me who—"

The bedspread suddenly collapsed. Florence stared at it awhile, then leaned over to pick it up.

She reared with a gasp as a hand caressed her buttocks. Angrily, she looked around the room. There was a chuckling—low-pitched, sly. Florence drew in a shaking breath. "You've proved your sex to me, at any rate," she said. The chuckling deepened. Florence shook her head in pity. "If you're all that clever, why are you a prisoner in this house?"

The chuckling stopped, and all three blankets flew from the bed as though someone were pulling them away in rage. The sheets went next, the pillows, then the mattress cover. In seven seconds, all the bedclothes lay in scattered heaps across the rug, the mattress shifted to the side.

Florence waited. When nothing more occurred, she spoke. "Feel better now?"

Smiling to herself, she started gathering up the bedclothes.

Something tried to pull a blanket from her hands. She jerked it back. "That's enough! I'm not amused!" She turned to the bed. "Go away, and don't come back until you're ready to behave."

As she started to remake the bed, the corridor door was opened. She didn't even look around to watch it shut.

DECEMBER 22, 1970

7:01 A.M.

I'm afraid not." Barrett drew his foot from the water. "Maybe it'll be warm enough by tomorrow morning." He dried the foot and pulled his slipper on again. Pushing to his feet, he looked at Edith with a rueful smile. "I could have let you sleep."

"That's all right."

Barrett looked around. "I wonder if the steam room works."

Edith pulled the heavy metal door and held it open for him. Barrett limped inside and turned to watch her follow. The door thumped shut. Barrett raised his candle and peered around, then leaned forward, squinting.

"Ah." Setting down his cane and candle, he eased himself into a kneeling position. He reached underneath and tried to turn the tap wheel of the steam outlet.

Edith sat across from him and leaned against the tile wall, straightening as the chill of it pierced her robe. She stared at Lionel sleepily. The flickering of their candles and his bobbing shadow on the walls and ceiling seemed to pulse against her eyes. She closed them momentarily, then opened them again.

She found herself beginning to appraise the shadow hovering on the ceiling over Lionel. It seemed, somehow, to be expanding. How could that be? There was no movement of air in the room; the candle flames burned straight up now. Only Barrett's shifting as he labored with the tap wheel was reflected on the walls and ceiling.

She blinked and shook her head. She could swear the edges of the shadow were extending like a spreading inkblot. She shifted on the bench. The room was still except for Lionel's breathing. Let's go, she thought. She tried to speak the words aloud, but something kept her from it.

She stared at the shadow. It hadn't gone across that corner before, had it? Let's get out of here, she thought. It's probably nothing, but let's go.

She felt her body going rigid. She was sure she'd seen a patch of lighted wall go black. "Lionel?" The sound she made was barely audible, a feeble stirring in her throat. She swallowed hard. "Lionel?"

Her voice came so abruptly that Barrett jerked around with a gasp. "What *is* it?"

Edith blinked. The shadow on the ceiling looked normal now.

"Edith?"

She filled her lungs with air. "Let's go?"

"Nervous?"

"Yes, I'm . . . seeing things." Her smile was wan. She didn't want to tell him. Still, she had to. If it did mean something, he would want to know. "I thought I saw your shadow start to grow." He stood and picked up his cane and candle holder, turning back to join her. "It's possible," he said, "but following your sleepless night in this particular house, I'm more inclined to think it was imagination."

They left the steam room and started back along the pool

edge. It *was* imagination, Edith thought. She repressed a smile Who ever heard of a ghost in a steam room?

7:33 A.M.

Florence knocked softly on the door to Fischer's room. When there was no answer, she knocked again. "Ben?" she called.

He was sitting up in bed, eyes closed, head leaning back against the wall. On the table to his right, his candle was almost guttered. Florence drifted across the room, protecting the flame of her candle with an upraised hand. Poor man, she thought, stopping by the bed. His face was drawn and pale. She wondered when he'd gotten to sleep. Benjamin Franklin Fischer: the greatest American physical medium of the century. His sittings in Professor Galbreath's house at Marks College had been the most incredible display of power since the heyday of Home and Palladino. She shook her head with pity. Now he was emotionally crippled, a latter-day Samson, self-shorn of might.

She returned to the corridor and shut the door as quietly as possible. She looked toward the door to Belasco's room. She and Fischer had gone there yesterday afternoon, but its atmosphere had been curiously flat, not at all what she'd expected.

She crossed the corridor and entered it again. It was the only duplex apartment in the house, its sitting room and bath located on the lower level, its bedroom on a balcony reached by a curved stairway. Florence moved to it and ascended the steps.

The bed had been constructed in seventeenth-century French style, its intricately carved columns as thick as telephone poles, the initials "E. B." carved in the center of the headboard. Sitting down on it, Florence closed her eyes and opened herself to impressions, wanting to verify that it had not been Belasco in her room the night before. She released her mind as much as possible without going into a trance.

A tumble of images began to cross her consciousness. The room at night, lamps burning. Someone lying on the bed. A figure chuckling. Lucid, staring eyes. A calendar for 1921. A man in black. A smell of pungent incense in her nostrils. A man and woman on the bed. A painting. A cursing voice. A wine bottle hurled against the wall. A sobbing woman flung across the balcony rail. Blood oozing on the teakwood floor. A photograph. A crib. New York. A calendar for 1903. A pregnant woman.

The birth of a child; a boy.

Florence opened her eyes. "Yes." She nodded. *"Yes."*

She went down the stairs and left the room. A minute later, she was entering the dining hall, where Barrett and his wife were breakfasting.

"Ah, good, you're up," Barrett said. "Breakfast just arrived."

Florence sat at the table and served herself a small portion of scrambled eggs, a piece of toast; she wouldn't be sitting until later in the day, since they had to wait for a cabinet to be built. She exchanged a few remarks with Mrs. Barrett, answered Barrett's questions by saying that she felt it would be better to let Fischer sleep than wake him up, then, finally, said, "I think I have a partial answer to the haunting of the house."

"Oh?" Barrett looked at her with interest that was clearly more polite than genuine.

"That voice warning us. That pounding on the table. The personality that approached me in my room last night. A young man."

"Who?" asked Barrett.

"Belasco's son."

They looked at her in silence.

"You recall that Mr. Fischer mentioned him."

"But didn't he say that no one was sure whether Belasco had a son or not?" Barrett said.

Florence nodded. "But he did. He's here now, suffering, tormented. He must have gone into spirit at an early age—just past twenty, I feel. He's very young and very frightened—and, because he's frightened, very angry, very hostile. I believe if we can convince him to go on, a portion of the haunting force will be eliminated."

Barrett nodded. Don't believe a word of it, he thought. "That's very interesting."

Florence thought, I know he doesn't believe me, but it's better that I tell him what I think.

She was about to change the subject when there was a loud knocking on the front door. Edith, who was drinking coffee, spilled some as her hand jerked. Barrett smiled at her. "Our generator, I imagine, And a carpenter, I hope."

Standing, he picked up his candle holder and cane and started toward the great hall. He stopped to look back at Edith. "Well, I guess it's safe to leave you long enough to answer the door," he said after a few moments.

He crossed the great hall and moved into the entry hall. Opening the front door, he saw Deutsch's representative standing on the porch, coat collar raised, an umbrella in his hand. To Barrett's surprise, he saw that it was raining.

"I've got your generator and your carpenter," the man said.

Barrett nodded. "What about the cat?"

"That too."

Barrett smiled with satisfaction. Now he could move.

1:17 P.M.

The lights went on, and, in unison, all four uttered sounds of pleasure. "I'll be damned," said Fischer. They exchanged spontaneous smiles. "I never thought electric lights could look so good," Edith said.

Bathed with light, the great hall was another place entirely. Now its size seemed regal rather than ominous. No longer black with looming shadows, it was a massive chamber in some art museum, and not a haunted cavern. Edith looked at Fischer. He was obviously pleased, his posture different, apprehension cleansed from his eyes. She looked at Florence, who was sitting with the cat on her lap. The lights on, she thought. That cat resting peacefully. She smiled. It didn't seem like a haunted house at all now.

She gasped as the lights flickered, went out, then on again. Immediately, they began to dim. "Oh, no," she murmured.

"Easy," Barrett said. "They'll get it."

A minute later, the lights were bright and steady. When another minute passed without a change, Barrett smiled. "There, you see?"

Edith nodded. Her relief had ended, though. From relaxed assurance, she had fallen back to a nagging dread that, any second, they might once more be in darkness.

Florence looked at Fischer, caught his eye, and smiled at him. He did not return it. Idiots, he thought. Some bulbs go on, and they all think the danger's over.

1:58 P.M.

The cabinet had been constructed in the northeast corner of the great hall by the installation of an eight-foot-long round wooden bar between the walls. A pair of heavy green draperies was hanging from the bar on rings, forming a triangular enclosure seven feet high. Inside the enclosure was a straight-backed wooden armchair.

Barrett edged aside the draperies on each side until there was an opening in the middle large enough to accommodate a small wooden table he had asked Fischer to carry in. Pushing the table in front of the opening, he placed on top of it a tambourine, a small guitar, a tea bell, and a length of rope. He looked at the cabinet appraisingly for several moments, then turned to the others.

They watched as he rummaged through the contents of the wooden chest from which he'd gotten the rope, tea bell, guitar, and tambourine. He lifted out a pair of black tights and a black long-sleeved smock and held them out to Florence. "I believe they'll fit," he said.

Florence stared at him.

"You don't object, do you?"

"Well—"

"You know it's standard procedure."

"Yes, but"—Florence hesitated, then went on—"as a precaution against fraud."

"Primarily."

Florence's smile was awkward. "Surely you don't think I'm capable of perpetrating fraud with a form of mediumship I didn't even know I had before last night."

"I'm not implying that, Miss Tanner. It's simply that I must maintain a standard. If I don't, the results of the sitting are scientifically unacceptable."

Finally she sighed. "Very well." She took the tights and smock, looked around, then went inside the cabinet to change, pulling the draperies together. Barrett turned to Edith. "Would you examine her, my dear?" he asked. Bending over the box, he lifted out a spool of black thread with a needle pushed through the thread, and handed it to her.

Edith moved toward the cabinet, a discomfited look on her face. She'd always hated doing this, although she'd never indicated it to Lionel. Stopping by the cabinet, she cleared her throat. "May I come in?"

There was a momentary silence before Florence answered. "Yes." Edith pushed between the drapery edges, stepping into the cabinet.

Florence had removed her skirt and sweater and was leaning over, stepping from her half-slip. Straightening, she draped the slip across the chair back. As she reached back to unhook her white brassiere, Edith stepped aside. "I'm sorry," she murmured; "I know it's—"

"Don't be embarrassed," Florence said. "Your husband is quite right. It's standard procedure."

Edith nodded, keeping her eyes on Florence's face as the medium hung her brassiere across the chair back. Her gaze dropped as Florence bent forward to remove her underpants. She was startled by the fullness of the medium's breasts, and looked up quickly. Florence stood erect. "All right," she said. Edith saw a stippling of gooseflesh on the medium's arms.

"We'll make it quick so you can dress," she said. "Your mouth?"

Florence opened her mouth, and Edith looked inside. She felt ridiculous. "Well, unless you have a hollow tooth or something—"

Florence closed her mouth and smiled. "It's just a technicality. Your husband knows I'm not concealing anything."

Edith nodded. "Your hair?"

Florence reached up both hands to unpin her hair. The movement made her breasts hitch, so their hardened nipples brushed against Edith's sweater. Edith twitched back, watching the tresses of thick red hair as they rippled downward, spilling over Florence's creamy shoulders. She'd never examined a woman so beautiful before.

"All right," Florence said.

Edith started fingering through the medium's hair. It was warm and silky to the touch. The fragrance of Florence's perfume drifted over her. Balenciaga, she thought. She drew in a labored breath. She could feel the pressing weight of Florence's breasts against her own. She wanted to step back but couldn't do it. She looked into the medium's green eyes, looked down quickly. Turning Florence's head, she looked into her ears. I will not look up her nose, she thought. She drew her hands back awkwardly. "Armpits?" she said.

Florence raised her arms and caused her breasts to jut again. Edith edged away from her and glanced down at her shaved armpits. She nodded once, and Florence lowered her arms. Edith felt her heartbeat thudding. The inside of the cabinet seemed very close. She looked at Florence unhappily. It seemed as if the two of them were stopped in time. Then she noted Florence glancing down, and lowered her gaze. She started at the sight of Florence's hands cupped beneath her breasts, holding them up. This is ridiculous, she thought. She nodded once, and Florence took her hands away. That's enough, Edith decided. I'll just say I did the rest. Obviously she has no intention of committing fraud.

She watched as the medium sat in the chair, hissing at its coldness. She looked up at Edith. I'll just say I did the rest, Edith thought.

Leaning back, Florence spread her legs apart.

Edith stared down at the medium's body: the heavy, ovate loll of her breasts, the swell of her stomach, the milk-white fullness of her thighs, the parted tuft of glossy copper hair between her legs. She couldn't take her eyes away. She felt a drawing hotness in her stomach.

She jerked her head around so quickly, looking up, that it sent a shooting pain through her neck.

"What *is* it?" Florence asked.

Edith swallowed, staring up across the wooden rod. There was only ceiling visible. She looked at Florence. *"What?"* the medium asked.

Edith shook her head. "I think we can assume—" She broke off, gesturing with a trembling hand, then turned and pushed from the cabinet.

She nodded to Lionel and crossed to the fireplace. She was sure she looked completely disconcerted, but hoped he wouldn't ask her why.

She stared into the fire. There was something in her hand. She looked at it; the spool of thread. Now she'd have to bring it back. She closed her eyes. Her neck still hurt from the wrenching she'd given it. Had she really seen a movement? There'd been nothing there. Still, she could have sworn that someone had been looking down into the cabinet.

At her.

2:19 P.M.

"Too tight?" asked Barrett.

"No, it's fine," Florence answered quietly.

Barrett finished tying the gloves at her wrists. As he did, Florence looked across his shoulder at Edith, who was sitting by the equipment table, the cat resting on her lap.

"Put your palms on the chair plates," Barrett instructed. The gloves he'd fastened to Florence had metal plates attached to their palms. As Florence rested them on the plates nailed to the chair arms, a pair of tiny bulbs on the equipment table lighted.

"So long as your hands remain in place, the bulbs will burn," Barrett told her. "Break contact—" He lifted her hands, and the bulbs went out.

Florence watched as Barrett unrolled the wire for the shoe plates. It disturbed her that Edith had looked up the way she had, when she'd been conscious of nothing.

"Will the foot plates activate the same two bulbs?" she asked.

"Two others."

"Isn't that a lot of light?"

"The combined wattage of all four bulbs is less than ten," he answered as he connected the shoe plates.

"I'd assumed we'd be in darkness."

"I can't accept darkness as a test condition." Barrett glanced up. "Would you try the foot plates?"

Florence set the plates attached to the soles of her shoes on the pair of plates Barrett had placed on the floor. On the equipment table, two more small bulbs went on. Barrett pushed up, wincing. "Don't be concerned," he said. "There'll be just enough illumination to observe by."

Florence nodded. Barrett's words failed to reassure her, though. Why do I feel so upset? she thought.

Fischer sat looking at the medium, her luxuriant figure outlined by the skin-tight costume. The sight did not arouse him. Those damned black outfits, he was thinking. How many of them had he worn? The memory of his early teen years was of endless sittings like this, his mother and himself riding from city to city on buses, from one test to another.

He lit another cigarette and watched as Barrett connected wire leads to Florence's arms and thighs, roped her to the chair, then picked up a folded piece of mosquito netting to which tiny bells had been sewn. Shaking it open, Barrett fastened it to the wooden rod so that the netting hung down in the space uncovered by the draperies. He pulled the small table several inches toward himself. Now the netting filled the space between the table and Florence, weights on its bottom holding it taut.

Barrett arranged the infrared lights so they'd shine across the surface of the table in front of the cabinet. Switching on the invisible lights, he moved his hand across the cabinet table. There was a clicking noise as the synchronized shutters of the two cameras were activated. Satisfied, Barrett checked the dynamometer and the globe of the telekinetoscope. He set out modeling clay and briefly stirred the melted paraffin wax in its pot on the small electric stove.

"We're ready now," he said.

As if it understood his words, the cat jumped suddenly from Edith's lap and loped across the room, heading for the entry hall. "Isn't that encouraging?" she said.

"Doesn't mean a thing," Barrett told her. Adjusting the red and yellow lights to minimum illumination, he moved to the wall switch and depressed it. The great hall darkened. Barrett took his place at the table, switching on the tape recorder. "December 22, 1970," he said into the microphone. "Sitters: Doctor and Mrs. Lionel Barrett, Mr. Benjamin Franklin Fischer. Medium: Miss Florence Tanner." Quickly he recited the details of arrangements and precautions, then sat back. "Proceed," he said.

The three sat quietly as Florence spoke an invocation and sang a hymn. After she was finished, she began to take in deep breaths. Soon, her hands and legs began to twitch as though she were being subjected to a series of galvanic shocks. Her head began to loll from side to side, her face becoming flushed. Low-pitched groans quavered in her throat. "No," she muttered. "No, not now." Gradually her noises faded, until, following a wheezing inhalation, she relapsed into silence.

"Two-thirty-eight p.m.; Miss Tanner in apparent trance," Barrett said into the microphone. "Pulse rate: eighty-five. Respiration: fifteen. Four electric contacts maintained." He checked the self-recording thermometer. "No change in temperature. Steady at seventy-three-point-two degrees. Dynamometer reading: eighteen hundred and seventy."

Twenty seconds later, he spoke again. "Dynamometer reading decreased to eighteen hundred and twenty-three. Temperature lowering; now at sixty-six-point-six degrees. Pulse rate: ninety-four-point-five and rising."

Edith drew in her legs, pressing them together as she felt coldness underneath the table. Fischer sat immobile. Even sheltered, he could feel the power gathering around him.

Barrett checked the thermometer again. "Temperature drop now twelve-point-three degrees. Dynamometer tension reduced to seventeen hundred and seventy-nine. Pressurometer negative. Electric contacts still maintained. Rate of breath increasing. Fifty . . . fifty-seven . . . sixty; rising steadily."

Edith stared at Florence. In the feeble light, all she could make out was the medium's face and hands. She seemed to be lying back against the chair, eyes shut. Edith swallowed. There was a cold knot in her stomach, which even Lionel's assured tones could not dispel.

She started as the camera shutters clicked. "Infrared rays broken, cameras activated," Barrett said. He looked at the dark blue instrument and tightened with excitement. "Evidence of EMR commencing."

Fischer looked at him. What was EMR? Clearly it was something vital to Barrett.

"Medium's respiration now two hundred and ten," Barrett was saying. "Dynamometer fourteen hundred and sixty. Temperature—"

He broke off at the sound of Edith's gasp. "Ozone present in the air," he said. Remarkable, he thought.

A minute passed, then two, the smell and coldness steadily increasing. Abruptly Edith closed her eyes. She waited, opened them again, and stared at Florence's hands. It had not been her imagination.

Threads of pale white, viscous matter were oozing from the medium's fingertips.

"Teleplasm forming," Barrett said. "Separate filaments uniting into single filmy strand. Will attempt matter penetration." He waited until the teleplasm strand was longer, then said to Florence, "Lift the bell." He paused before repeating the instruction.

The viscous tentacle began to rear up slowly like a serpent. Edith drew back in her chair, staring at it as it glided forward through the air, penetrated the net, and headed for the table.

"Teleplasmic stalk through net and moving toward the table." Barrett said. "Dynamometer reading: thirteen hundred and forty, dropping steadily. Electric contacts still maintained."

His voice became a blur of meaningless sounds to Fischer as he watched the moist, glistening tentacle inch its way across the table like a giant worm. A photograph flared briefly in his mind: him, fourteen, deep in trance, a similar extrusion from his mouth. He shivered as the filmy member twined itself around the handle of the tea bell. The tentacle began to tighten slowly. Suddenly it raised the bell, and Fischer's legs twitched spastically as the bell was shaken.

"Thank you. Put it down, please," Barrett said. Edith looked at him, astounded by his casual tone. Her gaze returned to the table as the gray extremity put down the bell, uncurling itself from the handle.

"Will try for specimen retrieval," Barrett said. Standing, he set a porcelain bowl on the cabinet table; at his approach, the tentacle jerked back as though in startled retreat. "Leave a section in the bowl, please," Barrett said, returning to his chair.

The gray appendage started swaying back and forth like the stalk of some undersea plant undulating in the current. "Leave a section in the bowl, please," Barrett repeated. He looked at the EMR recorder. The needle had passed the 300 mark. He felt a glow of satisfaction. Turning back to the cabinet, he repeated his instruction once more.

He was forced to speak the words seven times more before the glistening filament began to move. Slowly it started toward the bowl. Edith stared at it, repelled yet fascinated. It looked like an eyeless, gray-scaled serpent. As it reached the bowl, it slithered up across the rim. She flinched as it recoiled. Again it advanced on the bowl, with perceptible caution in its movement. Once again it snapped back soundlessly.

On the fifth advance, the tentacle remained in place, coiling with a languid, spiraling movement, until it filled the bowl. Thirty seconds later it withdrew. Edith started as it disappeared from sight.

Barrett rose and transferred the bowl to the equipment table. Edith glanced at the transparent liquid inside it. "Specimen retained in bowl," Barrett said, looking at it. "No odor. Colorless and slightly turbid."

"Lionel." Edith's urgent whisper made him look up.

Across the bottom half of Florence's face, a cloudy mass was starting to form.

"Teleplasmic matter being generated across lower part of medium's face," Barrett said. "Issuance from mouth and nostrils."

As he continued speaking into the microphone, describing the materialization and noting the flux of instrument readings, Edith stared at the formation in front of Florence's face. Now it resembled a torn, grimy handkerchief, the lower part of which hung down in shreds. The upper part was starting to rise. It spread with a swaying movement, first obscuring Florence's nose, then her eyes, finally her brow, so that her face was cloaked entirely, the formation like a ragged veil through which her pale features could be seen.

"Teleplasmic veil beginning to condense," said Barrett.

This really was remarkable, he thought. For a mental medium to produce such striking teleplasm at her first physical sitting was almost unprecedented. He watched with mounting interest.

The texture of the mistlike veil looked curdled now; in less than half a minute, Florence's face had vanished behind it. Soon, her head, then upper shoulders, were concealed beneath folds of what appeared to be a soggy, grayish shroud. The bottom of this dingy fabric was descending toward her lap, lengthening into a solid strip several inches wide. As it descended, it began to take on coloration.

"Separate filament extending downward," Barrett said. "Reddish hue impinging on the grayness. Stretching tissue seems to be inflamed. Getting brighter . . . brighter. The color of open flesh now."

Fischer felt numb. His chair seemed to be tilting backward as he watched the altering vesture on Florence's head and body. Sudden panic struck him. He was going under! He dug his nails into his palms until pain overshadowed all else.

The shroud on Florence was becoming more albescent every moment, starting to resemble linen dipped in white paint, transparent in some places, solid in others. Veillike strips and patches were beginning to appear at other spots on her body—her right arm and leg, her right breast, the center of her lap. It looked as though a solid bedsheet had been dipped into some iridescent liquid, then torn apart, the fragments thrown across her indiscriminately, the largest piece settling on her head and shoulders.

Edith pressed back hard against her chair, unaware that she was doing so. She had witnessed physical phenomena before, but never anything like this. Her face was masklike as she watched the teleplasmic sections start to coalesce. Bit by bit, they started to assume a shape. The filament, now pale again, looked vaguely like an arm and wrist.

"Something taking form," said Barrett.

Twenty-seven seconds later, a white figure stood before the cabinet, garbed in a shapeless robe, sexless, incomplete, its hands like rudimentary claws. There was a mouth, and two dark spots for nostrils, and it had two eyes which seemed to gaze at them. Edith drew in a rasping breath. "Easy," Barrett said. "Teleplasmic figure formed. Imperfectly—"

He broke off as the figure chuckled.

Edith made a stricken noise. *"Easy,"* Barrett told her.

The figure laughed: a rolling laugh, deep and resonant, which seemed to gorge the air. Edith felt her scalp begin to crawl. *The figure was turning to look at her.* It seemed to be coming closer. A frightened whimper filled her throat. *"Hold still,"* Barrett whispered.

Suddenly the figure reached for her, and Edith screamed, throwing her arms across her face. With a noise that sounded like the snapping of a giant rubber band, the figure vanished. Florence cried out hoarsely, making Edith jump again. Fischer struggled to his feet. "Hold it!" Barrett ordered.

Fischer stood beside the table rigidly as Barrett drew up the netting and shone the red beam of his pencil flashlight into Florence's face. Immediately he turned it off and checked his instruments. "Miss Tanner coming out of trance," he said. "Premature retraction, causing brief systemic shock." He looked at Fischer.

"Help her now," he said.

4:23 P.M.

Edith woke with a start. She checked her watch and saw that she'd been sleeping more than an hour.

Lionel was sitting at the octagonal table, looking into his microscope and making notes. Edith dropped her feet across the mattress edge and worked them into her shoes. Standing, she walked across the rug. Barrett looked up, smiling. "Feeling better?"

She nodded. "I apologize for what I did before."

"No problem."

Edith made a pained face. "I caused a 'premature retraction,' didn't I?"

"Don't worry, she'll get over it; I'm sure it's not the worst thing that's ever happened to her during a sitting." Barrett looked at her a moment, then asked, "What was it that upset you before the sitting? The examination?"

Edith was aware of restraining her reply. "It was a little awkward, yes."

"You've done it before."

"I know." She felt herself tensing. "I just felt awkward this time."

"You should have told me. I could have done it."

"I'm glad you didn't." Edith managed a smile. "Compared to her, I look like a boy."

Barrett made a scoffing noise. "As if that would matter."

"Anyway, I'm sorry I ruined the sitting." Edith was conscious of changing the subject.

"You didn't ruin anything. I couldn't be more satisfied."

"What are you doing?"

Barrett gestured toward the microscope. "Take a look."

Edith peered into the eyepiece. On the slide, she saw groups of shapeless forms and groups of oval and polygonal bodies. "What am I looking at?" she asked.

"A specimen of that teleplasm prepared in water. What you see are conglomerates of etiolated, lamellar, cohesive bodies, as well as single laminae of varied forms resembling epithelium without nuclei."

Edith looked up chidingly. "Now, do you really think I understood what you just said?"

Barrett smiled. "Just showing off. What I'm trying to say is that the specimen consists of cell detritus, epithelium cells, veils, lamellae, filmy aggregates, isolated fat grains, mucus, and so on."

"Which means—?"

"Which means that what the Spiritualists refer to as ectoplasm is derived almost entirely from the medium's body, the remainder being admixtures from the air and the medium's costume—fibrous vegetable remains, bacterial spores, starch grains, food and dust particles, et cetera. The bulk of it, however, is organic, living matter. Think of it, my dear. *An organic externalization of thought.* Mind reduced to matter, subject to scientific observation, measurement, and analysis." He shook his head in wonderment. "The concept of ghosts seems dreadfully prosaic compared to that."

"You mean Miss Tanner made that figure from her own body."

"Essentially."

"Why?"

"To prove a point. That figure was undoubtedly supposed to be Belasco's son—a son who, I'm convinced, never existed."

4:46 P.M.

The cat lay warmly indolent beside her. Its body throbbed with purrs as Florence stroked its neck.

When she'd come upstairs, she'd found it cowering outside her door and, despite her wretchedness, had picked it up and carried it inside. She'd held it in her lap until its trembling had stopped, then had put it on the bed and taken a hot shower. Now she was lying in her robe, the bedspread pulled across her.

"Poor puss," she murmured. "What a place to bring you." She ran the edge of a finger along the front of its neck, and the cat raised its head with a languid movement, eyes still closed. Barrett had said that he needed it as an additional verification of "presence" in the house. It seemed a harsh measure, though, merely to acquire a slight scientific validation. Maybe she could get it taken away by the couple who brought their meals. She'd ask Barrett to let her know the moment the cat had served its purpose.

Florence closed her eyes again. She wished she could sleep, but things kept nagging at her mind. Mrs. Barrett's strained embarrassment—the way she'd jerked around, as though someone were looking at her; Barrett's overzealous safeguards against fraud; the onset of physical mediumship in herself; her inability to go inside the chapel; her concern for Fischer; her feeling of dissatisfaction with herself; her fear that she was giving more importance to Belasco's son than he warranted. After all—

She jolted, gasping, as the cat leaped from the bed. Sitting up, she saw it rushing to the door and crouching there, back arched, fur on end, its pupils expanded so completely that its eyes looked black. Hastily she stood and crossed to it. The instant she opened the door, it darted out into the corridor and disappeared.

Something flapped behind her, and she whirled, to see the spread and blankets landing on the rug.

There was something underneath the sheet.

Florence stared at it. It was the figure of a man. She started toward the bed, tightening as she saw that the figure was nude. She could make out every body contour, from the swelling broadness of the chest to the bulge of genitals. She felt a stir of sensual awareness in her body. No, she told herself; that's what he wants. "If you're here only to impress me with your cleverness again, I'm not interested," she said.

The figure made no sound. It lay immobile underneath the sheet, chest expanding and contracting in a perfect simulation of breath. Florence peered at its face. "Are you Emeric Belasco's son?" she asked. She edged along the side of the bed. "If you are, you said that nothing changes. Yet, with love, all things are possible. This is true of life, and true of life beyond life." She leaned across him, trying to make out his features. "Tell me who you are," she said.

"Boo!" the figure shouted. Florence jumped back with a cry. Instantly the sheet collapsed, and there was nothing on the bed. The air began to ring with mocking laughter. Florence tightened with resentment. "Very funny," she said. The laughter rose in pitch, taking on a frenzied quality. Florence clenched her hands. "If practical jokes are all you're interested in, stay away from me!" she ordered.

For almost twenty seconds, it was deathly still inside the room. Florence felt her stomach muscles slowly tightening. Suddenly the Chinese lamp was pitched to the floor, shattering its bulb; only the light from the bathroom kept the room from total darkness. Florence twitched as footsteps thudded across the rug. The door to the corridor was flung open so hard that it crashed against the wall.

She waited for a while before she crossed the room to shut the door. Switching on the overhead light, she moved to the fallen lamp and picked it up. Such anger, she thought. Yet it wasn't only anger; that was clear.

It was a plea as well.

6:21 P.M.

Florence walked into the dining hall. "Good evening," she said.

Fischer's smile was cursory. Florence sat down. "Have you

seen this couple yet?" she asked, gesturing toward the table, which was set for supper.

"No."

She smiled. "Funny if there wasn't any couple."

Fischer showed no sign of amusement. Florence glanced toward the great hall. "I wonder where the Barretts are," she said. She looked back at him. "Well, what have you been doing?"

"Scouting." Fischer lifted the cover from one of the serving dishes and eyed the heap of lamb chops. He replaced the cover.

"You should eat," she said.

He pushed the dish toward her. "Maybe we should wait," she said.

"Go ahead."

Florence waited a few more seconds. Then she said, "I'll have some salad." She served her plate and looked at him. He shook his head. "A little?" Fischer shook his head again.

Florence ate some salad before she spoke again. "Were you in contact with Belasco's son when you were here before?"

"All I was in contact with was a live wire."

The sound of footsteps made them look around. "Good evening," Florence said.

"Good evening." Barrett smiled politely; Edith nodded. "Are you feeling better?" Barrett asked.

Florence nodded. "Yes, I'm fine."

"Good," Barrett and his wife sat down, served themselves, and started eating.

"We were talking about Belasco's son," Florence said.

"Ah, yes; Belasco's son."

Something in Barrett's tone made Florence bristle. Suddenly the thought of having been subjected by him to the indignity of a physical examination galled her. The costume, those ridiculous precautions: ropes and nets and infrared lamps, hand and foot plates turning lights on, cameras. She tried to repress a mounting anger but couldn't. How dare Barrett treat her this way? Her position in this project was just as vital as his.

"Will it never end?" she said.

The others looked at her. "Were you addressing me?" inquired Barrett.

"I was." Again she tried to quell her anger, but again the vision of the physical examination flashed across her mind, the costume, the absurd safeguards against fraud.

"Will what never end?" asked Barrett.

"This attitude of doubt. Distrust."

"Distrust?"

"Why should mediums be expected to produce phenomena only under conditions which science dictates?" she demanded. "We're not machines. We're human beings. These rigid, unyielding demands by science have done more harm than good to parapsychology."

"Miss Tanner—" Barrett looked confused. "What brought this on? Have I—"

"I'm not a medium for the fun of it, you know." Florence cut him off. The more she spoke, the more infuriated she became. "It's often painful, often unrewarding."

"Don't you think—?"

"It just so happens I believe that mediumship is God's manifestation in man." She couldn't stop herself. " 'When I speak with thee,' " she quoted angrily. " 'I will open thy mouth, and thou shalt say to them: Thus saith the Lord.' "

"Miss Tanner—"

"There is nothing in the Bible—not a single recorded phenomenon—which does not occur today, whether it be sights or sounds, shaking of the house, or coming through closed doors: rushing winds, levitations, automatic writing, or the speaking in tongues."

There was a heavy silence. Florence glared at Barrett, conscious of Fischer and Edith staring at her. Somewhere, deep inside her mind, she heard a warning cry, but fury stilled it. She watched Barrett pour himself some coffee, watched him pick up his cup. He looked at her. "Miss Tanner," he said, "I don't know what's bothering you, but—"

He broke off as the cup exploded in his hand. Edith jerked back, gasping. Barrett, frozen, gaped at the shard of handle still in his fingers. Blood was starting to drip from the cut in his thumb. Florence felt a pounding at her temples. Fischer looked around in startlement. "What in God's name—?" Barrett started.

He was drowned out as the glass beside his plate burst apart, its fragments scattering across the table. Edith jerked her hands back as her plate leaped from the table, flipping over rapidly and dumping food across the floor before it landed, shattering. She recoiled as the top part of her glass broke off with a cracking noise and jumped across the table toward her husband. Barrett, pulling out a handkerchief, twisted to the side. The glass top thudded off his arm and tumbled to the floor. Fischer's glass exploded, and he lurched back, flinging an arm in front of his face.

Florence's plate somersaulted, scattering salad over the table. She reached out to grab it, then jolted back as the plate went flying across the table. Barrett jerked his head aside. The plate scaled past his ear and landed on its edge, rolling rapidly across the floor, to break against the wall. Edith cried out as a heavy serving dish began to slide across the table toward him. Barrett jumped up, toppling his chair. He almost fell, then leaned against the table. The serving dish slid off the table edge and crashed to the floor. Mashed potatoes splattered over his shoes and trouser cuffs.

Fischer was on his feet now. He tried to turn from the table, but was slammed against it as his chair lurched hard against his legs. He saw his cup go leaping from the table, gouting coffee over Barrett's shirt front as it struck him in the middle of the chest. Edith's scream choked off as Fischer's plate was catapulted from the tabletop, flying closely over her head. The chair slid back from Fischer, and he crumpled to his knees, his face a mask of shock.

Barrett tried to twist the handkerchief around his bleeding thumb. The silver pot fell over and began to spin across the table at him, spouting coffee. Barrett lurched aside to avoid it, slipped on the potatoes, flailed for balance, then went crashing onto his right side. The coffeepot fell off the table, bouncing off his left calf. He cried out at the burning impact. Edith tried to stand to help him, but her chair rocked backward, throwing her off balance. A knife and spoon went flying past her cheek.

Florence shrank into her chair as another serving dish began to skid across the table, headed for Barrett. Barrett scrabbled aside with a gasp. The serving dish crashed down beside him, the edge of its cover striking his shin. Edith struggled to her feet. "Under the table!" Fischer cried. Florence slid from the chair, falling to her knees. Fischer flung himself beneath the table. Overhead, the hanging lamp began to pendulum, the length of its swings increasing rapidly.

They were barely in the shelter of the table when the objects on the monastery table against the east wall came to life. A heavy silver chafing dish arced across the room and hit their table with a deafening impact. Edith cried out. Barrett started reaching for her automatically, then went back to wrapping his thumb. A silver bowl came hurtling at them, struck a table leg, and spun around in a blur of movement. Florence glanced at Fischer. He was on his knees, eyes staring, face a frozen mask of dread. She wanted to help him but felt too dazed. There was a churning coldness in her stomach.

All of them looked up in shock as the dining table started rocking back and forth. The silver creamer landed nearby, contents splattering across the floor like a gout of ivory paint. The silver sugar bowl fell beside it as the table rocked with mounting violence, legs crashing down like pounding horse hooves. The table shifted suddenly, and Barrett had to jerk his hand away to keep from getting it crushed. The chairs began to overturn, banging one by one against the floor, the noise like rifle shots.

Suddenly the table surged away from them, sliding fast across the polished floor. It smashed against the fire screen and bent it out of shape. Above them, all the sanctuary lamps were swinging violently. One of them tore loose and hurtled sideways, creating a shower of sparks as it collided violently with the stone mantel, then crashed to the tabletop. A silver candelabrum flew across the room and landed on the floor by Barrett, thudding against his side. He fell with a gasp of pain. Florence cried out. *"No!"*

All movement ceased abruptly, except for the decreasing arcs of the remaining sanctuary lamps. Edith bent over Barrett anxiously. "Lionel?" She touched his shoulder. He managed to nod.

"Ben, you've got to leave this house."

Fischer turned to Florence, startled by her words.

"You aren't up to it," she told him.

"What the hell are you talking about?"

Florence turned to Barrett for support. "Doctor—" she began, then stopped, seeing how he looked at her as Edith helped him to his feet. "Are you all right?" she asked.

He didn't answer, leaning against the table with a groan. Edith looked at him in fright. "Lionel?"

"I'll be all right." He tightened the handkerchief around his thumb. The cut was deep; it stung. There were islands of pain all over his body—his arm, his chest, his shin, his ankle, mostly his side. His leg ached horribly.

Florence stared at him. Why had he looked at her that way? Suddenly she thought she knew. "I'm sorry I spoke so angrily," he said. "But please support me in this. I think it's important that Ben—that Mr. Fischer leave the house."

Barrett clenched his teeth against the pain. "Trying to get us both out now?" he muttered. Florence looked at him in surprise. "Help me to our room, please?" Barrett asked his wife. Edith nodded faintly, handed him his cane, and took his arm.

Florence didn't understand. "What do you mean, Doctor Barrett?"

He threw a glance around the wreckage of the hall. "I should think that was obvious," he said.

Stunned into silence, Florence watched the Barretts leave. After they were gone, she looked at Fischer. "What is he saying?" she asked. "That *I*—?"

Fischer turned away from her.

"Ben, it isn't true!"

He lurched away. Still moving, he glanced back at her. "You're the one who'd better leave," he said. "You're the one who's being used, not me."

6:48 P.M.

Barrett sat down gingerly. "My bag," he murmured. Edith let go of his arm and hurried to the Spanish table, lifting off the small black bag in which he kept his codeine and first-aid kit. Returning quickly to the bed, she set the bag beside him. Lionel was removing the handkerchief from his thumb with slow, careful movements, his teeth clenched at the pain.

The sight of the deep, blood-oozing cut made Edith hiss. "It's all right," Barrett told her. Reaching into the bag, he took out the first-aid kit and opened it. Removing a packet of sulfa powder, he tore it open. "Would you get me a glass of water, please?"

Edith turned to the bathroom. Barrett drew a box of gauze from the first-aid kit and started to break the seal on its cover. When Edith returned, he handed her the box. "Would you bandage it?" he asked. She nodded, giving him the glass of water. Taking his container of pills from the black bag, he got one out and washed it down.

Edith winced as she started bandaging. "This needs stitches."

"I don't think so." Barrett gritted his teeth, eyes narrowing, as she wrapped the gauze around the thumb. "Make it tight."

When the thumb was bandaged and taped, he eased up his left trouser leg. There was a dark-red burn on the calf. Edith looked at it in dismay. "You have to see a doctor."

"Put some Butesin picrate on it."

She looked at him for several moments indecisively. Then, kneeling beside him, she spread the yellow cream across the burn. Barrett hissed and closed his eyes. "It's all right," he muttered, knowing she was looking at him.

Edith wrapped some gauze around his leg, then helped him lie down. Barrett groaned and shifted onto his left side. "I am one gigantic mass of bruises," he said, trying to make it sound like a joke.

"Lionel, let's go home."

Barrett took another sip of water and handed her the glass. He slumped back on the pillows she had propped behind him. "I'm all right," he said.

"What if it happens again?"

He shook his head. "It won't." He looked at her a moment. "You could go, though."

"*Leave* you here?"

Barrett raised his right hand as though making a pledge. "Believe me, it won't happen again."

"Then why should I leave?"

"I just don't want you hurt."

"You're the one who's hurt."

Barrett chuckled. "That I am. It had to be that way, of course. I'm the one who angered her."

"You're saying"—Edith hesitated—"*she* did all that?"

"Making use of the power in the room," he said. "Converting it to poltergeist-type phenomena directed at me."

Edith thought about the violence of what had happened. The gigantic table rocking back and forth, then hurled across the floor like an express train. The whipping movement of those massive hanging lamps. "My God," she said.

"I made a mistake," Barrett told her. "I accepted her genial attitude toward me at face value. You can never do that with a medium. You never know what's underneath. It might be absolute hostility, and if it is"—he blew out breath—"by making unconscious use of their power, they can inflict tremendous damage. Especially when that power can be amplified a hundredfold by the kind of energy that fills this house." His smile was grim. "I'll not make that mistake again."

"Is it so important that we stay?" she asked.

Lionel answered quietly. "You know it means everything to me."

Edith nodded, trying to suppress the rise of panic in herself. *Five more days of this,* she thought.

8:09 P.M.

As she paced restlessly, her mind kept going over it again and again. Was Barrett right? She couldn't make herself believe it. Yet the evidence was there. She *had* been furious with him. The poltergeist phenomena *had* been directed primarily at him. Her body *did* feel enervated, as it always did after psychic use.

She turned and crossed her room again. I was angry with him, yes, she thought, but I wouldn't try to hurt him just because our views are different.

No. She wouldn't accept it. She respected Dr. Barrett; loved him as a fellow human being, as a fellow soul. She'd die before she'd harm him. Truly. Truly!

With a faint sob, Florence knelt beside the bed and bowed her head to rest it on tightly clasping hands. Dear God, please help me. Show me the path to follow. I am yours to lead. I consecrate my heart and soul to your exalted works. Dear Lord, I beg you for an answer. Reach down your hand and lift my spirit, help me to walk in your light, along your blessed way.

She looked up suddenly, eyes opened. For several moments she was frozen to the spot, her expression one of indecision. Then a radiant smile pulled back her lips, and standing eagerly, she crossed the room and went into the corridor. She glanced at her wristwatch; they would still be awake. Walking to the door of the Barretts' room, she knocked four times in quick succession.

Edith opened the door. Across her shoulder, Florence could see Dr. Barrett sitting up in bed, his legs beneath the covers.

"May I speak to you?" she asked.

Barrett hesitated, his face drawn with pain.

"I'll only be a moment," she said.

"Very well."

Edith stepped aside, and Florence crossed the room to Barrett's bed. "I know what happened now," she said. "It wasn't me. It was Belasco's son."

Barrett looked at her without response.

"Don't you see? He wants to separate us. Disunited, we are far less of a challenge to him."

Barrett didn't speak.

"Please believe me," Florence said. "I know I'm right. He's trying to turn us against each other." She looked at him with anxious eyes. "If you don't believe me, he'll have succeeded; can't you see that?"

Barrett sighed. "Miss Tanner—"

"I'll sit for you first thing in the morning," she broke in. "You'll see."

"There'll be no further sittings."

Florence stared at him, incredulous. "No further sittings?"

"It isn't necessary."

"But we've barely begun. We can't stop now. We've so much to learn."

"I've learned everything I wish to learn." Barrett was trying to control his temper, but the pain was making it difficult.

"You're cutting me off because of what happened before," Florence objected. "It wasn't my fault. I've told you that."

"Telling me is not convincing me," Barrett answered in a tightly restrained voice. "Now, if you don't mind—"

"Doctor, we can't stop the sittings!"

"I am doing so, Miss Tanner."

"You think it was me who—"

"Not only think it, Miss Tanner, but know it," he interrupted. "Now, *please*, I'm in considerable pain."

"Doctor, I was not responsible! It was Belasco's son!"

"Miss Tanner, *there is no such person!*"

The sharpness of his voice made Florence shrink away from him. "I know you're in pain—" she started faintly.

"Miss Tanner, will you *go?*" he asked through gritted teeth.

"Miss Tanner—" Edith began.

Florence looked around at her. She wanted desperately to convince Barrett, but the look of concern on his wife's face stopped her. She looked back at him. "You're wrong," she said. Turning away, she started for the door. "I'm sorry," she murmured to Edith. "Please forgive me."

She held herself in check until she'd returned to her room. There she sat down on the edge of her bed and started to cry. "You're wrong," she whispered. "Don't you see? You're wrong. You're *wrong.*"

10:18 P.M.

Edith lay on her back, staring at the ceiling. She'd closed her eyes a dozen times, only to open them again in seconds. She couldn't conceive of falling asleep. It seemed an impossibility to her.

She turned her head on the pillow and looked at Lionel. He was heavily asleep. It was no wonder, after what he'd been through. She'd been appalled when she'd helped him undress and put on his pajamas. His entire body was discolored by bruises.

She closed her eyes again, a terrible uneasiness inside her—nervousness with no apparent source. It was probably the house that made her feel it. What in God's name was this power Lionel kept talking about? That it was present was undeniable. What had happened in the dining hall had been terrifying proof of its existence. The thought that Miss Tanner could utilize that power against them was unnerving.

Edith sat up, turning back the bedclothes. Frowning, she slid her feet into her slippers and stood. She wandered across the rug and stopped by the octagonal table, looking at the box in which Lionel kept his manuscript. Abruptly she turned and walked across the room. Stopping in front of the fireplace, she looked inside. There was a low-burning fire, mostly glowing wood coals. She thought of putting on another log, sitting in the rocking chair, and staring at the fire until sleep came. She glanced uneasily at the rocking chair. What would she do if it started moving by itself again?

She rubbed a hand across her face. There was a tingling underneath the skin. She drew in a shaking breath and looked around. She should have brought a book to read. Something light and undemanding. A mystery novel would be good. Better still, some humor; that would be perfect. Some H. Allen Smith or Perelman.

She moved to the cabinet to the right of the fireplace and opened one of its doors. "Oh, good," she murmured. There were shelves of leatherbound volumes inside. None of them were titled. She pulled one out and opened it. It was a treatise on *Conation and Volition*. She frowned and slid it back onto its shelf, drew out another. It was printed in German. "Wonderful." She replaced it on the shelf, pulled out a third book. It dealt with eighteenth-century military tactics. Edith's smile was pained. Water, water everywhere, she thought. Sighing, she pushed the book back onto its shelf and pulled out a larger volume bound in blue leather with gold-edged pages.

The book was false, its center hollowed out. As she opened the cover, a pack of photographs fell out and spilled across the rug. Edith started, almost dropping the book. Her heartbeat quickened as she stared down at the fading photographs.

Swallowing, she stooped and picked one up. A shudder rippled through her flesh. The photograph was of two women in a sexual embrace. All the photographs were pornographic—men and women in a variety of poses. Some of them made it evident that the men and women were performing on the huge round table in the great hall while other men and women sat around the table, watching avidly.

Edith pressed her lips together as she picked up all the photographs and pressed them into a bundle. What an ugly house this is, she thought. She put the photographs into the hollow book and thrust it back onto its shelf. As she closed the cabinet door, she saw, on one of the upper shelves, a decanter of brandy on a silver tray with two small silver cups beside it.

She walked across the room and sat on her bed again. She felt uncomfortable and restless. Why did she have to look in that cabinet? Why, of all the books inside it, did she have to pick out that one?

She lay down on her side and drew her legs up, crossing her arms. She shivered. *Cold,* she thought. She stared at Lionel. If only she could lie beside him; not for sex, just to feel his warmth.

Not for sex. She closed her eyes, a look of self-reproach on her face. Had she ever wanted sex with him? She made a pained sound. Would she have even married him if he hadn't been twenty years her senior and left virtually impotent by the polio?

Edith twisted on her back and glared up at the ceiling. What's the matter with me, anyway? she thought. Just because my mother told me sex is evil and degrading, do I have to fear it all my life? My mother was a bitter woman, married to an alcoholic woman-chaser. I'm married to another kind of man entirely. I have no reason to feel like this; no reason at all.

She sat up suddenly and looked around in terror. *Someone's watching me again,* she thought. She felt the skin on the back of her neck begin to crawl. Her scalp was covered with an icy tingling. Someone's looking at me, knowing what I feel.

Pushing up, she walked to Lionel's bed and looked at him. She mustn't wake him up; he needed rest. Turning hurriedly, she moved to the octagonal table and dragged its chair beside Lionel's bed. She sat on the chair, and carefully, so as not to wake him, put her hand on his arm. There couldn't be anyone looking at her. There were no such things as ghosts. Lionel had said so; Lionel knew. She closed her eyes. There are no such things as ghosts, she told herself. No one is looking at me. There are no such things as ghosts. *Dear God in heaven, there are no such things as ghosts.*

11:23 P.M.

Fischer broke the seal on the bottle and unscrewed its cap. He poured two inches of bourbon into a glass and set down the bottle. Picking up the glass, he swirled the liquor around. He hadn't had a drink in years. He wondered if it was a mistake to start again. There had been a time when he couldn't stop once he'd started. He didn't want to sink to that again. Especially here.

He took a sip, grimacing as he swallowed. He coughed, and his eyes watered; he rubbed a finger over them. Then he leaned against the cupboard and began to take tiny sips of the bourbon. It felt comfortingly warm as it trickled down his throat and settled in his stomach.

Better thin it down, he thought. He walked around the steam table and over to the sink, where he turned on the cold water. After it had cleared, he held the glass of bourbon underneath the faucet and added an inch of water. That was better. Now the relaxation could come without the danger of his getting drunk.

Fischer lifted himself onto the sink counter and took judicious sips of his drink as he thought about the house. What was it doing this time? he wondered. There *was* a plan; of that he had no doubt. That was the horror of the place. It was not amorphously haunted. Hell House had a method. It worked against invaders systematically. How it did this, no one had ever found out. Until December 1970, he thought, when B. F. Fischer, moving just as systematically—

His right hand twitched so violently as the corridor door was opened that he spilled half his drink across the floor. Florence came into the kitchen, looking harried and exhausted.

"Why aren't you in bed?" she asked.

"Why aren't you?"

"I'm looking for Belasco's son."

He didn't speak.

"You don't think he exists either, do you?"

Fischer didn't know what to say.

"I'll find him," she said, turning away.

Fischer watched her go. He wondered if he should offer to accompany her. He shook his head. Things always happened around her, because she was too open. He didn't want to experience anything more today. He watched her push through the swinging door and disappear into the dining hall. Her footsteps faded. It was still again.

All right, the house, he thought; his plan. Two days had passed. He had the feel of the place now. It was time to start figuring what his approach was going to be. Obviously, it could not consist of working in tandem with Barrett or Florence. He'd have to function on his own. But how?

Fischer sat immobile, staring at the floor. After a while, he took a sip of his drink. It had to be something clever, he thought, something different, something that would circumvent the house's method.

He tapped the fingers of his left hand on the drainboard.

Clever. Different. Florence was right about the multiple-haunting idea; that much he could agree on. Belasco and a host of others were in this house. How to best them, though?

After several minutes Fischer put the drink down, jumped abruptly to the floor, and started toward the entry hall. A walk around the house, he thought. All by himself this time, without Florence Tanner to distract his train of thought. Those things she'd "felt." Jesus Christ. He shook his head, a mirthless smile on his lips. Those Spiritualists were too damn much.

He was crossing the entry hall when he froze in his tracks, his heartbeat leaping. A figure was drifting down the staircase. Fischer blinked his eyes and squinted, trying to see who or what it was; there were no lights on the stairs.

He started as the figure reached the foot of the steps and started toward the front door. It was Edith in a pair of light blue ski pajamas, her eyes staring straight ahead. Fischer stood motionless as she glided like a wraith across the entry hall and pulled open the front door.

She went outside, and Fischer, starting, ran across the entry hall. He dashed through the open doorway, gasping in shock as he saw that she had disappeared into the mist. He ran across the porch and down the steps, hearing a crackling of frost beneath his tennis shoes as he ran along the path. He saw a blur of movement ahead. *Is it really her?* he thought in sudden horror. Or was he being tricked? He started slowing down, then caught his breath. The figure was headed toward—

"No!" He bolted forward, grabbing. Two emotions flared in him at once—relief that it was flesh and skin he clutched, and fierce elation that he'd thwarted the will of the house. He pulled Edith away from the edge of the tarn. She looked at him without a sign of recognition, eyes like glass.

"Come back inside," he said.

Edith held back stiffly, face expressionless.

"Come on. It's cold out here." He turned her toward the house. "Come on."

Edith began to shiver as he led her. For several frightening moments he thought he'd lost his sense of direction; that they were going to walk into the freezing night to die of exposure. Then he saw, through the swirling mist, the nebulous rectangle of the front doorway, and hurried toward it, one arm around Edith, drawing her along beside him. He led her up the porch steps and into the house, pushing the door shut as they went inside. As quickly as he could, he guided her across the entry hall and into the great hall. Standing Edith before the hearth, he bent over and picked up a log, tossing it onto the coals. He grabbed a poker and jabbed at the log until it caught fire. Tongues of flame leaped upward cracklingly. "There we go," he said. He turned to look at Edith. She was staring at the mantel, her expression taut, unreadable. Fischer turned and looked. There were pornographic carvings on the mantel he hadn't noticed before.

Edith's groan was one of such revulsion that Fischer looked back sharply. She was shivering. He pulled off his sweater and held it out to her. She didn't take it. Her eyes were fixed on his face. "I'm not," she said.

Fischer stiffened as she reached up and began to remove her pajama top. "What are you doing?" he asked. His heartbeat quickened as she pulled the pajama top over her head and dropped it on the floor. Her skin was covered with gooseflesh, but she didn't seem aware of being cold. She started to work the pajama bottoms over her hips. Her blank expression was unnerving. "Stop it," Fischer told her.

She didn't seem to hear. She pushed down hard, and the pajama bottoms slipped down her legs. She stepped out of them and moved toward Fischer. "No," he muttered, as she stepped up close to him. She pressed against him with a moan and slid her arms around his back. She pushed her loins against him. Fischer started as she kissed his neck. She started reaching down to touch him. Fischer pulled back. Edith's eyes were blank. He braced himself and slapped her as hard as he could.

Edith spun around with a gasp and almost fell. Fischer grabbed her arm and pulled her back to her feet. She stared at him in shock. Suddenly she looked down at herself, gasping in horror. She yanked free of his grip so violently that it made her stagger backward. She almost fell again. Regaining her balance, she snatched her pajamas off the floor and held them in front of herself.

"You were walking in your sleep," he told her. "I found you outside, starting to go into the tarn."

She didn't respond. Her eyes were wide with fear. She backed away from him, heading toward the archway.

"Mrs. Barrett, it was the house—"

He broke off as she whirled and ran across the room. He started after her, then stopped and listened. After almost a minute, he heard a door being closed upstairs. His shoulders slumped. Turning, he stared into the fire.

Now the house was getting to her as well.

11:56 P.M.

Something kept drawing her to the cellar. Florence descended the stairs and pushed through the swinging metal door that opened on the swimming pool. She remembered the feeling she'd had when she and Fischer had looked into the steam room yesterday: a sense of something perverted, something unwholesome. She could not resign that feeling to what she felt about Belasco's son. Still, she had to be sure.

Her footsteps echoed and re-echoed as she walked along the edge of the pool. She blinked. Her eyes were tired. She felt badly in need of sleep. But she couldn't go to bed the way things were. Before she slept, she had to prove—to herself, at least—that Belasco's son was not imagination.

She pulled open the door to the steam room, looked inside. The pipe valve had been fixed, she saw. The room was filled with steam. She stared into the curling depths of it. There was something in there, without a doubt, something terribly malignant. But Belasco's son was not that way. His fury was defensive. He was desperately in need of help, and desperately desired that help, yet, at the same time, had such scarified malaise of soul that he fought against help in almost suicidal fashion.

She turned from the steam room and walked back along the length of the pool. She'd better warn Dr. Barrett not to use the steam room. She looked around. If Belasco's son was not here, why had she felt a compulsion to come to the cellar? There was only the pool and steam room. No, that wasn't true; she remembered now. There was a wine cellar across the corridor.

The moment she remembered it, it seemed as though a burst of cognizance exploded through her. An excited smile beginning on her lips, she hurried to the swinging door and pushed it open. Running across the corridor, she opened the wine-cellar door and felt around for a light switch. After a moment she found it, pushed it up. The light was dim, the overhead bulb filmed with dust and grime.

Florence walked into the room and looked around. The feeling was intense. Her gaze jumped from wall to wall, across the empty wine racks. Suddenly it froze on the wall across from the door. She stared at it. *Yes*, she thought. She started toward it.

She cried out as unseen hands clutched her by the throat. She reached up and began to grapple with the hands. They were cold and moist. She yanked them away and staggered to the side. Regaining direction, she lunged for the wall. The hands grabbed her arm and slung her sideways. She reeled across the floor and crashed against a wine rack. "Don't!" she cried. She turned and looked around the room. "I'm here to help!"

She pushed away from the wine rack, started for the wall again. Again the hands were on her, clutching at her shoulders. She was turned and hurled away. She almost hit the door before she caught her balance, whirling. *"You will not deter me."* She started forward slowly, praying in a soft, determined voice. The hands grabbed hold of her again. They jerked free as she spoke out loudly: "In the name of the Father, the Son, and the Holy Ghost!" Florence rushed to the wall and pressed herself against it. She was flooded with awareness. "Yes!" she cried. A vision leaped across her mind: a lion's den—a young man looking at her pleadingly. She sobbed with joy. "Daniel!" She had found him! *"Daniel!"*

DECEMBER 23, 1970

6:47 A.M.

The distant scream cut like a knife into Edith's sleep. She twitched awake, staring upward in confusion. A sound of rustling made her jerk around. Lionel was propped on his left elbow, looking at her.

"What *was* it?" she asked.

Barrett shook his head.

"I mean, was it real?"

Barrett didn't answer.

The second scream made her gasp. Barrett caught his breath. "Miss Tanner." He dropped his legs across the mattress edge and felt for his slippers. Edith started sitting up. She gasped again as Lionel's legs gave way. He fell against his bed, hissing at the pain in his thumb.

"Are you all right?" she asked.

He nodded once and pushed erect again, grabbing for his cane. Edith stood up, pulling on her quilted robe. She followed Lionel quickly to the door. He pulled it open, and they moved into the corridor, Lionel hobbling badly. Edith walked beside him, buttoning her robe. She glanced toward Fischer's room. Surely he had heard.

Barrett stopped at Florence Tanner's door and knocked three times in quick succession. When she failed to answer, he opened the door and went inside. The room was dark. Edith felt herself stiffen with anticipation as Lionel flicked up the wall switch.

Florence Tanner was on her back, arms clutched across her chest. Barrett limped to her bed, Edith close behind him. "What is it?" he asked.

Florence stared at him with narrowed, pain-glazed eyes. He leaned down, wincing at the pull of stiffened muscles. "Miss Tanner?"

She shuddered, digging teeth into her lower lip to keep from crying. Slowly she withdrew her arms, and Edith started as she saw him begin to unbutton the medium's gown. There were two damp patches on it, one above each breast. Florence closed her eyes as Barrett drew aside the edges of the gown. Edith shrank back.

There were deep teeth marks ringing the nipples on Florence's breasts.

Abruptly Florence pulled the blankets to her chin. Despite her will, a sob convulsed her throat; she tried in vain to check it. "Don't fight it," Barrett told her. Florence sobbed again, tears spilling down her cheeks.

Edith stared at Florence as she cried. For the first time since they'd met, the medium seemed vulnerable, and Edith felt a rush of sympathy. "Is there anything I can do?" she asked.

Florence shook her head. "I'll be all right."

Edith glanced aside as Fischer entered the room and joined them by the bed. "What happened?" he asked.

Florence hesitated before drawing down the covers briefly. Edith tried not to look, but couldn't help herself. Her breath shook as she saw the bites on Florence Tanner's breasts again.

"He's punishing me," Florence said.

Edith's face went blank. She glanced at Lionel, who was looking at the medium without expression.

"I found him last night," Florence told him. "Daniel Belasco."

There was heavy silence. Barrett looked embarrassed. Florence managed a smile. "No, I'm not imagining it." She laid a hand on her breasts. "Did I imagine these?"

Barrett gestured inconclusively.

"His body is in the wine cellar."

Edith could see how awkward Lionel felt. She knew that he wanted to be sympathetic but didn't know what to say that wouldn't hurt her further.

"Will you help exhume the body?" Florence asked.

"I would, but after last night, I'm afraid I'm in no condition for heavy labor."

Florence stared at him in disbelief. "But, Doctor, he's *there*. Doesn't that mean anything to you?"

"Miss Tanner—"

Florence turned to Fischer. "Will you help me, then?"

Fischer looked at her in silence. He *had* heard her scream, Edith realized abruptly; heard but been afraid to come until Lionel had arrived. Now he was afraid to offer help. It was not surprising. Whenever something violent occurred, Miss Tanner was always there.

When he didn't answer, Florence clenched her teeth, forcing back a sob. "All right, I'll do it myself." The pain of the bites seemed to overwhelm her, and she closed her eyes.

"I'll help you," Fischer said.

Florence opened her eyes and tried to smile. "Thank you."

Barrett put his hand on Edith's arm and started turning.

"Are you so afraid I might be right, Doctor?" Florence asked him.

Barrett looked at her appraisingly. At last he nodded. "Very well. We'll go downstairs with you. I can't dig, however, if that's what you intend to do."

"Ben and I will do that," Florence told him.

Edith glanced at Fischer. He was standing at the foot of the bed, looking at Florence without expression. Suddenly she felt a shiver plaiting up her back.

Was there really something down there?

7:29 A.M.

Fischer drove the crowbar edge into the cleft, and, straining, levered out another chunk of brick and mortar. It had taken him more than twenty minutes to gouge away an opening no larger than his fist. His pants and tennis shoes were streaked with mortar stains; there was a film of powder on his hands. He sneezed as mortar dust got up his nostrils. Turning, he withdrew his handkerchief and blew his nose. He looked at Florence, who was watching him with anxious eyes. She forced a smile. "I know it's hard."

Fischer nodded, drawing in a ragged breath. He almost sneezed again, controlled it, then, raising the crowbar, jammed its edge into the breach. It slipped as he began to pry away another clump of brick, and, losing balance, he pitched against the wall. "Damn!" he muttered. He straightened up, teeth set on edge, and once more drove the crowbar edge into the wall gap.

He jimmied out another piece of brick, which bounced across the floor, then looked at Florence. "This could take all day," he said.

"I know it's hard," she said again. Fischer stretched his back. "Let me do it for a while," she offered. Fischer shook his head and raised the crowbar.

"Before you continue—" Barrett said.

Fischer turned.

"Since this is clearly going to take a long time," Barrett said to Florence. "you won't mind if I go upstairs and get off this leg. It's rather painful."

"Yes, of course," she said. "We'll call you when we've found him."

"Quite." Barrett took hold of Edith's arm and turned for the door. Florence exchanged a look with Fischer as he turned back to the gap in the wall.

He was about to thrust the crowbar when he saw it. *"Wait."* Barrett and Edith looked around as he picked up his flashlight and shone the beam of light into the opening.

"What is it?" Florence was unable to contain her eagerness.

Fischer squinted through the haze of dust. He blew into the gap, then pointed the flashlight beam again. "Looks like a rope," he answered.

Florence came over, and Fischer handed her the flashlight. "Keep pointing it in there." She nodded quickly. Fischer reached into the opening and clamped his fingers on the dusty rope. He pulled down, but there was no give. He pulled up, felt the rope grow slack, then tauten as he let go. "I think there's a weight on the end of it," he said.

Florence caught her breath. "A *counterbalance.*"

Fischer grabbed the crowbar and started jabbing its beveled edge at the sides of the hole, widening it as quickly as he could. After a minute of forceful digging he dropped the crowbar, and before the clanging resonance had faded, had both hands through the opening. Clutching at the rope, he started pulling upward. The resistance was too strong. He braced himself and pulled with all his might, forehead pressed against the wall, eyes closed, teeth gritted. Move, you bastard, *move,* he thought.

Suddenly the rope lurched upward, slamming the edge of his right wrist against the jagged brick edge. Fischer jerked his hands back. He was examining his wrist when a rumbling noise began inside the wall. He looked up, startled.

A section of wall was hitching slowly to the right. Fischer braced himself for what they'd see—or wouldn't see. He was conscious of Florence standing beside him tensely as the wall section creaked and shuddered to the side.

Edith made a gagging noise and turned away. Fischer's lips pulled back in a grimace. Florence's sigh of relief fell strangely on his ears.

Shackled to the wall inside the narrow passage were the mummified remains of a man.

Barrett murmured, "Shades of Poe."

"I told you he was here," Florence said.

Fischer stared at the grayish, parchmentlike features of the corpse. Its eyes were like dark, hardened berries, its lips drawn back and frozen in a soundless scream. Obviously, he'd been tied behind the wall while still alive.

"Well, Doctor?" Florence asked.

Barrett drew in a faltering breath. "Well, what?" he asked. "I see the mummy of a man. How do you know it's Daniel Belasco?"

"I *know*," she said.

"Beyond a doubt? Beyond the slightest doubt?"

"Yes." She looked incredulous.

Barrett smiled. "I think more proof than that is called for."

Florence stared at him. "You're right," she said abruptly.

Turning to the opening, she reached out for the left hand of the shackled figure. Fischer watched her remove a ring. "Here." She held it out to Barrett.

Barrett hesitated before taking it. Fischer glanced at Edith.

She was staring at her husband with a look of apprehension. He looked at Barrett. The physicist was handing back the ring, a forced smile on his lips. "Very good," he said.

"Do you believe me now?"

"I'll think it over."

"*Think it over?*" Florence gaped at him. "Are you telling me—?"

"I'm telling you nothing," Barrett cut her off. "I'm saying that I need more time to digest this information and work out my interpretation of it. I must advise you, however, not to presume that one cadaver with a ring can reverse the scientific convictions of a lifetime."

"Doctor, I'm not *trying* to reverse your convictions. All I'm asking is that we work together. Can't you see that both of us can be right?"

Barrett shook his head. "I'm sorry, no. That I cannot see; and never will." He turned abruptly, limping toward the corridor. "My dear?" he said.

Edith looked at Florence for a moment, then turned to follow her husband across the room. Fischer took the ring from Florence. It was made of gold, with an oval crest.

Across the crest, in scroll-like letters, were the initials "D. B."

8:16 A.M.

They had eaten in silence for almost twenty minutes now. Barrett pushed aside his plate and drew his cup of coffee in front of himself. He stared across the table at the EMR indicator. Awkward that they had to take their meals at the same table on which his equipment was placed. Still, there was no help for it, since the dining hall was wrecked.

He glanced at Edith. She was sitting motionless, both hands wrapped around her coffee cup, as if for warmth. She looked like a frightened child.

He thrust aside his thinking on the problem. "Edith?" She looked at him, and Barrett smiled. "Disturbed?"

"Aren't you?"

He shook his head. "No, not at all. Is that why you think I've been quiet?"

Edith seemed to hesitate, as if afraid to bring up points he might not be able to refute. "There *was* a figure," she finally said.

"Quite a dreadful one."

Edith gazed at him uneasily.

"Not necessarily *the* figure, however," he said.

"But the ring."

"D. B. doesn't *have* to stand for Daniel Belasco."

She did not look reassured.

"It could stand for David Bart," he said. "Donald Bascomb." He smiled. "Doctor Barrett."

"But—"

"On the other hand, it might actually *be* Daniel Belasco—assuming such a person existed at all."

"Doesn't that prove her story, then?"

"It would appear to."

"I don't understand, then."

"The point is not the evidence or what it seems to prove, but *who found* that evidence."

Edith still looked bewildered. Barrett smiled. "My dear," he said, "Miss Tanner is a sensitive of considerable development. Add to that the vast power residuum in this house to which she, as a medium, has access. The result is a loaded psychic situation in which she is enabled to create any number of effects to validate her views. She was responsible for that 'poltergeist' attack on me last night, later claiming its source as Daniel Belasco. Next she became 'aware' of his body and 'discovered' it this morning, thus verifying her story even further. The fact that those may actually be the remains of Daniel Belasco is irrelevant. The point is simply that Miss Tanner is manipulating her power and the power in the house to build a case for herself."

Edith looked at him anxiously. Barrett knew she wanted to believe him but was still thrown off by what had happened. "What about the teeth marks, though?" he said.

She started.

"That *is* what you're thinking, isn't it?"

Her smile was faint. "You must be psychic, too."

Barrett chuckled. "Not a bit. It has to be the only point remaining on which you're still uncertain."

"Isn't it proof?"

"To her it is."

"They *were* teeth marks."

"They appeared to be."

"Lionel—" Edith looked more confused than ever. "Are you telling me they *weren't* teeth marks?"

"They may have been," he said. "All I'm saying is that they most certainly were not inflicted by Daniel Belasco."

Edith grimaced. "She did it to herself?"

"Perhaps not directly, although I can't discount the possibility," he said. "More likely, though, it falls under the category of stigmata."

Edith looked a little ill.

"Stranger things have happened." Barrett hesitated, then went on. "I never did tell you what happened to Martin Wrather that time; if you recall, I merely said he'd suffered injury while sitting. What happened was that his genitals were nearly severed. He did it to himself in a moment of hysteria. To this day, however, he remains convinced that 'forces from the other side' attempted to emasculate him." He smiled somberly. "Which is a far cry from a few small bites on female breasts—although I'm sure the pain she's suffering is considerable.

"You see how she's rounding out her case, though," he continued. "She comes upon the body last night—and this morning, in a rage at having his secret discovered, Daniel Belasco punishes her, tries to frighten her away."

"But you"—she gestured weakly—"don't believe any of it."

"None."

She sighed, as if surrendering. "What's going to happen, then?"

"What's going to happen is that my machine will arrive this morning, and by tomorrow I'll end the so-called curse of Hell House by purely scientific means."

They looked around as Fischer entered the great hall and walked over to the table, wearing his pea jacket, his clothes and hands streaked with earth stains. He said nothing as he sat and poured himself a cup of coffee, lit a cigarette.

"Are the services completed?" Barrett asked, the faintest edge of gibing in his voice.

Fischer glanced at him, then lifted the silver cover from the platter of bacon and eggs and looked at them before he dumped the cover back in place.

"Isn't Miss Tanner having breakfast?" Barrett asked.

Fischer shook his head, then drank some coffee. Barrett studied him. The man was obviously under pressure. He'd never given it much thought, but for Fischer to have come back to this house after what had happened must have required a tremendous act of will.

"Mr. Fischer," he said.

Fischer raised his eyes.

"I didn't respond to Miss Tanner last night because I was in pain and . . . well, to be quite frank, angry with her, too.

But I do think she was right when she suggested that you leave."

Fischer eyed him coldly.

"Please don't take this as criticism. I simply think that, for your own good, it might be wise for you to go."

Fischer's smile was bitter. "Thanks."

Barrett laid his napkin on the table. "Well, I've given you my feelings on the matter. The decision is yours to make, of course." He took out his pocket watch and raised the lid. As he put the watch back into its pocket, he noticed Edith glancing away from Fischer. "Perhaps we should bring some food to Miss Tanner," he suggested.

"She wants to be alone right now," Fischer said.

Barrett nodded, then pushed to his feet, flinching as he set his weight down on his burned leg. "My dear?" he said. She nodded with a faint smile, standing.

"He seems particularly tense today," he said as they started across the entry hall.

"Mmm."

He looked at her. "So do you."

"It's the house."

"Of course." He smiled. "Wait until tomorrow. You'll notice quite a change."

He looked around with an elated smile as someone knocked on the front door. "My machine," he said.

8:31 A.M.

So this broken body has released the spirit which shall never return to it again. This body has served its purpose, it can serve that purpose no more. Earth to earth, ashes to ashes, dust to dust. Amen."

She had spoken the words of the funeral service three

times now, the first time when she and Fischer had laid Daniel Belasco's body to rest, twice more upon returning to her room. Now his soul could rest.

It had been bitterly cold outside, the ground as hard as iron. Fischer's attempt to dig a pit finally had to be abandoned. They had searched the area around the house until they'd found a hollow in the earth, placed the body in that, and covered it with leaves and stones. Then she had recited the words of the funeral service, both of them standing beside the makeshift grave, heads bowed, eyes closed.

Florence smiled. She'd see to it that Daniel had a proper burial as soon as possible. What mattered now was that he was released from this house.

Reaching into the pocket of her sweater, she drew out Daniel's ring and held it in her palm, closing her fingers over it.

The images began immediately. She saw him: dark-haired, handsome, imperious in attitude, yet, underneath the superficial arrogance, as defenseless as a child. She saw him laughing at the table in the dining hall, saw him in the ballroom, waltzing with a beautiful young woman. There was only youth and tenderness in his smile.

The visions darkened. Daniel in the theater, looking at a play, face taut, eyes glittering. Florence tightened. This was not what he desired; but he was young, impressionable. Everything degrading was available. She saw him reeling down a corridor, a drunken woman on his arm. She saw him in this very bedroom, trying, in spite of everything, to find a sense of beauty in the sex act.

The corruption deepened. Drunkenness. Despair. A brief escape, then, helplessly, retreat to Hell House, never to escape again. Florence winced. She saw him in the great hall, naked, sitting at the huge round table, watching avidly. She saw him sliding a hypodermic needle into his arm, saw him venting sexual desires that made her tremble in the darkness. Yet, always, behind the mask—the face that Hell House had created—cowered the boy; wanting to flee, but incapable of doing so; wanting love, but finding only license.

She caught her breath, seeing him approach his father. She could not make out the face of Emeric Belasco; the figure stood in shadows, giant, menacing. She moved her lips in prayer, the ring gripped tightly in her hand. The shadows started to contract. In a moment she would see him. Something cold began to fill her chest; the vision faltered. Florence groaned. She mustn't lose it! She descended deeper with a surge of will. If only she could see the father, get inside the father, understand the father. Sweat broke out across her brow. She felt a snake uncoiling in her stomach, cold and wet. "No," she murmured. She must not surrender. There was meaning here, an answer.

She cried out as a violent shock coursed through her body. Instantly her hand unclasped, the ring slipped off. She heard it thumping on the rug, a vast distance below. She felt as though she lay in some great cavern, wounded. She could not perceive the walls or ceiling; in every direction lay only darkness and distance. She tried to open her eyes but couldn't. Blackness trickled sluggishly across her mind, blotting out awareness. Power, she thought. Dear God, the *power*.

She started slipping down the wall of a gigantic pit, moving downward toward a darkness which was blacker than any she had ever known. She tried to stop herself but couldn't. The sensation was physical—her body sliding down and down, the walls of the pit adhesive enough to keep her from pitching into space, not enough to stop her inexorable descent toward the darkness below. The darkness that waited had a character, a personality. It's him, she thought. He waits for me.

Oh, God, he waits for me!

She fought against it, praying to her guides, her spirit doctors, all those who had helped her in the past. Keep me from falling deeper, she entreated them. Take my hand and bear me up. I ask this in the name of our eternal God. Help me, help me!

Abruptly she was back inside the room, the pit and cavern gone. She was asleep, yet not asleep. She knew that she was on the bed, unconscious; knew she was aware, as well. She heard the opening and closing of a door. Was it the door of her room, or some imagined door within her mind? All she knew was that her eyes were fastened shut; that she slept, yet was awake. She heard footsteps drawing near.

She saw a figure. With her eyes closed, she could see it coming toward her like a silhouette cut from black paper. Did she imagine it? Was the figure in the room, or in her mind?

It reached the bed and sat beside her; she could feel the mattress yielding as it sat. Suddenly she knew that it was Daniel, and a groaning noise enveloped her. Was it a real groan, issuing from her lips, or a thought sound which expressed the shock she felt? *It could not be him.* He was at rest. She and Fischer had placed his body in a consecrated grave. He could not be back again; it was impossible. Asleep, awake, she saw him sitting on the bed beside her, a figure in black. Was he looking at her? Were there eyes in that dark head?

"Is it you?" she asked. She heard her voice but couldn't tell if it was thought or real.

"It is."

"Why?" she asked, she thought. "You should have gone on."

"I cannot."

She tried to wake herself, unable to endure this limbo of fragmentary awareness. "You have to go," she told him. "You were given your release."

"It's not the release I seek."

"What *is*, then?" She became more conscious of the battle to awaken. She had to separate herself before it was too late.

"You know what it is," he said.

She did know, suddenly. The knowledge was a chilling wind across her heart. *"You must go on,"* she said.

"You know what you must do," he answered.

"No."

"I need it, or I cannot leave."

"No!" she answered. *Wake!* she thought.

Daniel said, "Then I must kill you, Florence."

Icy hands were clamped around her neck. Florence cried out in her sleep. She reached up, clawing at them. Suddenly she woke. The hands were gone. She started pushing up, then froze in shock, her heartbeat staggering.

There was a hideous sound beside her on the bed; an eerie sound, half-animal, half-human, liquid, and deranged. She couldn't move. What was it? Very slowly Florence turned her eyes. The bathroom door was open slightly, faint illumination clouding through the room.

It was the cat.

She watched it staring at her. Its eyes were glittering, insane. It kept making the wavering, unnatural sound in its throat. She began to lift her hand. "In the name of God," she whispered.

With a savage yowl, the cat leaped at her face. Florence jerked back, both arms flung before her. The cat thrashed into her, its sharp claws hooking deep into her arms. She cried out as she felt its teeth dig brutally into her head. She tried to push it loose but couldn't; it was sprawled across her face, its hot fur in her eyes and mouth. Its teeth dug deeper, front claws buried in her arms, the harsh, demented sound still bubbling in its throat. Florence jerked her left arm free and dug her fingers into fur and skin, trying to pull its head back. The teeth pulled loose. Instantly the cat's head lunged berserkly at her throat. Florence blocked its way with her right arm, and the cat's teeth sank into her flesh again. She sobbed in pain and tried to jerk its head away. The cat began to kick its rear legs. Florence grabbed its throat and started squeezing. It began to make a gurgling noise, its rear legs thrashing, clawing at her chest and stomach through the sweater. Suddenly the teeth pulled free. Florence hurled the cat to the floor.

She sat up quickly, gasping for breath. In the faint light from the bathroom she could see the cat roll over and regain its feet. She jumped from the bed and lunged toward the bathroom. The cat hurled itself against her legs, digging teeth and claws into her calves. She cried out, almost falling. Struggling to regain balance, she toppled against the Spanish table, right arm crashing on the telephone. Instantly she snatched up the receiver, swung down at the cat with it. The first blow smashed against her knee. She sobbed and swung again, hitting the cat's head. She began to hit it again and again, battering at its skull until, abruptly, the teeth jerked out. Kicking the cat away, she spun around and dashed for the bathroom. The cat raked to a halt, then darted after her. Lurching through the doorway, Florence slammed the door and fell against it as the cat crashed against the other side and started clawing frenziedly at the wood.

Florence stumbled to the sink and looked at her reflection in the mirror. She gasped in shock, seeing the deep holes in her forehead, blood oozing from the cavities. Tugging up her sweater, she pulled it over her head, groaning at the sight of her chest and stomach crisscrossed with a network of bleeding lacerations, her torn bra spotted with bloodstains.

She looked at her arms, wincing at the perforations the cat's teeth had dug into her flesh. She whimpered, turning on the cold water. Dragging a washcloth off its rack, she held it underneath the faucet until it was soaked, then began to pat it on the bites and scratches. She started crying at the pain, digging teeth into her lower lip. Hot tears blurred her sight.

As she washed the wounds, she heard the cat outside the door, raking its claws through the wood and making the horrible noise in its throat.

9.14 A.M.

"It's big," Edith said.

Barrett grunted as he jimmied the end of a plank from the side of a plank from the side of the crate stamped FRONT. His movements were excited, overquick. The crowbar slipped.

"Don't overdo it, now."

He nodded, prying at the other end of the plank. She hadn't seen him so worked up in years. "Can I help you?"

Barrett shook his head.

Edith watched uneasily as he leaned forward in his chair and pried the boards loose, cracking several of them, pulling off jagged pieces with his left hand, and tossing them onto the floor. "They packed it well enough," he muttered. She couldn't tell if he was pleased or annoyed by the fact.

The crate was eight by ten feet in width and length, and taller than Barrett by a foot. What was in it? Edith wondered. His machine, yes; but what was his machine, and how was it supposed to end the haunting of a house?

"Damn!"

She twitched as Barrett cursed and dropped the crowbar with a hiss of pain to clutch at his bandaged thumb.

"Lionel, please don't overdo it."

"All *right*," he said impatiently. He picked up the crowbar and returned to the crate.

"Why don't you ask Fischer to help you?"

"Do it myself," he muttered.

Edith flinched as he drove the crowbar in between two planks and started jimmying out one of them. "Lionel, *take it easy,*" she said. "You look as though you mean to tear that crate apart with your teeth."

Barrett stopped and looked at her, his chest rising and falling heavily, a dew of perspiration on his forehead. He made a sound which might have been amusement. "It's just that this is—well, the culmination of all my years in parapsychology," he said. "You can understand why I'm excited."

"And you can understand why I'm concerned."

He nodded. "I'll restrain myself," he promised. "I guess I can spare a few more minutes after twenty years."

Edith leaned back in her chair, relieved. Maybe if she kept him talking while he worked, he wouldn't get too overwrought.

"Lionel?"

"Yes?"

"Should we report that body to the police?"

"We will," he said, "when the week is up."

Edith nodded, wondering what to talk about next.

"Was Fischer really a powerful psychic?" she asked, wondering why the question came to mind.

"At one time, it was generally conceded that he ranked with Home and Palladino."

"What did he do?"

"Oh"—Barrett pried away another plank end from the front of the crate and set the board aside, revealing a line of glass-fronted dials—"the usual: levitation, direct voice, biological phenomena, imprints, percussion, materialization—that sort of thing. At one sitting, a table that weighed almost five hundred pounds was raised to the ceiling in full light, him with it, and the combined strength of six men couldn't pull it down.

"Later, when the lights were out in the testing room—

full controls in operation—a group of seven perfectly formed faces floated around the room. One of the testers—Doctor Wells, the famous Harvard chemist—had his face blown into by one of them, and another tried to kiss him. I believe he was rather a cynic about the entire subject until that night."

"What else?" Edith prompted as he fell silent again.

"Oh, a . . . dark shadow in the shape of a man walked around the testing room with a tread that shook the walls. Green phosphorescent lights, like outsize butterflies, fluttered around the table and nested in the sitters' hair. A mandolin floated near the ceiling, playing 'My Bonny Lies Over the Ocean.' Professor Mulvaney of the Pittsburgh Parapsychological Association held a perfectly formed materialized hand for more than ten minutes, describing it as possessing bones, skin, hair, nails, and warmth. It dissolved in his grip in less than a second.

"Finally, a mass of teleplasm flooded from Fischer's mouth and formed the figure of a Chinese mandarin, seven feet tall, complete to the finest detail. It spoke to the group for twenty minutes before being retracted into Fischer's body." Barrett set aside another plank. "Fischer was all of thirteen at the time."

"He was genuine, then."

"Oh, yes, completely." Barrett started working on the final plank. "Unfortunately, that was long ago. It's like a muscle, you see. Fail to use it, and it atrophies." He set aside the final plank and stood with his cane. *"Now,"* he said.

Edith rose and walked over to him. He was peeling off a large envelope that was taped to the front of the machine. As he opened it and slid out his blueprints, Edith looked at the control panel with its array of switches, dials, and knobs. "What did this cost to build?" she asked.

"I'd say in excess of seventy thousand dollars."

"My God." Edith ran her gaze over the dials. "EMR," she

murmured, reading the metal plate fastened below the largest dial. The numbers on it ranged from zero to 120,000.

"What *is* EMR, Lionel?"

"I'll explain it later, dear," he said distractedly. "I'll tell all of you exactly what the Reversor is designed to do."

"The Reversor," she said.

He nodded, looking at the top blueprint. Pulling the pencil flashlight from his pocket, he shone its thin beam through a grille-like opening on the side of the machine. He frowned and, limping to the table, set down the blueprints, and picked up a screwdriver. Returning to the machine, he began to unfasten a plate.

Edith moved to the fireplace and held her hands toward the flames. She'd stood right here, she thought after a moment. She could remember nothing before being slapped from sleep, to find herself naked in front of Fischer. She shuddered, trying not to think about it.

She was moving back toward Lionel when Fischer suddenly came dashing in. Edith started as he called out, "Doctor!"

Barrett whirled.

"It's Miss Tanner!"

Edith froze. My God, what's happened now? she thought.

"She's been hurt again."

Barrett nodded once and, limping to the table, grabbed his black bag. "Where?" he asked.

"In her room."

The three moved hurriedly across the great hall, Barrett setting the pace as best he could. "How bad is it?" he asked.

"She's scratched—torn—bitten."

"How did it happen?"

"I don't know; the cat, I think."

"The *cat?*"

"I was bringing her some food. When she didn't answer

my knock, I opened the door. The second I did, the cat shot out and disappeared."

"And Miss Tanner?"

"She was in the bathroom," Fischer said. "At first she wouldn't come out. When she did—" He stopped, grimacing.

She was lying on her bed when they came in; she opened her eyes and turned her head as they crossed the room. Edith made a sound of shock. The medium's skin was as pale as wax, deep, blood-encrusted indentations on her head, puffy scratches on her face and neck.

Barrett put his bag by her bed and sat down beside her. "Have you disinfected these?" he asked, looking at the bites on her head.

She shook her head. Barrett opened his bag and removed a small brown bottle and a box of Q-Tips. He glanced at the rips in Florence's sweater. "Your body, too?"

She nodded, tears welling in her eyes.

"You'd better take the sweater off."

"I've washed myself."

"That's not enough. There could be infection."

Florence glanced at Fischer. Without a word, he turned and walked to the other bed, sitting down on it, his back to them. Florence started to remove her sweater. "Would you help her, Edith?" Barrett asked.

Edith moved to the side of the bed, wincing as she saw the pattern of the jagged slashes across Florence's chest and stomach, the bites and lacerations on her arms. She reached behind the medium to unhook her bra, stepping back as Florence slipped it off. The medium's breasts were covered with scratches as well.

Barrett unscrewed the cap of the bottle. "This is going to hurt," he said. "Would you like a codeine?"

Florence shook her head. Barrett dipped a Q-Tip into the bottle and began to swab out one of the puncture wounds in her forehead. Florence hissed and closed her eyes, tears pressing out beneath the lids. Edith couldn't watch. She turned away and looked at Fischer. He was staring at the wall.

Several minutes passed, the only sound Florence's hissing and an occasional murmur of apology from Barrett. When he was done, he drew a blanket across her chest. "Thank you," she said. Edith turned back.

"The cat attacked me," Florence said. "It was possessed by Daniel Belasco."

Edith looked at her husband. His expression was unreadable.

The medium tried to smile. "I know, you think—"

"It doesn't really matter what I think, Miss Tanner," Barrett cut her off. "What matters is your being mauled."

"I'll be all right."

"I wonder if that's so, Miss Tanner. I wonder if it might not be advisable for *you* to leave rather than Mr. Fischer."

Edith was aware of Fischer twisting around to look at them.

"No, Doctor." Florence shook her head. "I don't think it would be advisable at all."

Barrett looked at the medium for several moments before he spoke again. "Mr. Deutsch needn't know," he said.

Florence looked confused.

"I mean"—he hesitated—"you've more than contributed your share to the project."

"And you'll see to it that I get paid off, is that it?"

"I'm only trying to help. Miss Tanner."

Florence started to reply, then held back. She averted her eyes before she looked at Barrett again. "All right," she said, "I'll accept that. But I'm not going to leave."

Barrett nodded. "Very well. It's up to you, of course." He paused, then added, "But I would feel derelict in my responsibility toward you if I didn't urge, no, *warn* you to leave this house while you can." He paused again. "Furthermore, if I think your life is in danger, I may *see* to it that you go."

Florence looked appalled.

"I don't intend to stand by knowingly and allow you to become yet one more victim of Hell House," Barrett told her. He snapped his bag shut, picked it up. "My dear?" he said. Struggling to his feet, he turned for the door.

10:43 A.M.

Edith turned onto her right side and looked at the other bed. Lionel was asleep. She should never have let him work on that crate. They should have asked Fischer to open it.

She thought about what Lionel had said before he'd gone to sleep: that Florence Tanner was becoming so anxious to prove her case that she was sacrificing her bodily well-being to do it.

"Dissociation of mind resulting in a modification of self is the basic cause of mediumistic phenomena," he had said. "I don't know if there really was a Daniel Belasco or not, but the personality Miss Tanner claims to be in touch with is nothing more than a division of her own personality."

Edith blew out a harried breath and turned onto her back. If only she could understand as Lionel did. All she could think of were those horrible teeth marks around Florence Tanner's nipples; the scratches and bites which Florence claimed the cat had inflicted. How could she have done those things to herself, even unconsciously?

Edith slipped her legs across the mattress edge and sat up. She stared at her shoes for several minutes before pushing her feet into them. Standing, she moved to the octagonal table and looked at the manuscript. She ran a finger over the title page. Would it really hurt? she thought. It was ridiculous to have this almost mindless dread of alcohol. Just because her father's drinking had made her childhood miserable was no reason to condemn liquor per se. All she was contemplating was one small drink in order to relax.

She moved to the cabinet and opened the door. Lifting out the decanter and one of the small silver cups, she carried them to the table. She pulled a tissue from her purse and cleaned out the silver cup before she poured it full of brandy. It was very dark. She wondered suddenly if it could be poisoned. That would be a grisly way to end things.

She dipped a finger into the brandy, touched it to her tongue. Would she know if it was poisoned? Her tongue began to burn, and she swallowed nervously. The warmth spread delicately to the tissues of her throat. Edith raised the silver cup and held it underneath her nostrils. The aroma was pleasing. How could it be poisoned? Surely someone had tasted it before this.

She took a tiny sip, closing her eyes as it trickled down her throat. The inside of her mouth grew warm. She made a sound of pleasure as the brandy reached her stomach and a tiny core of heat began expanding there. She took another sip. It's what I need, she thought. I'm not a potential drunk just because I sip a little brandy. She moved to the rocking chair, hesitated, then sat down. Leaning back, she closed her eyes and drank the brandy with deliberate sips.

When the cup was empty, she opened her eyes and looked toward the table. No, she thought. One was enough. She felt relaxed now; that was all she wanted. She held the cup before her eyes, examining the intricacies of its silverwork. Maybe she'd take it home as a souvenir when the week was over. She smiled. There; that was better. She was planning ahead.

She thought about Fischer. She really should apologize to

him for avoiding him so rudely this morning. She should thank him for saving her life. She shivered, thinking of the stagnant water in the tarn, and stood up, wavering slightly as she crossed the room. She opened the door and stepped into the corridor, closing the door behind herself as quietly as possible.

A wave of dread swept over her for an instant as she realized that she was alone for the first time since they'd entered the house. She scoffed away the dread. She was being foolish. Lionel was just inside the room. Florence was probably in her room, Fischer in his. She moved along the hallway to his door. Was she making a mistake? No, she thought; I owe him an apology, I owe him thanks.

She knocked on Fischer's door and waited. There was no sound inside the room. After several moments she knocked again, but there was no response. Edith turned the knob and pushed at the door. What am I doing? she thought. She couldn't stop herself. Opening the door, she looked inside.

The room was considerably smaller than the one she and Lionel were in. There was only one massive bed with a high, square-cut canopy. To its right was a table with a French telephone and an ashtray on it. Edith looked at the ashtray filled with mashed cigarette butts. He smokes too much, she thought.

She drifted to the armchair beside the table. Fischer's tote bag was on it, its zipper undone. Edith looked inside and saw some T-shirts and an open carton of cigarettes. She swallowed, reaching down to touch the bag.

She whirled with a gasp.

Fischer was standing in the doorway, looking at her.

For a terribly extended time, it seemed to her, they stared at each other. Edith's heartbeat raced; she felt a licking heat across her face.

"What is it, Mrs. Barrett?"

She tried to get control of herself. What must he be thinking to find her here like this? "I came to thank you," she managed.

"Thank me?"

"For saving my life last night."

She drew back unconsciously as Fischer walked over to her. "You shouldn't have left your husband."

She didn't know what to say.

"Are you all right?"

"Of course."

Fischer looked at her closely. "I think you should go back to your room now," he said.

He moved beside her as she crossed the rug. "Try tying your wrist to the bed at night," he told her.

Edith nodded as he followed her into the corridor and to her room. She turned to face him. "Thank you."

"Don't leave your husband again," he said. "You should never—"

He broke off, leaning forward suddenly as though to kiss her. Edith twitched and drew back. "Have you been drinking?" he asked.

She tightened. "Why?"

"Because it isn't safe to drink here. It isn't safe to lose control."

"I am not losing control," she told him stiffly. She turned and went inside her room.

11:16 A.M.

Florence started as someone knocked on the door. "Come in."

Fischer entered.

"Ben." She tried to rise.

"Don't get up," he told her. He started across the room. "I'd like to talk to you."

"Of course." She patted the bed. "Sit here beside me."

Fischer settled on the mattress edge. "I'm sorry you're in pain."

"It will pass."

He nodded, unconvinced, then looked at her in silence, until Florence smiled. "Yes?" she asked.

He braced himself for her reaction. "I agree with Doctor Barrett. I think you should leave."

"Ben."

"You're being torn to pieces, Florence. Can't you see that?"

"You don't think I'm doing these things to *myself*, do you?"

"No, I don't," he answered. "But I don't know who *is* doing them, either. You say it's Daniel Belasco. What if you're wrong? What if you're being fooled?"

"Fooled?"

"There was a woman medium here with us in 1940. Grace Lauter. She became convinced that a pair of sisters haunted the house. She built a very convincing case for it. The only trouble was, she was wrong. She cut her throat the third day we were here."

"But Daniel Belasco *does* exist. We found his body, found his ring with his initials on it."

"We also put him to rest. *Why isn't he at rest, then?*"

Florence shook her head. "I don't know." Her voice was faltering. "I just don't know."

"I'm sorry." He patted her hand. "I'm not trying to pick at you. I'm just concerned, that's all."

"Thank you, Ben." After several moments she smiled at him. "Benjamin Franklin Fischer," she said. "Whoever gave you such a name?"

"My father. He was nuts for Benjamin Franklin."

"Tell me about him."

"There's nothing to tell. He left my mother when I was two. I don't blame him. She must have driven him mad."

Florence's smile faded.

"She was a fanatic," Fischer said. "When I started showing signs of mediumship at nine, she devoted her existence to it." His smile was humorless. "My existence, too."

"Do you regret it?"

"I regret it."

"Truly, Ben?" She looked at him with deep concern.

Fischer smiled abruptly. "You said you were going to tell me about Hollywood when we settled down." His smile went wry. "Not that things have settled down much."

"It's a long story, Ben."

"We have time."

She gazed at him in silence. "All right," she finally said. "I'll tell you briefly."

Fischer waited, looking at her.

"Perhaps you read about it," Florence said. "The gossip columns made a lot of it at the time. *Confidential* even did a story on the Spiritualist meetings I held in my home. They made it sound like something else, of course.

"It wasn't, Ben. It was exactly what I claimed. As for the stories about me never marrying because I wanted to 'play the field,' as they called it, they weren't true either. I never married because I never met a man I wanted to marry."

"How did you become an actress?"

"I loved to act. When I was a child, I put on little shows for my parents and relatives. Later on, I joined the high-school drama club, a local theater group, majored in dramatics at college. The progression was remarkably smooth; it happens that way sometimes. A God-given appearance, a combination of fortunate events." She smiled a little ruefully. "I was never a great success at it. I didn't apply myself enough. But there was never anything questionable, either. No dark past, no scars covering childhood wounds. I had a wonderful childhood. My parents loved me, and I loved them. They were Spiritualists; I became a Spiritualist."

"Were you an only child?"

"I had a brother. David. He died when he was seventeen—spinal meningitis." She looked into the past. "It was the only real sorrow of my life."

She smiled again. "It was the 'waning' of my career, they said, that made me 'flee' from Hollywood, 'turning to religion' for comfort. They always neglected to mention that I'd been a Spiritualist all my life. Actually, I blessed my fading career. It gave me the opportunity to do what I always knew I should do—devote myself exclusively to mediumship.

"I didn't fear Hollywood—or flee from it. There's nothing fearful about it. It's a location and an enterprise, nothing more. What those involved in it make of their lives is their own choice. The so-called 'corrupting' influences are no greater than similar influences that exist in any line of work. It isn't the business that matters, but the corruptibility of those who enter it.

"Not that I was unaware of the moral vacuum which usually surrounded me. On crowded sets, at parties, I was often overwhelmed by the atmosphere of unwholesome tension in the air." She smiled, remembering. "One night, when I went to bed, I said the Lord's Prayer as I always do. Suddenly I realized that what I'd said was 'Our Father which art in heaven, Hollywood be thy name.' " She shook her head in amusement. "I left within the month and came East to stay."

Fischer began to speak, then broke off as somewhere, faintly, in the distance, the cat yowled. *End of pleasant interlude*, he thought. Florence looked pained. "The wretched thing." She started to rise.

Fischer pressed her back against the pillows. "I'll look."

"But—"

"Rest." he told her, standing.

"Before you go, would you get my purse?"

Fischer walked across the room and got it for her. Florence opened it and removed a medallion, holding it out to him. Fischer took it. There was a single word engraved on it: BELIEVE.

"It's all within you if you do," she said.

He started to hand it back to her. "No, keep it," she said. "From me to you, with love."

Fischer forced a smile. "Thank you." He slipped the medallion into his pocket. "I'm really all right, though. Worry about yourself, not me."

"Will you sit with me after I rest?" she asked. "I've got to contact Daniel Belasco, and trance is the quickest way. But I don't want to sit alone."

"You won't consider leaving, then?"

"I can't, Ben, you know that." She paused. "Will you sit with me?"

Fischer looked at her uneasily. Finally he nodded. "Right."

He left the room without another word.

12:16 P.M.

The cool water rippling against his face felt good. The skin of his burned calf had contracted, making it painful to kick, but he didn't want to stop. Every time he lifted his right hand from the water, the pain in his thumb intensified. I need this, though, he thought. He hadn't been swimming for almost a week.

He reached the shallow end of the pool and stopped, holding on to the coping with his left hand. Edith was sitting on a wooden bench near the steam-room door. "Don't overdo," she said.

"I won't. I'll just do two more laps."

Twisting around, Barrett began to swim again. He closed his eyes and listened to the splashing sounds his arms and feet made.

He wondered how badly the atmosphere of the house was affecting Edith. When he'd waked up, he'd tried to rise without disturbing her, but the moment he'd stirred, her eyes had opened. There'd been a smell of brandy on her breath, and when he'd gotten up he'd seen a decanter of it on the table, a small silver cup beside it. She'd told him that she'd found them in the cabinet and taken one cupful to relax. He'd put the decanter back in the cabinet, telling her she'd taken a serious risk drinking anything in this house. She'd promised not to touch any more.

Barrett's hand touched the far end of the pool and, turning, he started swimming back. We should be out of here by tomorrow night, he thought. If he could get the Reversor functioning without delay, he was certain they could leave by then. He smiled to himself, wondering if Edith had any concept at all how the Reversor was going to change the atmosphere of the house.

He reached the shallow end and stood up, hissing at the coldness of the air on his body. Edith helped him up the steps and wrapped a towel around his shoulders. "Can you stand a few minutes in the steam room?" he asked.

She nodded, handing him his cane.

"I think it would do me good."

"Yes. Go in." She pulled open the heavy door.

"You'd better remove your outer clothes," he told her.

"All right."

Barrett tossed the towel onto the wooden bench and limped inside the steam room as Edith let the door thud shut.

He groaned in pleasure at the feeling of the wet heat on his body. Breathing through his teeth, he felt around until he found a bench. The top of it was burning hot. He eased around the room, feeling with his cane, until it touched the hose. Moving his left hand along its length until he reached the wall, he turned the spigot once. Cold water gushed from the end of the hose. Barrett washed it over the bench top and sat down, putting aside his cane. Reaching down, he worked the bathing suit across his hips. It slithered down his legs, and he shook it off.

He looked toward the door. Edith was taking rather a long time. He frowned. He didn't want to stand again. Still, he mustn't leave her alone for more than seconds.

He was on the verge of getting to his feet when the door opened and he saw the outline of her figure. He was surprised to see that she had taken all her clothes off. As the door jarred shut, he said, "Over here." He'd have to remember to put in a brighter bulb. The one overhead was either deficient in wattage or covered with grime; probably both.

Edith moved cautiously across the steam-obscured room. She made a faint sound as she walked through the gush of cold water. Barrett pulled the hose until the end was in his hand, then washed off the bench beside himself, wincing as some of the water sprayed against his leg. He tossed down the hose, and Edith sat beside him. Barrett heard her drawing in erratic breaths, trying not to let the hot air down her throat. "All right?" he asked.

She coughed. "I never could get used to breathing in steam rooms."

"Try putting water on your face and taking a breath as you do."

"I'm all right."

Barrett closed his eyes and felt the damp heat seeping into

his flesh. He twitched as Edith's hand settled on his leg. He covered it with his. After several moments she leaned over and kissed his cheek. "I love you," she said.

Barrett put his arm across her shoulders. "I love you, too," he said. She kissed him on the cheek again, then on the corner of his lips. He felt a stirring in his body as she pressed her lips to his, moving her head as she kissed him. Barrett opened his eyes as one of her hands ran down his stomach. Edith? he thought.

After several moments she swung around and straddled him, her lips never leaving his. He felt her hot, slick stomach thrust against his. Reaching down, she took hold of his sex and began to rub it against herself. Barrett's breath began to labor. The hot air seared his throat and chest. He made a startled sound as she dug her teeth into his lower lip. He could smell the brandy on her breath.

Her lips ran across his cheek, her tongue trailing over the skin. "Make it hard," she whispered in his ear. Her voice was almost fierce. Barrett caught his breath as she grabbed his injured hand and pulled it up against her breast. He jerked it back as fiery pain ran up his wrist. *"Don't!"* she ordered, clutching it again.

"My thumb!" he cried. The pain was so severe, his vision started blurring. He could hardly breathe, his lungs struggling with the scalding air. Edith didn't seem to hear. She clutched at his organ, groaning so loudly it made Barrett's heartbeat leap. "For Christ's sake, make it hard!" she cried. She jammed her lips on his again.

Barrett couldn't breathe. Gagging, he jerked his head back, slamming it against the tile wall. He cried out in new pain, his face contorted. Edith fell against him, sobbing. Barrett tried to catch his breath. "Edith," he gasped.

She wrenched to her feet and turned away. "Don't," he

muttered, reaching for her dazedly. He felt a rush of cold air as she opened the door, saw her outline vaguely. Then the door thumped shut again.

Wincing, he bent over, feeling for the hose. He rubbed cold water on his face, drawing in a breath through clenched teeth. My God, what's come over her? he thought. He knew that the curtailment of their sex life must have had a damaging effect on her, but she'd never shown desire like this. The house *must* be affecting her. Standing groggily with his cane, he inched his way across the steam-filled room, grimacing at the increase of heat on his face. The ceiling bulb had all but disappeared from view now, no more than a spot of pale light overhead. Barrett reached the door and felt for the handle. Finding it, he closed his fingers over it and pushed. The door held fast. He pushed it harder. The door wouldn't move. His features tightened. Clutching the handle as hard as he could, he pushed again.

The door refused to budge.

A flicker of uneasiness oppressed him. Barrett willed it off. "Edith?" he called. He hit the door with the palm of his left hand. "Edith, the door is stuck!"

There was no reply. *My God, she didn't go upstairs*, he thought with sudden dread. He pushed at the handle again. The door was wedged in its frame. The heat and dampness, he told himself; the door had warped, expanded. "Edith!" he called. He pounded on the door with his fist.

"What *is* it?" he heard her answer faintly.

"The door is stuck! Try to open it from your side!"

He waited. There was a thump on the door, and he felt it stir. He grabbed the handle again and pulled with all his strength as she thrust her weight against the door on the other side.

The door held.

"What are we going to do?" he heard her ask. She sounded frightened.

Could she possibly use the bench to batter open the door? No, it was too heavy. Barrett scowled. The heat seemed to be getting worse. He'd better turn it off.

"Lionel?"

"I'm all right!" He lowered himself gingerly to his left knee to get below the worst of the heat. He made a worried sound. Well, there was no other way. He couldn't stay in here. "You'd better get Fischer!" he called.

"What?" He couldn't tell if she hadn't heard or was appalled by what he'd said.

"You'd-better-get-Fischer!"

Silence. Barrett knew the thought of going alone through the house was terrifying to her. "It's the only way!" he shouted.

Edith didn't answer for a long time. Then he heard her call. "All right! I'll be right back!"

Barrett remained motionless for a while. He hoped to God she didn't run into anything. In her mental state, it could be catastrophic. He scowled. I can't just stay like this, he thought. I'd better turn off that steam.

He looked abruptly to his right; he thought he'd heard a sound. There was nothing but swirling steam. He stared at it with slitted eyes. It was thick and white and coiling, and made shapes. A person with an uncontrolled imagination might see all sorts of things in it.

Barrett hissed. "Ridiculous." He stood and edged his way across the floor until his shins bumped against the edge of the wooden bench. Kneeling again, he reached beneath the bench for the tap wheel. He couldn't find it and began to crawl along the bench, feeling for it.

He froze. He was certain that he'd heard something this

time, a kind of—*slithering* noise? Barrett shivered despite the heat. "Ri*dic*ulous," he muttered. He continued crawling. No wonder this house had claimed so many victims. Its atmosphere was incredibly conducive to delusions. The sound he'd heard was probably coming from the tap wheel he was searching for—an escape of steam, probably too much pressure. It was getting awfully hot in here.

His hand came in contact with the tap wheel, and he felt a burst of relief. He tried to turn the wheel, but it stuck. He fought off premonition, gritting his teeth against the pain in his leg as he wrapped both hands around the wheel. "Stuck," he said aloud, as though to convince somebody in the room that the problem was a normal one. He strained the muscles of his arms and back, trying to revolve the wheel.

It wouldn't move.

"Oh, no." He swallowed, flinching at the scorch of air in his throat and chest. This is not good, definitely not good, he thought. Still, it was a physical problem: a door stuck in its frame, a steam valve stuck—things to be expected in an old house. Edith would be back with Fischer in a few moments. If worse came to worst, he could lie on the floor and wash his face off with the water while—

He jerked around. The noise again, too definite to be imagination. It *was* a slithering noise, no doubt of it, like the stirring of some torpid serpent on the floor. Barrett's face hardened. Come *on,* he told himself; don't go childish on me now. He turned around slowly, leaning his back against the bench and trying to see through the steam. If it *was* some phenomenon, he had only to keep his wits about him. There was nothing in the house that could harm him so long as he didn't panic.

He listened carefully, wincing at the throb of pain in his thumb. After what seemed to be a minute or more, he heard the sound again, a liquid, sliding noise. He imagined lava pouring slowly down a coal chute, splattering like smoky gruel into a bin. He shuddered. "*Stop* it," he ordered himself. He was reacting as credulously as Miss Tanner now.

The hose! he thought abruptly. If wet heat could cause the door to warp out of shape, wet coldness might reverse the process. He began to feel around for the hose.

He heard the sound again, ignored it this time. *Psi phenomena abound in realms of credulity*. The sentence flashed across his mind. Precisely, he thought. He gulped in breath without thinking, groaning at the fire of it in his throat and chest. Where the hell was that damned hose, anyway? The tile floor was beginning to hurt both legs now.

He felt the gush of water then and made a sound of gruff satisfaction. He reached for the hose, edging his hand across the floor.

He cried out, jerking back his hand. It had touched what felt like hot slime. Barrett held his hand to his face and looked at it. The light was very dim; he had to squint. He felt his heartbeat catch. There seemed to be a kind of darkish ooze clinging to his palm and fingers. With a gagging sound, he reached down quickly, rubbing his palm on the floor. What in God's name? Melted grout from between the tiles? Some sort of—?

He jerked around so fast it made his neck hurt. He stared into the roiling steam, heartbeat jolting. The sound had started up again, louder now, moving toward him. Barrett drew back unconsciously, trying to see. He rubbed his hand across his eyes without thinking, smearing some of the slime on his face. He made an angry, sickened noise and rubbed it off with his left hand. It had a vaguely familiar smell. Where the hell *is* she? he suddenly thought. For an instant he felt a rush of panic as he imagined her not telling anyone, leaving him imprisoned here because of what had happened between them.

"No," he muttered. That was ludicrous. She'd be back

any moment. He'd better get to the door and wait. He wavered to his feet and moved haltingly away from the sound, visualizing a gigantic jellyfish heaving its transparent, quivering bulk across the floor at him. "That's enough," he muttered, furious at himself. He had to get to the door. He stared into the steam but couldn't see which way the door was. The noise continued—a dragging, soggy noise. Barrett felt a chill of dread lace up his back. He'd best prepare himself. He mustn't panic.

He cried out in shock as his feet sank into hot, thick slime. He started jumping back and slipped, landing on his left elbow and crying out again as jagged pain shot up his arm. He writhed in agony on the floor.

Suddenly he felt the slime push up against his side like heated gelatin. He thrashed away from it, the odor welling over him. It was the smell of rot—*the odor of the tarn!* It's come inside! his mind cried, terrified. He flung himself to his knees. The door; where was the door? He guessed and, shoving to his feet, hobbled clumsily in that direction.

Something blocked his way—something near the floor that had size and bulk and was alive. With a cry of horror, Barrett fell across it. It reared up, shoving him onto his back, hot and jellylike, reeking of stagnation. Barrett screamed as it flopped across his legs. He struck out wildly with his left foot, feeling it sink into muculent slime, then strike what felt like skin the texture of cooked mushroom.

Suddenly it was before his eyes, bulbous, glistening darkly. "No!" he screamed. He kicked at it again, thrashing back across the floor, until his back slammed violently against the door. He felt the ropy form start oozing up his legs adhesively. Shrieks of terror flooded from his lips. The room began to swirl and darken. He could not dislodge the glutinous weight. He felt the hotness of it sucking at his flesh.

Suddenly the door was shoving in behind him, pushing

him directly into the gelatinous form. It struck his face; his screaming mouth was filled with turgid jelly. Coldness washed across his side. He felt hands slip beneath his arms. He thought he heard Edith screaming. Someone started dragging him across the floor. Looking up, he made out Fischer's face above him, pale and indistinct. Just before he lost consciousness, Barrett saw his body. There was nothing on it.

12:47 P.M.

Fischer gulped down coffee, holding the cup with both hands. Once again the couple from Caribou Falls had come and gone, unseen.

He'd been in the theater, searching for the cat, when he'd heard Mrs. Barrett's shouting. Rushing to the entry hall, he'd met her, and she'd told him, frightenedly, that her husband was locked in the steam room.

In there; he'd suddenly remembered Florence's words. Without a word, he'd dashed downstairs, shoved through the swinging doors, and raced along the side of the pool, the rapid padding of his tennis shoes echoing off the walls and ceiling.

He'd heard Barrett's screams before he reached the steam-room door. He'd jarred to a halt and almost turned around when Mrs. Barrett had come running in. He'd been unable to retreat before her look of panic. Turning back, he'd sprinted to the steam-room door and thrown his weight against it, to no avail. Mrs. Barrett had come rushing up behind him, begging him to save her husband, her voice unnatural, shrill.

Grabbing one end of the wooden bench against the wall, he'd dragged it to the steam-room door and rammed it hard against it. Immediately the door had given, and dropping the bench, he'd shoved the door in. Inside, Barrett's screams had cut off suddenly, and Fischer had felt his weight against the door and reached around to grab him in the burning steam and pull him out, forced to strain every muscle because of Barrett's weight. By then Barrett's wife was shaking uncontrollably, her face almost gray. Somehow the two of them had managed to get Barrett upstairs and put him on his bed. Fischer had offered to help put Barrett's pajamas on, but Mrs. Barrett, in a tight, almost inaudible voice, had told him she could do it. He'd left immediately and come downstairs.

He set down the empty cup and covered his eyes with his left hand, mind a jumble of confusions. The unlocked door that had been locked by the time they'd reached the house. The restored electrical system that had failed to work. Florence's inability to enter the chapel. The record playing by itself. The cold breeze on the stairs. The tinkling chandelier. The pounding noises during the séance; Florence suddenly, inexplicably, becoming a physical medium. The figure at the séance; its hysterical warning to them. The poltergeist attack. Mrs. Barrett being led to the tarn in her sleep; removing her pajamas; acting so peculiarly this morning. The bites on Florence's breasts. The body in the wall; the ring. The attack on Florence by the cat. Now the attack on Barrett in the steam room.

He slumped back in the chair. Nothing fitted, he thought. Nothing added up. They were exactly nowhere in their quest. But Florence was being torn apart emotionally and physically. Mrs. Barrett was losing control. Barrett had been violently assaulted twice. And, as for himself—

His mind leaped back, remembering. Faces sprang before him: Grace Lauter's, Dr. Graham's, Professor Rand's, and Fenley's. Grace Lauter working by herself, convinced that she, alone, would solve the mystery of Hell House; not even talking to the rest of them. Him working with Dr. Graham and

Professor Rand, who, in turn, refused to work with Professor Fenley because he was a Spiritualist and not a "man of science."

Three demoralizing days before it ended. Grace Lauter with her throat cut by her own hand; Dr. Graham, dead drunk, wandering outdoors to perish in the woods; Professor Rand dying of a cerebral hemorrhage after an experience in the ballroom he'd been unable to describe before he died; Professor Fenley still in Medview Sanatorium, hopelessly insane. Himself found naked on the front porch, horror-ridden, old before his time.

"And now I'm back," he muttered in a trembling voice. "I'm *back.*" He closed his eyes and couldn't stop from shaking. *How?* he thought. I'm not afraid to try, but how do I begin? A rage of bewilderment clamped his muscles suddenly. Jerking open his eyes, he grabbed his cup and hurled it far across the room. *It's too damn complicated!* screamed his mind.

1:57 P.M.

She blinked her eyes. Lionel was awake. She put her hand in his. "Are you all right?"

He nodded, didn't smile. Edith forced control into her voice. "I'll pack our bags," she said. She waited. Lionel returned her look without expression.

"We'll go today," she said.

"I want you to go."

Edith stared at him. "We'll both go, Lionel."

"Not until I'm finished."

She couldn't believe it, even though she'd anticipated his response. Her lips twitched, words unspoken stammering in her mind.

"You go into Caribou Falls," he told her. "I'll join you tomorrow."

"Lionel, I want both of us to go."

"Edith—"

"No. I don't want to hear a word. You can't convince me, anymore, you know what's happening. You would have died down there if Fischer hadn't come. You would have been killed by . . . *what?* By *what?* We have to go before this house destroys us all. *Now,* Lionel. *Now.*"

"Listen to me," he said. "I know it's gone beyond the point of endurance for you. It hasn't for me, however. I'm not going to let what happened frighten me away. I've waited twenty years for this. Twenty long years of work and research, and I'm not about to lose it all because of—something in a steam room."

Edith stared at him, a pulsing at her temple.

"It was a shock," he said. "I admit it. It was a terrible shock. I've never experienced anything remotely like it in my life. But it was not the dead. You hear me, Edith? *It was not the dead.*"

He closed his eyes. "Please," he said. "Go into Caribou Falls. Fischer will drive you there. I'll join you tomorrow."

He opened his eyes after a while and looked at her. "Tomorrow, Edith. After twenty years, there's only one more day before I prove my theory. *One more day.* I can't retreat when I'm so close. What happened was ghastly, yes, but I can't, I *won't* let it chase me away." His hand closed tightly over hers. "*I'd rather die than leave.*"

The room was still. Edith felt her heartbeat like a slow, erratic drumbeat in her chest.

"Tomorrow," she said.

"I swear to you I'll end the reign of terror in this house by then."

She stared at him, feeling lost and helpless. She had no

faith of her own remaining. She could only cling to his. God help us if you're wrong, she thought.

2:21 P.M.

"O Spirit of Immortal Truth," Florence began, "help us, this day, to rise above the doubts and fears of this life. Open our natures to mighty revelations. Give us eyes to see, and ears to hear. Bless us in our efforts to lift the darkness from the world."

The bathroom light cast dim illumination on the place where they sat. Florence sat in the chair beside the table, eyes closed, hands on her lap, knees and feet pressed tightly together. Fischer had pulled the other chair across the floor and sat facing her at a distance of four feet.

"The sweetest expression of spiritual life is service," Florence was saying. "We offer ourselves for the service of the spirits. May they find us ready, and may they, so that naught may impede our free expression, commune with us this day and reveal their light to us. Most of all, may they impart to us the power to communicate with that tortured soul who still hovers in this place, unsanctified, imprisoned: Daniel Belasco." She raised her face. "Attend us, ministering angels. Help us in our effort to lift the burden from this soul. All this we ask in the name of the Eternal and Most Everlasting Spirit. Amen."

There was momentary silence. Fischer heard the crackling noise his throat made as he swallowed. Then Florence began to sing: " 'Sweet souls around us, watch us still. Press nearer to our side. Into our thoughts, into our prayers, with gentle helpings glide.' "

When the song was ended, Florence began to take in deep breaths, drawing air into her lungs convulsively through clenched teeth as she rubbed both hands over her body. Soon her month fell open, and her head began to loll back. The heavy breathing continued. Florence slouched down in the chair, head rolling from side to side. At last she was still.

Minutes passed. Fischer began to shiver. Coldness was starting to gather between them, rising slowly like ice water, until he felt as though he were submerged to the waist in it.

He twitched as faint spots of light began to appear in front of Florence. *Focuses of condensation*; the phrase drifted across his mind. He stared at the spots as they grew in size and number, hovering in the air in front of Florence like a galaxy of pale, miniature suns. His legs felt almost numb now. Soon, he thought.

His fingers dug into the chair arms as teleplasm started oozing from the medium's nostrils. The viscous filaments resembled twin gray serpents gliding downward from her nose. As Fischer watched in dry-mouthed silence, they joined to form a heavier coil, which started to unravel, then began to rise and cover Florence's face. Fischer lowered his eyes. He heard a sound like rustling paper, closed his eyes.

The smell of ozone penetrated his nostrils like the odor of a badly chlorinated swimming pool. Compelled, he opened his eyes and looked up, wincing. The teleplasm had covered Florence's head, hanging over it like a wet, filmy sack. As he stared at it, he saw it being shaped as though by some invisible sculptor, the eye pits pressed in, a ridge of nose appearing, nostrils, ears, a line of mouth. In less than a minute, it was complete; the face of a young man, dark-haired, handsome, grave in its expression.

Fischer cleared his throat. His heartbeat felt unreal. "Have you a voice?" he asked.

There was a labored, gurgling noise like the sound of a death rattle. Fischer felt his skin crawl. After half a minute, the sound stopped, and there was silence again.

"Can you speak now?" Fischer asked.

"I can." The voice was undeniably masculine.

Fischer hesitated, then drew in a quick breath. "Who are you?"

"Daniel Belasco." The lips of the face did not move, but the voice was coming from the pallid features of the young man.

"Was it your body we found behind the wall of the wine cellar this morning?"

"It was."

"We gave you proper services outside. Why are you still here?"

"I cannot leave."

"Why?"

There was no answer.

"Why?"

No answer. Fischer clutched his hands together on his lap. "Did you have anything to do with the attack on Doctor Barrett in the steam room?"

"No."

"Who did it, then?"

There was no answer.

"Did you attack Doctor Barrett in the dining hall last night?" Fischer asked.

"I did not."

"Who did?"

Silence.

"Did you bite Miss Tanner this morning?"

"I did not."

"Who did?"

Silence.

"Did you possess the cat to attack her?"

"I did not."

"Who did, then?"

Silence.

"Who did, then?" Fischer persisted. "Who attacked Doctor Barrett? Who bit Miss Tanner? Who possessed the cat?"

Silence.

"Who?" demanded Fischer.

"Cannot say."

"Why not?"

"Cannot."

"Why?"

Silence.

"You have to tell me. Who attacked Doctor Barrett in the dining hall and steam room? Who bit Miss Tanner? Who possessed the cat?"

He heard a quickening of breath.

"Who?" he demanded.

"Cannot—"

"You have to tell me."

The voice began to plead. "Cannot—"

"Who?" asked Fischer.

"Cannot say—"

"Who?"

"Please—"

"Who?"

He heard something like a sob.

"Him," said the voice.

"Who?"

"Him."

"Who?"

"Him. Him!"

"Who?"

"Him!" cried the voice. "The Giant! Him! Father, Father!"

Fischer sat in rigid silence as the face lost form, the teleplasm rippling. Suddenly it began to steam back into Florence's nostrils. As it vanished, Fischer heard her moan with pain. In less than seven seconds it was gone.

He sat immobile for almost a minute before standing. He felt numb as he walked into the bathroom, ran some water into a glass, and carried it back into the bedroom, standing motionless beside the chair until she opened her eyes.

After she had drunk the water in one long swallow, he moved to the wall switch and turned on the hanging lamp beside her bed.

He sank down heavily on the chair across from hers.

"Did he come through?" she asked.

As he told her what had happened, her expression tensed to one of deep excitement.

"Belasco," she said. "Of course. Of *course.* We should have realized it."

Fischer did not respond.

"Daniel would never have hurt me. He would never have hurt Doctor Barrett. I *knew* it couldn't have been him, despite the evidence; it simply didn't *feel* right. He's as much a victim of the house as anyone." She looked at Fischer's unconvinced expression. "Don't you see?" she said. *"He's being kept here by his father."*

Fischer regarded her in silence, wanting to believe what she was saying but afraid to commit his mind.

"Don't you *see?*" she asked him eagerly. "They're warring together, Daniel trying to escape from Hell House, his father doing everything he can to prevent it by trying to turn me against Daniel, trying to make me believe that Daniel means me harm, when he doesn't. When all he wants is—"

She stopped so quickly that Fischer's eyes narrowed. "Wants *what?*" he asked.

"My help."

"That's not what you were going to say."

"Yes, it was. I'm the only one who *can* help. I'm the only one he trusts. Don't you see?"

Fischer eyed her guardedly. "I hope I do," he said.

3:47 P.M.

Edith sat up and slid her legs across the mattress edge. Reaching out, she picked up Lionel's watch from the table and raised its lid. Nearly four o'clock. How could he possibly get his machine ready by tomorrow?

She stared at him as he slept, wondering if he still believed everything he said. Somehow, she had the uncomfortable feeling that he was no longer as confident as he claimed. Not that he would ever show it, not even to her. When it came to his work, he was a man of unrelenting pride, always had been.

Standing abruptly, Edith moved to the cabinet and opened the door. All right, both of them had warned her. Nothing had happened, had it? The brandy had relaxed her, nothing more. If she was going to stay in this house until tomorrow, she was damned well going to take a few steps to make that stay endurable.

She carried the decanter and one of the silver cups to the table. Setting down the cup, she pulled out the decanter top and poured the cup full of brandy. Picking up the cup, she drank its contents with a swallow. She threw her head back, eyes closed, mouth open wide, sucking at the air as brandy scalded down her throat. It was like pouring hot syrup into her chest and stomach. Heat pulsed outward, radiating through her veins.

She poured herself another cupful, took a sip of it, and eased herself onto the table, pushing aside the box with Lionel's manuscript in it. She took another sip of brandy, then swallowed the entire cupful, head laid back again, eyes closed, a look of sensual enjoyment on her face.

She thought about being in the steam room with Lionel, trying not to face the nagging qualm that, beyond a certain point, she'd been infuriated at his impotence, as if, somehow, it were his fault and not that of the polio. She tightened, thinking that the real reason he wanted her to go to Caribou Falls was that he didn't want to be annoyed by her needs; that he wanted to concentrate on his machine.

She blinked. That was a terrible thing to think of Lionel. If he'd been able to, he would have made love to her.

Would he? her mind demanded. Or did he really care at all whether they ever had sex?

With an impulsive movement, she reached around for the decanter, knocking the box off the table, spilling pages of the manuscript across the rug. She started to get up, then, with a frown, ignored it. Let it lie, she thought. I'll get it later. She closed her eyes, emptying another cupful of brandy into her mouth and swallowing it.

She slipped off the table, almost fell. I'm *drunk*, she thought. A momentary pang of guilt assailed her. Mom was right, I am like him, she thought. She fought it off. I'm *not!* she told her unseen mother; I'm a good girl. "*Hell—*" She scowled. I'm not a girl at all, I'm a woman. With desires. He should know that. He's not *that* old. Or that impotent. It was his damned religious mother, not the polio. It was—

She frowned away the thought, weaving across the bedroom toward the cabinet. Her limbs felt warm and silky, and there was a lovely numbness in her head. They were wrong; getting drunk was the only answer. She thought about the cabinet of liquor in the kitchen. Maybe she'd get a bottle of bourbon from it—maybe two bottles. Maybe she'd just drink herself insensible until tomorrow came.

She removed the hollowed book so quickly that it slipped

from her fingers and thudded on the rug, the photographs scattering. She sank to her knees and started looking at them one by one. She licked her upper lip unconsciously. She stared at a photograph of the two women lying on the great hall table, performing mutual cunnilingus. The room seemed to get hotter and hotter.

Abruptly she flung away the photograph as though it was burning her fingers. *"No,"* she muttered frightenedly. She started, looking back toward Lionel as he stirred, then pushed clumsily to her feet and looked around the bedroom like a cornered animal.

She walked across the room quickly. Opening the door, she moved into the hall and closed the door, flinching at the noise; she'd meant to be more quiet. Shaking her head to clear it, she walked to Fischer's room.

He wasn't there. Edith stared into his room and wondered what to do. Closing the door, she turned and started back along the hallway, drifting to her left until she reached the banister rail. She held on to it for balance as she headed for the staircase. For some strange reason, the house did not seem frightening to her. Further proof that alcohol was just the thing, she thought.

She had the sensation of floating down the staircase. Vaguely she recalled some film about the South she'd seen at a revival. All she could remember clearly was some woman in hoop skirts gliding down the stairs as though she were descending on a track. She felt the same way. She wondered why she felt so confident.

A glimmer, faint, too fleeting to be captured. Edith blinked and hesitated. Nothing. She continued down the stairs. He's in the great hall, she decided. He was always where the coffee was. She couldn't recall ever seeing him eat. No wonder he was so thin.

As she crossed the entry hall, she heard a sound of splintering wood. Again she stopped. She hesitated, then moved forward once again. Of course, she thought. She smiled. She'd never felt so fuzzy in her life. She closed her eyes. I'm floating, said her mind. Father and daughter, drunks forever.

She stopped in the archway and leaned against it dizzily. She blinked her eyes, refocusing with effort. Fischer had his back to her. He was using the crowbar to pry apart the crate. That's sweet, she thought.

She started as Fischer spun around, the crowbar raised as though to strike at some attacker. He whirled so quickly that the cigarette between his lips arced to the floor.

"Kamerad," she said. She raised her arms as though surrendering.

Fischer stared at her without a sound. She saw his chest rise and fall with agitated breath. "Are you angry?" she began to say.

He cut her off. "What the hell are you doing here?"

"Nothing." She pushed off from the archway and started toward him weavingly.

"Are you *drunk*?" He sounded stunned.

"I've had a few drinks, if that's any of your business."

Fischer dumped the crowbar on the table, moving toward her. "Lionel will be pleased that you—" She gestured airily toward the machine.

Fischer reached her, took her arm. "Come on."

She pulled away from him. "Come on, yourself." She staggered slightly, then regained her balance, turning toward the machine.

"Mrs. Barrett—"

"Edith."

Fischer took her arm again. "Come *on*. You shouldn't leave your husband."

"He's all right. He's sleeping."

Fischer tried to turn her, but she wouldn't do it. Snickering, she pulled away from him again. "For Christ's sake!" he snapped.

A teasing smile drew back her lips. "No, not for his sake." Fischer looked at her confusedly.

As she started toward the table, the room was nebulous around her, and she had the vague impression it was filled with people standing just beyond the limits of her vision. That's imagination, said her mind. All there is in here is mindless energy.

She reached the table and rubbed a finger on its surface. Fischer rejoined her. "You've got to go upstairs."

"No, I don't." She took hold of his right hand. Fischer pulled it away. Edith smiled and rubbed her finger on the table again. "This is where they met," she said.

"Who?"

"Les Aphrodites. Here. Around this table."

Fischer took her arm again. Edith jerked it in against herself so that his hand was pinned against her breast. "Here. Around this table," she repeated.

"You don't know what you're saying." Fischer pulled his hand away.

"I know exactly what I'm saying. Mr. Fischer." Edith snickered. "Mr. B. F. Fischer."

"Edith—"

He tightened as she pushed against him, sliding her arms around him. "Don't you like me at all?" she asked. "I know I'm not as beautiful as Florence, but I—"

"Edith, it's the house. It's making you—"

"The house is doing nothing," she broke in. "*I'm* doing it."

He tried to pull away her arms. She pressed against him harder. "Are you impotent too?" she teased.

Fischer wrenched her arms loose, pushing her away. "Wake up!" he shouted.

Fury burst inside her. "Don't tell *me* to wake up! *You*

wake up!—you sexless bastard." Edith stumbled back against the table, wriggled up on top of it, and yanked her skirt with clawing fingers. "What's the matter, little man?" she jeered. "Never had a woman?" Grabbing at her sweater front, she jerked it open, popping buttons. Dragging aside the edges, she undid the front hook of her bra and, clutching at her breasts with palsied fingers, held them up, a look of furious derision on her face. "What's the *matter*, little man?" she ranted. "Never had a tit before? *Try* it! It's delicious!"

Sliding off the table, she advanced on Fischer, fingers gouging at her breasts. "Suck them," she said, her voice trembling with hatred. Her face convulsed with sudden fury. "Suck them, you fairy bastard, or I'll get myself a woman who will!"

His head jerked sideways. Edith scanned the movement, and a sudden weight crashed down on her.

Lionel was standing in the archway.

A wave of darkness billowed up at her. Her legs gave way; she started falling. Fischer leaped to catch her. "No!" she screamed. She twisted to the left and fell against a marble statue on a pedestal. She caught at it; the cold stone pressed against her breasts. It seemed as though the face was leering at her Edith cried out as the weight of it fell backward from her grasp and shattered on the floor. She landed on her knees and toppled forward.

Darkness swallowed her.

4:27 P.M.

Somewhere there was music playing, slowly, tenderly; a waltz. She was dancing to the music, gliding through a kind of mist. Was she in the ballroom? She could not be sure. Her partner's face was indistinct, yet she felt certain it was Daniel's. She could feel his arm around her and his left hand holding out her right. It was warm. There was a scent of flowers in the air; roses, she decided. A summer dance. A small string orchestra performing. Florence danced in languorous circles with her partner.

"Are you happy?" he asked.

"Yes," she murmured. "Very."

Was she on a set? Was that it? Was she making a film? She tried to recall but couldn't. Still, how could it be a film? It was all too real; no camera, no banks of lights, no fourth wall missing and the crew in sight, the sound man at his board. No, it was a real ballroom. Florence tried again to see her partner's face, but couldn't focus her eyes. "Daniel?" she murmured.

"My dear?"

"It *is* you," Florence said.

She saw him then, his grave face very handsome, very gentle. His arm drew tight around her. "I love you," he said.

"And I love you."

"You'll never leave me? Always be beside me?"

"Yes, my darling, always; always."

Florence closed her eyes. The music quickened, and she felt herself being swept around the ballroom floor. She heard the rustling of a hundred skirts, the ballroom filled with dancers, lovers. Florence smiled. And she loved, too; loved Daniel. Daniel held her safely as they danced. She scarcely felt her feet; she seemed to float.

She felt a scented breeze across her face and smiled again. He'd danced her out onto the wide veranda. Overhead, the sky was filled with stars, like diamond fragments sprinkled on black velvet; she didn't have to look to know that they were there. The moon was full, pale silver, glowing. It shed soft radiance on the garden just beyond. She didn't have to look; she knew. Had she been drinking wine? She felt intoxicated. No; it was intoxication of the spirit. It was joy and love, sweet music playing in the distance as she waltzed with her beloved Daniel, around, around, dancing slowly toward—

He shouted. "No!"

Florence gasped in shock, all senses flooded. Daniel stood before her in the mist, white-faced, frightened, gesturing for her to stop. Icy water numbed her feet and ankles, cold wind scored her face, the smell of rot assailed her nostrils; crying out, she staggered back and fell. Something seemed to rush away behind her. Florence thrashed around and caught a momentary view of someone very tall and dressed in black vanishing into the mist.

She shuddered as the freezing air sliced deep into her flesh. She lay beside the tarn.

She had been walking into it.

With a sound of sickened dread, she pushed up, started running for the house. Her shoes were wet, the bottoms of her stockings. Shivering, she dashed along the gravel path. The blind face of the house loomed darkly from the mist. She ran across the gravel, up the steps. The doorway yawned. She ran inside and slammed the door, falling back against it.

She was shaking from the cold, from fright. She couldn't stop herself. *She'd almost walked into the tarn.* The knowledge horrified her.

She started as a figure hurried down the hallway from the kitchen. It was Fischer, with a glass in his hand. Seeing her, he stopped a moment, then advanced again. "What happened?" he asked.

"Is that whiskey?"

Fischer nodded.

"Let me have some."

He handed her the glass, and Florence drank, choking as the liquor scalded down her throat. She handed back the glass.

"What happened?" Fischer asked.

"He tried to kill me."

"Who?"

"Belasco," she said. She clutched at his arm. "I *saw* him, Ben. I actually caught a glimpse of him as he left me by the tarn."

She told him what had happened, how Belasco had made her think she was dancing in the ballroom with Daniel, while he'd led her to the tarn to drown her. How Daniel had warned her at the moment she was going in.

"How did Belasco get control of you?" he asked.

"I must have dozed off. I was tired after sitting, after everything that's happened today."

Fischer looked ill. "If he can get you in your sleep now—"

"No." She shook her head. "He won't again. I'm warned now. I'll retain my strength." She shivered. "Can we go in by the fire?"

When they were sitting in front of the fire, her shoes and stockings off, her feet propped on a stool, a new log crackling on the fire, Florence said, "I think I know the secret of Hell House, Ben."

Fischer didn't speak for almost half a minute. "Do you?" he asked then.

"It's Belasco."

"How?"

"He safeguards the haunting of his house by reinforcing it," she said. "By acting as a hidden aide for every other haunting force."

Fischer did not respond, but she could tell from the sudden flare of interest in his eyes that she had gotten through to him. He sat up slowly, as though uncoiling, his eyes fixed on hers.

"Think of it, Ben," she said. "*Controlled multiple haunting.* Something absolutely unique in haunted houses: a surviving will so powerful that he can use that power to dominate every other surviving personality in the house."

"You think the others are aware of it?" he asked.

"I don't know about the others. All I know is that his son is. If he weren't, he couldn't have saved my life.

"It all fits, Ben," she said. "It's been Belasco from the start. He's the one who's kept me from the chapel. He's the one who tried to keep me from discovering Daniel's body last night. He's the one who made it seem that Daniel had bitten me, the one who possessed the cat. He's the one who caused the poltergeist attack on Doctor Barrett, trying to turn us against each other. He's the one who's keeping Daniel's soul imprisoned here.

"Think of what fantastic power he possesses, Ben. To actually be capable of keeping another's spirit from progression, *despite* a consecrated burial. Maybe it's because Daniel is his son, but, even so, it's incredible."

She leaned back in her chair, looking at the flames. "He's like a general with his army. Never entering the battle, but always controlling it."

"How can he be hurt, then? Generals don't get killed in war."

"We'll hurt him by decreasing the size of his army until he has no one left, until he has to fight his war alone." She looked at him with challenge in her eyes. "A general without an army is nothing."

"But we have only till Sunday."

Florence shook her head. "I'm staying here until the job is done," she said.

She closed the door and moved immediately to her bed. Kneeling beside it, she offered up a prayer of gratitude for the enlightenment which had been given her, a prayer of request for strength to deal with what she had discovered.

When the prayers were ended, she rose and moved into

the bathroom to cleanse her ankles and feet; there was still a residue of odor from the tarn on them. As she washed and dried them, she thought about the massive project which lay ahead: to release the earthbound spirits from this house, against the will of Emeric Belasco. It almost seemed too much to accomplish.

"But I will," she said aloud, as though Belasco listened. She'd have to be alert, though. What Ben had said was true. "You've been fooled before," he'd said. "Make sure you aren't fooled again."

"I'll be careful," she'd replied.

She would. She recognized the sense in what he'd said. How thoroughly she had been fooled last night into believing that, perhaps, she'd been responsible for the poltergeist attack on Dr. Barrett. How thoroughly she had been fooled this morning into thinking that Daniel was responsible for the bites and for the cat's attack on her. She must not allow herself to be fooled again. Daniel had not been responsible for any of those things. He was tormented, not tormentor.

Florence closed her eyes, hands clasped in front of her. Daniel, listen now, she whispered in her mind. I thank you, with all my heart, for saving my life. But don't you see what it means? If you can thwart your father's will in that way, you can also thwart it by departing from this house. You don't have to stay here any longer. You're free to go if only you believe. Your father has no power to hold you prisoner. Ask for the help of those beyond, and it will come to you. You *can* leave this house. You *can!*

Florence opened her eyes abruptly. Moving to the Spanish table, she opened her purse. She took out a pad and pencil, laid the pad on the table, picked up the pencil, and held its point against the paper. Instantly it started moving. She closed her eyes and felt it writing by itself, tugging her hand this way and that. In seconds it stopped, and the feeling of control drained from her hand. She looked at the pad.

"No!" She tore the top sheet off and crumpled it into a ball, flinging it to the floor, "No, Daniel! No!"

She stood beside the table, trembling, staring at the paper, the words engraved on her mind.

One way only.

6:11 P.M.

Fischer stood at the edge of the tarn, shining his flashlight at the turbid surface of the water. Twice now, he was thinking. Edith first, then Florence. He moved the cone of light across the water, grimacing at the stench which hovered over it. Once when he'd been working in a hospital, an old man had died of gangrenous wounds on his back. The smell of his room had been like this.

He looked around. Footsteps were approaching through the mist. Abruptly he switched off his flashlight and turned. Who was it? Florence? Surely she would not be coming back after what had happened. Barrett or his wife? He couldn't believe that they'd come out here either. Who, then? Fischer tensed as the footsteps drew closer. He could not determine their origin in the mist. He waited, rigid, heartbeat thudding.

They were on him suddenly. Seeing the glow of a lantern, he flicked on his flashlight. There was a strangled gasp. Fischer stared with blank confusion at the two gaunt faces in his light.

"*Who's that?*" the old man asked. His voice was trembling.

Fischer caught his breath and lowered the beam of light. "I'm sorry," he said. "I'm one of the four."

The old woman released a breath which sounded like a groan. "Lord," she muttered.

"I'm sorry, I was startled, too," Fischer apologized, "I didn't realize what time it was."

"You scared the livin' breath from us," the old man said resentfully.

"Sorry." Fischer turned away.

The couple mumbled indistinctly as they trailed him to the house. Fischer held the door for them, then followed as they hurried across the entry hall, looking around uneasily. They were wearing heavy overcoats, the woman a woolen scarf on her head, the man a battered gray fedora.

"How are things in the world?" asked Fischer.

"Mmm," the man responded. The old woman made a sound of disapproval.

"No matter," Fischer said. "We have our own world here."

He moved behind them into the great hall, observing as they set the covered dishes on the table. He saw them looking at Barrett's machine, exchanging glances. Quickly they gathered up the lunch things and started toward the entry hall. Fischer watched their departure, fighting an urge to yell "Boo!" and see what would happen. If they thought a flashlight beam in the face was frightening, what would they think of what had happened in the house since Monday?

"Thank you!" he called as they moved beneath the archway. The old man grunted sourly, and he saw them exchange another look.

When the front door had shut, Fischer moved to the table and lifted the covers of the trays. Lamb chops, peas and carrots, potatoes, biscuits, pie, and coffee. *A Meal Fit for a King,* he thought. His smile was dour. Or was it *The Last Supper?*

Removing his pea coat, he tossed it onto a chair, setting the flashlight on top of it. He forked a lamb chop onto a plate, added a spoonful of carrots and peas, poured himself a cup of coffee. Community meals seem to have gone by the board since last night, he thought. He sat at the table and drank some coffee, then began to eat. He'd bring some food to Florence in a while.

He began to think of what she'd said. He'd been thinking of it constantly, trying to find loopholes in it. So far he'd been unable to; it made sense, there was no escaping it.

This time Florence was on the right track.

It was a strange, not altogether satisfying certainty he felt. They'd always known that Belasco was here—he and Florence had, at any rate—but the knowledge had been an unexplored one, at least on his part. That they would come to terms with Belasco himself had never really occurred to him. True, he had contacted him in 1940, but the juncture had been evanescent, a nonconnective tissue in the body of Hell House.

This was more than that. This was integral. He'd tried to pick it apart a dozen different ways without success. It was too logical. By using these anomalous means, Belasco could act in any area without his presence ever being known. He could create an all but incomprehensible tapestry of effects by manipulating every entity within the house, shifting from one to the other, always in the background—as Florence had said, a general with his army.

He thought about the record suddenly. It had been no coincidence. It had been Belasco greeting them upon their entrance into his home—his battlefield. He heard the eerie, mocking voice inside his mind again. *Welcome to my house. I'm delighted you could come.*

Fischer turned to see Barrett limping across the room, looking pale and solemn. He wondered if the older man were going to speak to him. He'd said nothing earlier, obviously suffering humiliation on humiliation by the fact that he'd been unable to carry Edith upstairs himself.

He waited. Barrett stopped and looked at his machine with a confused expression. He looked at Fischer then. "Did you do that?" he asked, his voice subdued.

Fischer nodded.

The faintest tremor raised the ends of Barrett's mouth. "Thank you," he murmured.

"You're welcome."

Barrett limped to the table and began to put food on two plates, using his left hand. Fischer glanced at his right and saw how awkwardly the thumb was held.

"I haven't thanked you for what you did this afternoon," Barrett said. "In the steam room," he added quickly.

"Doctor?"

Barrett looked up.

"What happened in here before—"

"I'd rather not discuss it, if you don't mind."

Fischer felt obliged to speak. "I'm only trying to help."

"I appreciate that, but—"

"Doctor," Fischer interrupted, "something in this house is working on your wife. What happened before—"

"Mr. Fischer—"

"—was not her doing."

"If you don't mind, Mr. Fischer—"

"Doctor Barrett, this is life and death I'm talking about. Did you know she almost walked into the tarn last night?"

Barrett started, looking shocked. "When?" he demanded.

"Near midnight. You were asleep." Fischer paused for emphasis. "So was she."

"She walked in her sleep?" Barrett looked appalled.

"If I hadn't seen her go outside—"

"You should have told me sooner."

"*She* should have told you," Fischer said. "The fact that she didn't is—" He broke off at the look of offense on Barrett's face. "Doctor, I don't know what you think is going on in this house, but—"

"What I think is going on is irrelevant to this conversation, Mr. Fischer," Barrett said stiffly.

"Irrelevant?" Fischer looked amazed. "What the hell do you mean, irrelevant? Whatever's going on is getting to your wife. It's gotten to Florence, and it's gotten to you. Or maybe you haven't noticed."

Barrett regarded him in silence, his expression hard. "I've noticed a number of things, Mr. Fischer," he finally said. "One of which is that Mr. Deutsch is wasting approximately a third of his money."

Picking up the plates of food and two forks, he turned away.

For a long time after he'd gone, Fischer sat without moving, staring across the great hall.

"Like hell," he muttered then. What in the name of God did Barrett expect him to do?—commit progressive suicide like Florence? If he wasn't handling things the way they should be handled, how come he was the only one unharmed so far?

The truth crashed over him so violently it made him catch his breath. "*No,*" he muttered angrily. It wasn't true. He knew what he was doing. Of the three of them, he was the only one who—

The defensive thought broke off in fragments. Fischer felt a wave of nausea rush through him. Barrett was right. Florence was right.

Those thirty years of waiting had been nothing but delusion.

Standing with a muffled curse, he strode to the fireplace. No, it was impossible. He couldn't deceive himself so completely. He struggled to remember what he'd done since Monday. He'd known the door would be locked, hadn't he? His mind rejected that. All right, he'd rescued Edith. Only because you couldn't sleep and happened to be downstairs, came the answer. What about saving Barrett, then? *Nothing,* said his mind. He'd been available, that was all—and even then he might have fled if it hadn't been for Mrs. Barrett's presence. What was left? He'd pulled the planking off the crate. Wonderful, he thought, in sudden rage. Deutsch hired himself a hundred-thousand-dollar handyman!

"Christ," he muttered. He shouted, "*Christ!*" He'd been the most powerful physical medium in the United States in 1940—and at fifteen. *Fifteen!* Now, at forty-five, he was a goddamned, self-deluding parasite, malingering his way through the week in order to collect a hundred thousand dollars. Him! The one who should be doing the most!

He paced back and forth in front of the fireplace. The feeling he had was almost unendurable, compounded of shame and guilt and fury. He'd never felt so meaningless. To walk around in Hell House like a turtle with its head pulled in, a blind shell seeing nothing, knowing nothing, doing nothing, waiting for the others to accomplish the work he should be accomplishing. He'd wanted to come back here, hadn't he? Well, he was back! Something—God only knew what—had seen fit to give him a second chance.

Was he going to let it pass him by, untouched?

Fischer stopped and looked around the great hall with a furious expression. Who the hell is Belasco? he thought. Who the hell are any of the goddamned dead who glut this house like maggots on a corpse? Was he going to let them terrify him to his dying day? They hadn't been able to kill him in 1940, had they? He'd been a child, a thoughtless, overconfident fool—and even so, they'd been unable to destroy him. Grace Lauter they'd destroyed—one of the most respected mental mediums of the day. Dr. Graham they'd destroyed—a hardheaded, dauntless physician. Professor Rand they'd destroyed—one of the nation's most noted chemistry teachers, head of his department at Hale University. Professor Fenley they'd destroyed—a shrewd, experienced Spiritualist who had survived a hundred psychic pitfalls.

Only he had lived and kept his sanity—a credulous boy of fifteen. Despite the fact that he had virtually begged to be annihilated, the house had been able to do no more than eject him, leaving him on its porch to die of exposure. It had not been able to kill him. Why had he never thought of it in just that way before? Despite the perfect opportunity, *it had not been able to kill him*.

Fischer moved to one of the armchairs and sat down hurriedly. Closing his eyes, he began to draw in deep breaths, starting to unlock the gates of consciousness before he had a chance to change his mind. Confidence suffused his mind and body. He was not a boy now, but a thinking man; not so blindly confident that he would make himself a vulnerable prey. He would open up with care, stage by stage, not allowing himself to be overwhelmed by impressions, as Florence did. Slowly, carefully, monitoring each step of the way with his adult intelligence, trusting only to himself, not allowing others to control his perception in any way.

He stopped his heavy breathing, waited, tense, alert. Nothing yet. A flatness and a vacancy about him. He waited longer, antennae feeling at the atmosphere. There was nothing. He drew in further breath, opening the gates a little wider, stopped again, and waited.

Nothing. Fischer felt a flicker of involuntary dread cross his mind. *Had he waited too long?* Had his power atrophied? His lips pressed hard together, whitening. *No*. He still possessed it. He breathed in deeply, inspiring further cognizance into his mind. He felt a tingling in his fingertips, the sensation of a spider web collecting on his face, his solar plexus drawing inward. He had not done this in years; too long. He had forgotten how it felt, that surging growth of awareness, all his senses widening in spectrum. Every sound was heard exaggeratedly: the crackling of the fire, the infinitesimal creaking of his chair, the sound of his breath soughing in and out. The smell of the house became intense. The texture of his clothes felt rough against his skin. He could feel the delicate waft of heat from the fire.

He frowned. But nothing else. What was happening? It made no sense to him. This house had to be gorged with impressions. The moment he'd walked in on Monday he'd sensed their presence like some cloud of influences, always ready to attack, take advantage of the slightest flaw, the least misstep in judgment.

It struck him suddenly. *Misstep in judgment!*

Instantly he started pulling back. But, already; something dark and vast was hurtling at him, something with discernment, something violent that meant to pounce on him and crush him. Fischer gasped and pressed back hard against the chair, recoiling his awareness desperately.

He was not in time. Before he could protect himself, the force swept over him, entering his system through the chink still open in his armor. He cried out loudly as it wrenched into his vitals, twisting, clawing, threatening to disembowel him, slice his brain to shreds. His eyes leaped open, staring, horror-stricken. Doubling over, he clapped both hands across his stomach. Something slammed against his back, his head, hurling him out of the chair. He crashed against a table edge, was flung back with a strangling gasp. The room began to spin around, its atmosphere a whirlpool of barbaric force. Fischer crumpled to his knees, arms crossed, trying to shut out the savage power. It tried to rip his arms apart. He fought it, teeth clenched, face a stonelike mask of agonized resistance, gurgling noises in his throat. You won't! he thought. You won't! You *won't!*

The power vanished suddenly, sucked back into the air. Fischer tottered on his knees, across his face the dazed expression of a man who'd just been bayoneted in the stomach. He tried to hold himself erect but couldn't. With a choking noise, he fell, landing on his side and drawing up his legs, bending forward at the neck until he had contracted to a fetal pose, eyes closed, body shivering uncontrollably. He felt the rug against his cheek. Nearby, he heard the pop and crackle of the fire. And it seemed as though someone were standing over him, someone who regarded him with cold, sadistic pleasure, gloating at the sight of his ravaged form, the helpless dissolution of his will.

And wondering, idly, casually, just how and when to finish him off.

6:27 P.M.

Barrett stood beside the bed, looking at Edith, wondering whether to wake her or not. The food was getting cold; but was it food she needed, or rest?

He moved to his own bed and sat with a groan. Crossing his left leg over his right, he touched the burn gingerly. He couldn't use his injured thumb. The cut should have been sutured. God knew how infected it was getting. He was afraid to remove the bandage and look.

He didn't see how he was going to work on the machine tonight. The least exertion brought on pain in his leg and lower back; just walking downstairs and up had been a strain. Grimacing, he eased off his left shoe. His feet were swelling too. He had to end it by tomorrow. He wasn't sure he could last beyond then.

The realization drained his waning confidence even further.

• • •

Noises had awakened him—the sound of something thumping on the rug. Slowly he had surfaced from a leaden sleep, thinking that he heard a door shut somewhere.

When he'd opened his eyes, Edith was gone.

For several groggy moments he had thought she was in the bathroom. Then, on the periphery of vision, he'd caught sight of something on the floor, and sat up, staring at the manuscript pages scattered across the rug. His gaze had shifted to the area beside the cabinet. Photographs were lying strewn about; a book had fallen.

Alarm had started rising in him then. Grabbing his cane, he'd stood, his attention caught by the brandy decanter on the table, the silver cup. Crossing to the cabinet, he'd looked down at the photographs, tensing as he saw what they were.

"Edith?" He'd turned toward the bathroom. "Edith, are you in there?" He'd limped to the bathroom door and knocked. "Edith?"

There'd been no reply. He'd waited several moments before turning the knob; the door was unlocked.

She was gone.

He'd turned in dismay, hobbling to the door as quickly as he could, trying not to panic; but everything about the situation was ominous: his manuscript thrown to the floor, those photographs, the brandy decanter back on the table, and on top of all that, Edith's absence.

He'd hurried into the corridor and moved to Florence Tanner's room. Knocking, he'd waited for several seconds, then knocked again. When there'd been no reply, he'd opened the door, to see Miss Tanner heavily asleep on her bed. He'd backed out, shut the door, and moved to Fischer's room.

There'd been no one there, and he'd begun to panic then. He'd moved across the corridor and looked into the entry hall below, thinking he heard voices. Frowning, he'd limped to the stairs and started to descend as quickly as he could, teeth set against the pain in his leg. He'd *told* her not to do this! What was the matter with her?

He'd heard her voice as he crossed the entry hall, her tone unnatural as she said, "It's delicious!" With renewed alarm, he'd hastened his steps.

Then he'd reached the archway and was frozen there, staring into the great hall with a stunned expression, watching Edith, sweater open, bra unhooked, advancing on Fischer, breasts in her hands, ordering him to—

Barrett closed his eyes and pressed a hand across them. He'd never heard such language from her in their married life, never seen a hint of such behavior, not even to himself, much less to any other man. That she was probably repressed, he'd always known; their sex life had been necessarily constrained. But this—

He dropped his hand and looked at her again. The pain was returning, the distrust, the anger, the desire for retaliation of some kind. He struggled against it. He wanted to believe that the house had done it all to her, but he could not expunge the nagging doubt that somewhere deep within her lay the real cause of what had happened. Which, of course, explained his sudden animosity toward Fischer's words, he recognized.

He stood and crossed to her. They had to talk; he couldn't stand this doubting any longer. Reaching down, he touched her shoulder.

She awakened with a gasp, eyes flung open, legs retracting suddenly. Barrett tried to smile but couldn't. "I've brought your supper," he said.

"Supper." She spoke the word as though she'd never heard it in her life.

He nodded once. "Why don't you wash up?"

Edith looked around the room. Was she wondering where

he'd put the photographs? he thought. He withdrew as she sat up, looking down at herself. He'd refastened her bra and closed her sweater with what buttons remained. Her right hand fluttered up the front of her sweater; then she stood and crossed to the bathroom.

Barrett limped to the octagonal table, picked up the boxed manuscript, and placed it on the library table against the wall. With great effort he pulled the chair beside her bed over to the octagonal table and sat down. He eyed the lamb chops and vegetables on his plate and sighed. He should never have brought her to this house. It had been a dreadful mistake.

He turned as the bathroom door opened. Edith, her face washed and hair combed, walked over to the table and sat. She did not pick up her fork, but sat hunched over, gaze deflected, looking like a chastened girl. Barrett cleared his throat. "The food is cold," he said, "but . . . well, you need something."

He saw her dig her teeth into her lower lip as it began to tremble. After several moments she replied, "You don't have to be polite to me."

Barrett felt a sudden need to shout at her, fought it off. "You shouldn't have had any more of that brandy," he said. "I examined it before, and unless I'm mistaken, it contains more than fifty percent absinthe."

She looked up questioningly.

"An aphrodisiac."

She gazed at him in silence.

"As for the rest," he heard himself say, "there *is* a powerful influence in this house. I think it's begun to affect you." Why am I saying this? he wondered. Why am I absolving her?

Still, the look. Barrett felt a tremor in his stomach.

"Is that all?" she finally asked.

"All?"

"You've . . . solved the problem?" There was an undertone of resentful mortification in her voice.

Barrett tensed. "I'm trying to be rational."

"I see," she whispered.

"Would you rather I ranted? Called you names?" He pulled himself erect. "I'm trying, for the moment, to blame it on outside forces."

Edith said nothing.

"I know I haven't provided sufficient . . . physical love," he said with difficulty. "There *is* the polio damage, but I suppose that's not a full excuse. Maybe it's my mother's influence, maybe my total absorption in my work, my inability to—"

"Don't."

"I'm blaming it on that," he said determinedly. "On myself and on the house." There was a sheen of perspiration on his brow. He took out his handkerchief and wiped it off. "Kindly permit me to do so," he said. "If there are other factors involved . . . we'll work them out later. After we've left this house."

He waited. Edith managed a nod.

"You should have told me what happened last night."

She looked up quickly.

"About your almost walking into the tarn."

She looked as though she were about to speak; but as he said no more, she changed her mind. "I didn't want to worry you," she said.

"I understand." He stood with a groan. "I think I'll rest my leg a bit before I go downstairs."

"You have to work tonight?"

"I have to finish by tomorrow."

She walked beside him to the bed and watched as he lay down, lifting his right leg with effort. He saw her trying not to show reaction to the swollen state of his ankles. "I'll be all right," he told her.

She stood beside the bed, looking at him worriedly. Finally she said, "Do you want me to leave, Lionel?"

He was quiet for a while before he answered. "Not if you'll stay with me all the time from now on."

"All right." She seemed to hold back, then, on impulse, sat beside him. "I know you can't forgive me now," she said. "I don't expect it—no, please don't speak. I know what I've done. I'd give twenty years of my life to undo it."

Her head dropped forward. "I don't know why I drank like that, except that I was nervous—frightened. I don't know why I went downstairs. I was conscious of what I was doing, yet, at the same time—"

She looked up, tears brimming in her eyes. "I'm not asking for forgiveness. Just try not to hate me too much. I need you, Lionel. I love you. And I don't know what's happening to me." She could hardly speak now. "I just don't know what's happening to me."

"My *dear*." Despite the pain, Barrett sat up and put his arms around her, pressing his cheek to hers. "It's all right, all right. It will all pass after we've left this house." He turned his face to kiss her hair. "I love you, too. But then, you've always known that, haven't you?"

Edith clung to him, sobbing. It's going to be all right, he told himself. It *had* been the house. Everything would be resolved after they left.

7:31 P.M.

Florence straightened with a groan. Leaning her elbow on the mattress edge, she levered to her feet. What time is it? she wondered. Declining her head, she raised her watch. *That late,* she thought, dismayed.

And still he was here.

Sighing wearily, she trudged into the bathroom and rinsed her face with cold water. As she dried her skin, she gazed at her reflection in the mirror. She looked haggard.

For more than two hours she'd been praying for Daniel's release. Kneeling beside the bed, hands clasped tightly, she had called upon all those in the spirit world who had helped her in the past, asking them to aid Daniel in breaking the bonds which kept him a prisoner of Hell House.

It hadn't worked. When the hours of prayer were ended and she'd sent out feelers of awareness, Daniel had been nearby.

Waiting.

Florence hung up the towel and left the bathroom. Crossing the bedroom, she went into the corridor and started for the stairs. More and more, her deepening involvement with Daniel was disturbing her. I should be doing more, she thought. There were so many other souls to be reprieved as well. Could she really manage to remain in Hell House for as long as it would take to do that? Without light or heat or food, how could she subsist? It was obvious that, after Sunday, Deutsch would want the house closed up.

What about the other entities she'd contacted since Monday?—and that only a small percentage of the actual number, she was convinced. Recollections tided through her mind as she descended the staircase. The "something" in her room; it might not have been Daniel. That sense of pain and sorrow she'd experienced while leaving the garage on Monday afternoon. The furious entity on the staircase to the basement who had called this house a "goddamn sewer." The perverted evil in the steam room. She still felt a terrible guilt for failing to warn Dr. Barrett. The spirit Red Cloud had described as like a caveman covered with sores. Whatever it was in the chapel which prevented her from entering; it might not be Belasco. The figure at the sitting which had reached for Mrs. Barrett. Florence shook her head. There were so many, she thought. Unhappy presences filled this house wherever she moved. Even now she felt that, if she opened herself, she would come upon many more of them. They were everywhere. In the theater and the ballroom, in the dining hall, the great hall—everywhere. Would a *year* be long enough in which to contact all of them?

She thought, with anguish, about the list which Dr. Barrett had. *Apparitions; Apports* . . . *Bilocation* . . . *Chemical phenomena* . . . *Clairsentience* . . . *Direct voice* . . . *Elongation* . . . *Ideoplasm* . . . *Imprints* . . . There must be more than a hundred items on the list. They had barely scratched the surface of Hell House. A massive sense of hopelessness assailed her. She tried to fight it off but found it impossible. It was one thing to speak of solving the enigma, step by step, if one had unlimited time. But a week. No, less. Only a little more than four days now.

Willfully, she thrust her shoulders back and walked erect. *I'm doing all I can,* she told herself. I can do no more. If all she did in the entire week was give Daniel peace, it would be enough. She walked determinedly into the great hall. She needed food. She wasn't going to sit anymore. She'd make sure she ate well for the rest of the week. Moving to the table, she began to serve herself some dinner.

She was about to sit at the table when she saw him. He was sitting before the fireplace, staring at the lowering flames. He hadn't even turned to look at her.

"I didn't see you," she said. She carried her plate of food over to him. "May I sit with you?"

He glanced at her as though she were a stranger. Florence sat down on another armchair and began to eat.

"What's wrong, Ben?" she asked when he gave no indication of accepting her company.

"Nothing."

She hesitated, then went on. "Has something happened?"

Fischer didn't answer.

"You seemed so hopeful before, when we were talking."

He said nothing.

"What's happened, Ben?"

"Nothing."

Florence started at the anger in his voice. "Have I done something wrong?"

He drew in breath, said nothing.

"I thought we trusted each other, Ben."

"I don't trust anyone or anything," he said. "And anyone who does, in this house, is a fool."

"Something *has* happened."

"A lot of things have happened," Fischer snapped.

"Nothing we can't handle."

"Wrong." He turned on her, his dark eyes filled with venom—and with fear, she saw. "There's nothing in this house we *can* handle. Nothing anyone is *ever* going to handle."

"That isn't true, Ben. We've made wonderful progress."

"Toward what? *Our mutual graves?*"

"No." She shook her head. "We've discovered much. Daniel, for instance; and the way Belasco works."

"Daniel," he said contemptuously. "How do you know there *is* a Daniel? Barrett thinks you made him up in your mind. How do you know he isn't right?"

"Ben, the body, the ring—"

"*A* body, *a* ring," he broke in. "Is that your proof? Your logic for putting your head on the block?"

Florence was shocked at the malevolence in his voice. What had *happened* to him?

"How do you know you haven't been deluding yourself from the first moment you entered this house?" he demanded. "How do you know Daniel Belasco isn't a figment of your imagination? How do you know his personality isn't exactly what you've made it, his problem exactly what you've made it? *How do you know?"*

He jarred to his feet, glaring at her. "You're *right,*" he said. "I'm obstructed, shut off. And I'm going to *stay* shut off until the week is over. At which time I'll collect my hundred thousand clams and never come within a thousand miles of this goddamned house again. I suggest you do the same."

Turning on his heel, he moved across the floor with angry strides. "Ben—!" she called. He ignored her. Florence tried to stand to follow, but she didn't have the strength. She sat slumped on the chair, gazing toward the entry hall. After a while she set her plate aside. His words had had a terrible impact on her. She tried to repress them, but they would not be repressed. All the uncertainties were returning. She'd always been a mental medium. Why should she have, suddenly, become a physical one? It made no sense, it was unprecedented.

It threatened her faith.

"No." She shook her head. It wasn't true. Daniel *did* exist. She had to believe that. He'd saved her life. He'd spoken to her, pleaded with her.

Pleaded. Spoken. Saved her life.

How do you know Daniel Belasco isn't a figment of your imagination?

She tried to repel the notion, but it wouldn't leave. All she could think was that if he *were* a product of her imagination, she would have had him save her life exactly as he did. In trance, she would have taken herself down to the tarn to prove

Belasco's murderous intent, then awakened herself at the moment of entering the tarn in order to prove that Daniel existed and wanted to save her life; even given herself the vision of him standing before her, blocking the way; the vision of Belasco fleeing.

"*No.*" She shook her head again. It wasn't true. Daniel did exist; he *did*.

Are you happy? she thought, the words rising unexpectedly to the surface of consciousness. *Yes. Very.* The words she'd exchanged with Daniel as she'd danced with him—or thought that she was dancing with him. *Are you happy? Yes. Very. Are you happy? Yes. Very.*

"Oh, my God," she murmured.

She'd spoken those words in a television play once.

Her mind strained desperately to resist the onrush of doubt—but now the dam of her resistance had fallen, and the dark waters were flooding in. *I love you. And I love you.* "No," she whispered, tears welling in her eyes. *You'll never leave me, will you? You'll always be beside me? Yes, my darling, always; always.*

She saw him as he'd looked that evening in the hospital, pale, drawn, eyes bright with the glitter of impending death; her beloved David. The remembrance chilled her. He had whispered to her earlier of Laura, the girl he loved. He'd never shared her physical love, and now he was dying, and it was too late.

He'd held her hand so tightly it had hurt, his face a lined, gray mask, his lips bloodless as he'd spoken those words to her: *I love you.* She had whispered back: *I love you, too.* Had he known, by then, that it was her in the room with him? Dying, had he thought that she was Laura? *You'll never leave me, will you?* he'd murmured. *You'll always be beside me?* And she had answered: *Yes, my darling, always; always.*

A sob of terror broke inside her. No, it wasn't true! She

started crying. But it *was* true. *She had made up Daniel Belasco in her mind.* There *was* no Daniel Belasco. There was only the memory of her brother, and the way he'd died, the loss he'd felt, the need he'd carried to his grave.

"No, no, no, no, no." Her hands were clutching at the arms of the chair, her head slumped forward, shaking, hot tears spilling from her eyes. She couldn't seem to breathe, kept gulping at the air, as if her lungs were bursting. No, it wasn't true! She could not have done this thing, this blinded, terrible, deluded thing! There had to be some way of proving that! There had to be!

She jerked her head up with a gasp, staring at the fire through gelatinous tears. It seemed as though someone had whispered in her ear: two words.

The chapel.

A trembling smile drew back her lips. She wavered to her feet and started toward the entry hall, rubbing at her eyes. There was an answer in the chapel; she had always known that. Now, in an instant, she knew it was the answer she needed; it was proof and vindication.

This time she would get in.

She tried not to run but couldn't help herself. She rushed across the entry hall and past the staircase, skirts rustling, shoes thudding on the floor. Turning the corner, she started down the side corridor, running as fast as she could.

She reached the chapel door and placed her hands against it. Instantly the rush of cold resistance filled her vitals, the grinding churn of nausea. She pressed both palms against the door and started praying. Nothing in this world or in the next was going to stop her now.

The force within the chapel seemed to waver. Florence pressed her weight against the door. "In the name of the Father, the Son, and the Holy Ghost!" she said in a loud, clear voice. The force began retreating, drawing backward and inward, as though it were shrinking. Her lips moved quickly as she prayed. "You cannot keep me from this place, for God is with me! We will enter now, together! Open! You cannot repel me any longer! *Open!*"

Suddenly the force was gone. Florence pushed the door and went inside, switching on the lights. Leaning back against the door, she closed her eyes and spoke. "I thank thee, Lord, for giving me strength."

After several moments, she opened her eyes and looked around. The dim illumination of the wall lights barely held the darkness at bay. She was standing in a shadow, only her face in light as she searched the room with her eyes. The silence was intense; she seemed to feel its pressure on her eardrums.

Moving forward abruptly, she drifted down the center aisle, averting her shocked gaze from the crucifix above the altar. This was the way; she felt it unmistakably. Unseen filaments were drawing at her.

She reached the foot of the altar and looked at it. A massive Bible with metal clasps was set on top of it. A Bible in this hideous place, she thought, shuddering. Her gaze shifted around the wall. The drawing power was so intense it seemed as though invisible threads were tied to her, pulling her toward . . . what? The wall? The altar? Surely not the crucifix. Florence felt herself drawn forward, forward.

She gasped, all movement frozen, as the cover of the Bible was flung back violently. As she stared at it, the pages began to turn so rapidly that they became a blur of movement. Florence felt a throbbing at her temples. Suddenly the pages stopped, and bending down, she looked at the page which had been uncovered.

"Yes!" she whispered joyously. "Oh, *yes!*"

The top of the page was titled BIRTHS. Below it was a single faded entry: "Daniel Myron Belasco was born at 2:00 A.M. on November 4, 1903."

9:07 P.M.

"There must be *something* I can do," she said. Barrett turned from the machine, where he was working on an uncovered circuit assembly, comparing its maze of wires and transistors with one of his blueprints. She had been watching him in restive silence for the past twenty minutes, noticing how tired he looked. Finally she'd had to speak.

"I'm afraid there isn't," he told her. "It's just too complicated. It would take ten times as long to explain what I wanted done as it does for me to do it myself."

"I know, but—" Edith broke off worriedly. "How much longer will it be?"

"Hard to say. I have to make certain everything's been done as specified. Otherwise there could be a malfunction, and all my work would be for nothing. I can't afford that." He tried to smile, but it was more like a grimace of pain. "I'll finish as soon as possible."

Edith nodded without assurance. She glanced at Lionel's watch on the table. He'd been at it for more than an hour now and had barely finished checking one circuit assembly. The Reversor was gigantic. At this rate it could take all night, and his energy simply wasn't up to it. She'd phone Dr. Wagman if she thought it would do any good, but she knew that Lionel would drop in his tracks before stopping now.

The cold weight in her stomach seemed to press down as she watched him work. He was not as confident as he had been. He'd been trying to conceal it from her but she knew his conviction had been badly shaken by the occurrence in the steam room. She knew how vulnerable she'd felt after what she'd done.

Despite his façade of certainty, Lionel must be feeling the same way.

She had to know. "What is your machine supposed to do?"

He looked across his shoulder. "I'd rather not explain it now, my dear. It's quite involved."

"Can't you tell me anything?"

"Well, in essence, I'm going to pull the plug on all the power in the house." He swallowed dryly, turned to get a drink of water. "I'll explain it in detail tomorrow," he continued, pouring water into a glass. "Suffice to say that any form of energy can be dissipated—which is what I plan to do."

She watched him take out a codeine pill and wash it down. He drew in a shaking breath and smiled. "I know it doesn't sound too satisfying at the moment, but you'll see." He set the glass down. "By this time tomorrow, Hell House will be drained, de-energized."

They looked around abruptly at the sound of measured clapping. Fischer stood in the archway, looking at them, a bottle underneath his right arm. "Bravo," he said.

Edith turned away, a dark flush on her face.

"Have you been drinking, Mr. Fischer?" Barrett asked.

"Have been, will continue to," said Fischer. "Not enough to lose control," he cut off Barrett's words. "Just enough to blunt the senses. Nothing in this goddamn house is going to get another crack at me. I've had it. I have *had* it."

"I'm sorry," Barrett said after a few moments. He felt, somehow, responsible for Fischer's black mood.

"Don't be sorry for me. Be sorry for yourself." Fischer pointed at the Reversor. "That goddamn pile of junk isn't going to do a goddamn thing but make a lot of noise . . . assuming that it works at all. You think this house is going to shape up 'cause you play your goddamn music box? The *hell* it is. Belasco's going to laugh in your face. They're all going to laugh in your face—the way they've been laughing all these years at any idiot who tries to come in here and . . . de-energize the place." He made a hissing sound. "De-energize, my ass." He glared at Barrett, gesturing toward Edith. "Get her out of here," he said. "Get yourself out. You don't have a chance."

"What about yourself?" asked Barrett.

"I'm all right. I know the score. You don't fight this place, it can't get at you. You don't let it get inside your skin, you're fine. Hell House doesn't mind a guest or two. Anyone can stay here if they don't mind fun and games. What it doesn't like is people who attack it. Belasco doesn't like it. All his people, *they* don't like it, and they fight back, and they kill you. He's a general, did you know that? A general with an army. He directs them!" Fischer gestured floridly. "Directs them like a—*mess of goddamn troops!* No one makes a move without him, not his son, not anybody."

Fischer pointed at Barrett, his expression suddenly rabid.

"I'm telling you," he said. "I'm *telling* you! Cut out this bullshit! Leave that damn machine alone, forget it! Spend your week here eating, resting, doing nothing. Then, when Sunday comes, tell old man Deutsch anything he wants to hear, and bank your money. Hear me, Barrett? Try anything more than that, and you're a dead man, *a-dead-man*." He looked at Edith. "With a dead wife by your side."

He jerked himself around. "Oh, hell, why bother anyway? No one listens. Florence doesn't listen. You don't listen. No one listens. Die, then. Die!" He stumbled off. "I was the only one who made it out alive in 1940, and I'll be the only one to make it out alive in 1970." He weaved across the entry hall. "You hear me, Belasco, you son of a bitch! I'm closed off! Try to get me! You never will! You *hear* me?"

Edith sat staring at her husband. He was watching Fischer's departure with a troubled look.

He looked at her. "Poor man. This house has really beaten him."

He's right; she heard the words in her mind. She hadn't the courage to voice them.

Barrett limped over, pulled a chair beside hers, and sat with a groan. He was silent for a while, then drew in a heavy breath and said, "He's wrong."

"Is he?" Edith's voice was faint.

He nodded. "What he calls a pile of junk"—he smiled at the words—"is nothing more or less than the key to Hell House." He raised a hand. "All right, grant you, things have happened which I don't quite comprehend—although I would if I had time." He rubbed his eyes. "That's not the point, however. Man controls electricity without understanding its true nature. What the details are of the energy inside this house is not as vital as the fact that I"—he pointed—"that *machine* . . . has the power of life and death over it."

He stood. "And *that* is *that*. I told you from the start that Miss Tanner is wrong in what she believes. I tell you now that Fischer is equally in error. And tomorrow I'll prove my case beyond a solitary doubt."

He turned away and hobbled back to the Reversor. Edith watched him go. She wished she could believe him, but Fischer's words had driven fear so deep inside her she could feel it in her blood, chill and acidic, eating at her.

10:19 P.M.

. . . Daniel, please. You have to understand. What you ask is inconceivable. You know that. It isn't that I have no sympathy. I do. I've opened up my heart completely to you. I believe in you and trust you. You saved my life. Now let me save your soul.

You don't have to stay in this house any longer. Help is present, if only you will ask for it. Believe me, Daniel. There are those who love you and will help you if you ask. Your father doesn't have the power to stop you. Not if you seek out those beyond, and take the hand they offer you. Let them help you. Take their hand. If you only knew the beauty which awaits you, Daniel. If you only knew how lovely are the realms which lie beyond this house. Would you keep yourself locked in a barren cell when all the beauties of the universe await you on the outside? Think! Accept! Don't close yourself to those who would so gladly help you. Try; only try. They wait for you with open arms. They will help you, give you comfort. Don't remain within these cheerless walls. You can be free. Believe that, Daniel. Believe it, and it will be so. I pledge you this. Trust me. Let go. Let go.

She could barely stand. Shuffling to the bathroom, she washed and changed into her nightgown with infirm movements. Her limbs were like iron. She had never felt such helpless enervation in her life.

Daniel wouldn't listen. He simply would not listen.

She returned to the other room and got into bed. Tomorrow, then, she told herself. He had to listen sooner or later. In the morning, she would start again. She slumped back heavily or the pillow, wincing at the flare of pain in her breasts. She lay on her back, staring at the ceiling with heavy-lidded eyes. Tomorrow, she thought.

She turned her head.

There was a figure standing by the door. She gazed at it without alarm. There was no menace in it.

"Daniel?"

The figure advanced. In the feeble light from the bathroom she saw its features clearly: youthful, handsome, the expression grave, the eyes filled with despair.

"Can you speak?" she asked.

"Yes." His voice was gentle, pained.

"Why won't you go?"

"I cannot."

"But you must."

"Not without—"

"Daniel, no," she said.

He turned his face away.

"Daniel—"

"I love you," he said. "You're the only woman I've ever said that to. I never met another like you. You're so good . . . so good . . . the kindest person I have ever known."

His face turned back to her, dark eyes searching her face. "I need—" He broke off, twisting toward the door. "I *will* speak to her!" he said frightenedly. "You can't stop me!" He looked back at her. "I can't remain much longer; he won't let me," he said. "I beg of you. Please give me what I ask. If I am driven from this house without fulfillment . . ."

"Driven?" Florence tensed.

"Your Doctor Barrett has the means."

She gazed at him, stunned.

"He knows the mechanism of my being in this house and can drive me from it," he said. "But that is *all* he knows. Whatever else I am—my heart, my mind, my soul—he knows nothing of, cares nothing for. He's going to drive me from one hell to another, don't you see? Only you can help me. I can leave this house tonight if you'll help me. Please." His voice began to fade. "If you care for me at all, have pity. Please have pity. . . ."

"Daniel—"

For several moments she could hear his wretched sobbing; then the room was still. She stared at the spot where he'd been standing. "You know I can't," she said. "Daniel, please. You know I can't. *You know I can't.*"

10:23 P.M.

Barrett's eyes were slitted as he climbed the stairway slowly, his arm across Edith's shoulders. He tried not to put too much weight on her, tried not to make any sounds of pain. She'd had enough distress today; and it was only temporary, after all. Another pill, a good night's sleep, and he'd be fit enough by morning. He could endure the pain another day or so. The Reversor was almost ready for use. Another hour's work tomorrow, and he'd be prepared to prove his theory. After all these years, he thought, the final proof. What was a little pain compared to that?

They reached the top of the stairs, and Barrett tried to walk by himself, despite the throbbing in his leg and back. Hobbling weakly, he made a sound which he intended to be wry amusement but which, instead, emerged as one of pain. "After we're home," he said, "I'm going to take a month's vacation. Finish up the last few pages of the book. Relax. Enjoy your company."

"Good." She didn't sound convinced. Barrett patted her shoulder. "It's going to be all right," he said.

Edith opened the door and helped him to the bed. She watched in concern as he sank down heavily on the mattress. "Lie back," she told him. She propped pillows against the headboard, and Barrett hitched himself against them as she lifted his legs onto the bed. He slumped back. "*Oh.*" He forced a smile. "Well, no one can say we aren't earning our money."

"*You* are." Edith flinched as she pulled off his shoes; they were on so tightly. Peeling off his socks, she began to massage his feet and ankles. Barrett saw that she was trying not to show distress at the swollen look of them.

"I'd better take another codeine," he said.

Edith stood and moved to his bag. Barrett tried to shift his weight on the mattress, hissing at the effort. He felt as heavy as a statue. He wouldn't mention it to Edith, of course, but it might not be amiss for him to undergo a short period of hospitalization after they got home.

He was winding his watch when Edith returned with the pill and a glass of water. Reaching out, he set the watch on the bedside table, then washed down the pill. Edith started to unbutton his sweater.

"That's all right," he said. "I'll sleep in my clothes tonight. It'll be simpler."

She nodded. "All right." She unbuckled his belt and loosened the top of his trousers. "I'll sleep in my clothes, too."

"You may as well."

Edith sat beside him on the bed and, leaning over, pressed herself against him. Her weight on his chest made it hard to breathe, but Barrett said nothing.

"If only today had never happened," she murmured.

"We can work it out." Barrett rubbed her back, wishing he cou'd think of some excuse to get her up that wouldn't hurt her feelings.

"Would you get my tie?" he asked after several moments.

Edith sat up, looking at him curiously.

"It's hanging in the closet."

She rose and got the tie, handing it to him.

"You want to wash up, brush your teeth before you go to bed?" he asked.

"All right."

Barrett lay, half-sitting, on the bed, listening to the sounds she made in the bathroom—the splashing of water as she washed, the brushing of her teeth, the rinsing of her mouth. Symphonie Domestique, he thought.

In hell.

He stared across the room. It was difficult to believe that they had been here only three days. He looked at the rocking chair. Two nights ago, it had moved by itself. For all the sense of time he felt, it might have been two weeks ago, two months.

His gaze moved lingeringly around the room. Grotesque, he thought. It could be a display room in some museum; the house was a treasure trove of art works. Thousands upon thousands of creations conceived and executed in the name of beauty—ending up in this house, which had to be the epitome of ugliness.

He blinked, refocusing his eyes as Edith came back into the room. "Can you stand to lie beside me in this tiny bed for one night?" he asked.

"I'd love to."

When she was lying beside him, both of them covered, Barrett started to fasten one end of the tie to her wrist. "I'm doing it so you won't sleepwalk." He tied the other end of the tie to one of the headboard posts. "That should give you enough freedom of movement."

Edith nodded, then, as Barrett put his arm around her, pressed against him, cradling her head in the hollow between his arm and chest. She sighed. "I feel safe now."

11:02 P.M.

If only I could sleep, she thought. Her smile was barren. The human mind, she thought. This afternoon she'd wanted to stay awake until their stay in Hell House was ended. Now she wanted nothing more than to drift into unconsciousness, eliminating eight or nine hours of their remaining time here.

She closed her eyes again. How many times had she closed and opened them now? Forty, fifty, a hundred? She drew in a long, slow breath. That smell; always that fetid smell.

Hell House should be burned to the ground.

She opened her eyes and looked at Lionel. He was deeply asleep. Moving her right hand, she felt the tug of the tie on her wrist. Had he really done it because she'd walked in her sleep last night? Or was it Fischer he was worried about? Did he really fear she'd go to Fischer again? She couldn't fathom what had driven her to him the first time. Had it truly been the house? Or was it something in herself? She'd never had such overt sex desires before—not even about Lionel, much less other men. Or women; she shuddered at the thought. She was frightened and appalled by the things she'd said and done.

She pressed her lips together. It was more than just herself; it had to be. Something had invaded her, some virus of corruption which, even as she lay here, might be spreading its disease throughout her mind and body. She would not believe it was herself alone, some unsuspected evil in her nature starting to emerge. It had to be the house. It had affected others. She could scarcely hope to be immune.

Her chin jerked up. She stared across the room.

The rocking chair had started moving.

"Lionel," she murmured. *No.* He needed sleep. It's force, she told herself; unguided, unintelligent; kinetics taking the path of least resistance—slamming doors, winds, footsteps, rocking chairs.

She wanted to close her eyes but knew that, even if she did, she'd hear the rhythmic squeaking of the chair. She stared at it. Dynamics. Force. Residuum. Her mind repeated the words again and again.

Yet all the time, she knew, she really knew, that it was someone sitting in the chair—someone whom she couldn't see. Someone cruel, implacable, waiting to destroy her, waiting to destroy them all. Was it Belasco? she thought in horror. What if he were suddenly to appear, gigantic, terrifying, smiling at her as he rocked? There's no one there! she forced herself to think. No one there at all!

The chair rocked slowly back and forth. Back and forth.

11:28 P.M.

The room felt hot. Groaning, Florence peeled aside the top blanket and dropped it to the floor. She turned on her side and closed her eyes again. Sleep, she told herself. Tomorrow we'll get back to it again.

A few minutes later she thrashed onto her back and looked at the ceiling again. No use, she thought. She wasn't going to sleep tonight.

Daniel's words had stunned her. She had always thought in terms of working with Dr. Barrett, but it had never occurred to her that such an alliance was an absolute necessity.

She'd almost gone to see him, tell him that they had to solve the problem of Daniel Belasco together. Then she'd realized that it would be a waste of time. As far as Dr. Barrett was concerned, there *was* no Daniel Belasco; he was a product of her own subconscious. What good would talking to him do? He hadn't accepted the body or the ring. Why should a Bible entry make any difference to him?

She drew aside the covers restlessly and sat up. *What was she to do?* She couldn't just stand by and let Dr. Barrett force Daniel from the house, without giving him peace. The thought appalled her. To plunge his desolate soul into limbo would be a crime against God.

Yet how could she prevent it? She mustn't even consider what Daniel had asked. She mustn't.

She stood with a mournful sigh and crossed the room. Entering the bathroom, she ran a glass of water. What other way *was* there, though? her mind probed. She'd been praying steadily since morning, pleading, importuning; all to no avail.

And, by tomorrow, Dr. Barrett would be ready with his machine.

For a moment she had the wild urge to run downstairs and damage the machine. She shook that off, angry at herself for even thinking it. She had no right to stand in Dr. Barrett's way. He was an honest, conscientious man who had devoted his life to his work. That he was so close to the truth was incredible. It was not his fault that the answer he'd found was only partial. He didn't even believe in the existence of Daniel Belasco. Obviously, he could not feel responsible for persecuting him.

Florence put down the glass and turned from the sink. There has to be an answer, she thought; there *has* to be. She started back into the bedroom.

She stopped with a gasp and looked toward the Spanish table.

The telephone was ringing.

It can't, she thought. It hasn't worked in more than thirty years.

She wouldn't answer it. She knew what it was.

It kept on ringing, the shrill sounds stabbing at her eardrums, at her brain.

She mustn't answer it. She wouldn't.

The telephone kept ringing.

"No," she said.

Ringing. Ringing. Ringing. Ringing.

With a sob, she lunged across the room and jerked up the receiver, dumping it on the table. She leaned against the edge of the table, suddenly weak, palms pressing on its surface. She could scarcely breathe. She wondered dazedly if she were going to faint.

She heard a thin voice coming from the earpiece. She couldn't hear what it said—a single word repeated—but she knew that it was Daniel's voice.

"No," she mumbled.

The voice kept speaking the same word, over and over. She jerked up the receiver, spoke into it desperately. "No!"

"Please," said Daniel.

Florence closed her eyes. "No," she whispered.

"Please." His voice was pitiful.

"No, Daniel."

"Please."

"No. No."

"Please." She had never heard such anguish in a voice before. *"Please."*

"No." She could barely speak now. Tears were trickling down her cheeks. Her throat felt clogged.

"Please," he begged.

"No," she whispered. "No, no."

"Please." The voice of someone begging for his very existence. *"Please."* She was his only hope. *"Please."* Tomorrow he would be thrust into horror by Dr. Barrett. *"Please."* There was only the one way. *"Please."* He started crying. *"Please. Please."* The world was gone. There were only the two of

them. *"Please."* She had to help him. *"Please."* He was sobbing. *"Please!"* Dear God, her heart was breaking! *"Please! Please! Please!"*

She hung up suddenly, a violent shudder racking through her body. All right! she thought. It was the only way. Her spirit guides would help her and protect her; God would help her and protect her. It was the only way; the only way. She believed in Daniel, she believed in herself. There was only the one way; she could see that now with vivid clarity.

Moving to the bed on trembling legs, she sank to her knees beside it, bowed her head, and clasped her hands together tightly. Closing her eyes, she began to pray: "Dear God, reach down your hand and give me your protection. Help me, this night, to bring to your care the tortured soul of Daniel Belasco."

For five minutes she prayed without cease. Then, slowly, she rose and undid her robe. Removing it, she laid it across the other bed. She shivered as she drew the flannel nightgown over her head. She looked down at her body. Let this be the temple, then, she thought.

Drawing aside the bedclothes, she lay on her back. The room was almost dark, the bathroom door nearly shut. She closed her eyes and started breathing deeply. *Daniel,* she called in her mind. *I give you, now, the love you never knew. I do this freely so that you will gain the strength to leave this house. With God's love and with mine, you shall rest, this night, in Paradise.*

She opened her eyes. "Daniel," she said, "your bride is waiting."

There was a movement near the door. A figure drifted toward her.

"Daniel?"

"Yes, my love."

She held out her arms.

He crossed the room, and Florence felt the drawing from her body as he neared. She could just make out his features, gentle, frightened, filled with need for her. He lay beside her on the bed. She turned to face him. She could feel his breath, and pressing close, she gave her lips to him.

His kiss was long and tender. "I love you," he whispered.

"And I love you."

She closed her eyes and turned onto her back again, feeling his weight shift onto her. "With love," she murmured. "Please, with love."

"Florence," he said.

She opened her eyes.

In an instant, she lay petrified, heartbeat staggering as she gasped at what was lying on her.

It was the figure of a corpse, its face in an advanced state of decomposition. Livid, scaly flesh was crumbling from its bones, its rotted lips wreathed in a leering smile that showed discolored jagged teeth, all of them decayed. Only the slanting yellow eyes were alive, regarding her with demoniacal glee. A leaden bluish light enveloped its entire body, gases of putrefaction bubbling around it.

A scream of horror flooded from her throat as the moldering figure plunged inside her.

11:43 P.M.

Fischer jerked up, gasping, at the sound of screaming in the next room.

For several moments he sat frozen, bound by dread. Then something drove him to his feet and carried him across the room. Flinging open his door, he lunged into the corridor and rushed to the door of Florence's room, twisted the knob, and pushed.

The door was locked.

"Oh, my God." He looked around in panic, the sound of Florence's mindless screams draining him. He glanced at the door to the Barretts' room as it opened suddenly and Edith peered out, her expression taut and stricken.

Lurching across the corridor, Fischer grabbed a heavy wooden chair and dragged it to the door. He started crashing it against the wood. The screaming broke off. He kept slamming the chair against the door. One of its legs snapped off. "Damn!" He battered at the door dementedly, seeing, on the edge of vision, Barrett and Edith hurrying toward him.

Suddenly the jamb was splintered and the door flew open. Hurling the broken chair aside, Fischer reached inside and switched the light on, then rushed into the room.

The sight of Florence made him gag. He heard the sound of Edith being sick. "Dear God," Barrett muttered.

She was naked, lying on her back, her legs spread far apart, her eyes wide open, staring upward with a look of total shock.

Her body was bruised and bitten, scratched, gouged, and running with blood.

Fischer looked at her face again, the face of a woman who had just been driven mad. Her lips stirred feebly. Compelled, he leaned over to hear. At first there were only rattling noises in her throat. Then she whispered, *"Filled."* She stared at him with wide, unblinking eyes. *"Filled."*

He was unable not to ask. "With what?"

With hideous abruptness, she began to smile.

DECEMBER 24, 1970

7:19 A.M.

Fischer sat slumped in an armchair, staring at Florence. He hadn't closed his eyes all night. When Barrett's pills had finally put her to sleep, he'd dragged the heavy armchair to her bedside; and Barrett and Edith had gone back to their room, Barrett with the promise that he'd return in several hours to take over watching. He'd never returned. Fischer had not expected it. He knew how badly Barrett had been physically and mentally abused the last two days in Hell House.

He shivered as a chill ran through him. Sitting up, he rubbed his eyes and yawned, wondering what time it was. He could use some coffee. Straining to his feet, he trudged into the bathroom, twisted the cold-water faucet, and cupped his right hand underneath the icy stream. Bending over, he splashed the water into his face, hissing at the sting of it. He straightened up and gazed at his reflection in the cabinet mirror. Water was dripping from his chin. He puffed out breath and misted drops of water on the mirror surface. Reaching out, he slid a bath towel from its rack and patted it against his face.

He went back into the bedroom and stood beside the bed,

looking at Florence. She looked at peace; a beautiful woman, asleep. It had not been that way during the night. Despite the sleeping pills, she had dozed erratically, limbs twitching, whimpering at times as though in pain, trembling periodically with paroxysmal seizures. He had been tempted to wake her from whatever terrors she had been experiencing. It had proven unnecessary. At unexpected intervals, she had jolted awake on her own, eyes staring, face disfigured by a look of dread. Each time, he'd held her hand, trying not to wince when her grip became painful, her clutching fingers as white as bone. She'd never spoken. After a while her eyes had fallen shut, and in seconds she had gone to sleep again.

Fischer blinked, refocusing his eyes. Florence was awake and looking at him. Her face had no expression. It was as though she'd never seen him before.

"How are you?" he asked.

She made no reply, gazing at him fixedly, her eyes those of a doll, glasslike, unmoving.

"Florence?"

There was a crackling sound in her throat as she swallowed. Fischer rose and walked into the bathroom, returning with a glass of water. "Here." He held it out.

Florence didn't stir. Fischer held the glass awhile, then set it on the bedside table. Florence's gaze shifted to the place where he had put it, then sprang back to his face.

"Can you speak?" he asked.

"Have you been here all night?"

Fischer nodded.

Her gaze shifted again, moving to the chair, then back again to probe at Fischer's eyes. "There?" she asked.

"Yes."

She made a noise of cynical amusement. "*Stupid.*" She ran an appraising gaze over his body. "You could have slept with me."

Fischer waited guardedly.

She pulled the covers down from her chest. "Who put on my nightgown?"

"I did."

Florence smiled with derision. "Fun?" she asked.

"After we cleaned you off."

Something flared in her eyes—a nova of awareness. Her body was convulsed by a wrenching shudder. "Oh, my God," she whispered. Tears welled in her eyes. "He's inside me." She reached out tremblingly for him.

Fischer took her hand and sat beside her on the bed. "We'll get rid of him."

She shook her head.

"We *will*." He squeezed her hand.

Florence pulled her hand away so fast he couldn't hold it. She began unbuttoning the front of her nightgown.

"What are you doing?"

Florence paid no attention. Breathing hard, she yanked aside the edges of her gown, exposing her breasts. Fischer winced at the sight of them. The teeth marks around her nipples looked purplish and infected. Florence clutched a hand around each breast, compressing and pulling them erect, their nipples hardening. "Look at them," she said.

Fischer grabbed her hands and forced them to her sides. In the instant that he did so, Florence lost rigidity and, with a faint groan, turned her head on the pillow. Fischer pulled the covers to her chin. "I'm taking you out of here this morning," he said.

"He lied to me." Her voice was strengthless. "He said it was the only way."

Fischer felt ill. "You still believe there's a Daniel—"

"Yes!" She turned back suddenly. "I know there is. I found the entry of his birth inside the chapel Bible." She saw his look of startlement. "He let me in to prove that he existed.

He's the one who always kept me out. He learned about my brother, picked it from my mind—just as you said. He knew I'd believe him, because the memory of my brother's death would make me believe." She clutched at Fischer's hand again. "Oh, God, he's *inside* me, Ben; I can't get rid of him. Even as I'm speaking to you, I can feel him in there, waiting to take over."

She began to shake so violently that Fischer drew her up and put his arms around her. "Shhh. It's going to be all right. I'll take you out of here this morning."

"He won't let me go."

"He can't stop you."

"Yes he can; he *can*."

"He can't stop me."

Florence jerked away from him and thrashed back, thumping hard against the headboard of the bed. "Who the fucking hell are you?" she snarled. "Maybe you were hot stuff when you were twelve, but now you're shit. You hear me? Shit!"

Fischer stared at her in silence.

A flickering in her eyes revealed the change, like the evanescent shimmer of sunlight across a cloud-darkened landscape. Instantly she was herself again; but not emerging from amnesia. It was, instead, a sudden, brutal surfacing to self, with total memory of every vileness she'd been forced to utter.

"Oh, God, please help me, Ben."

Fischer held her tightly, sensing the congested turmoil in her mind and body. If only he could dig inside her like some psychic surgeon, rip away the cancerous mass, and fling it from her. He couldn't, though; he didn't have the power or the will.

He was as much a victim of this house as she was.

Fischer drew back. "Get dressed. We'll leave."

Florence stared at him.

"Now."

She nodded; but it seemed the jerk of a marionette's head as the operator moved the string from overhead. Drawing aside the bedclothes, Florence rose and walked to the bureau. Fischer watched as she drew some clothes from its drawers and started for the bathroom.

"Florence—"

She turned to face him. Fischer braced himself. "You'd better dress in here."

The skin grew taut across her cheekbones. "I have to *piss*. Is that all right?"

"Stop it!" Fischer shouted.

Florence jerked so hard she dropped her clothes. She looked at him bewilderedly.

"Stop it," he repeated quietly.

Florence looked painfully embarrassed. "But I have to . . ." She couldn't finish.

Fischer stared at her sadly. What if she became possessed in there, did something harmful to herself?

He sighed. "Don't lock the door."

She nodded once and turned. Entering the bathroom, she closed the door. Fischer listened for the sound of the lock, relaxing gradually when it didn't come. Standing, he walked across the room and picked up the clothes she'd dropped.

He looked around with relief as Florence opened the bathroom door and came out. Without a word he handed her her clothes and turned away. He sat on the bed with his back to her. "Keep talking while you dress."

"All right." He heard the rustle of her nightgown as she took it off. He closed his eyes and yawned. "Did you sleep at all?" she asked.

"I'll sleep when you're out of here."

"You're going too, aren't you?"

"I'm not sure. I don't think I'm vulnerable as long as I'm

shut off from the house, not fighting it. I might stay. I have no qualms about lifting a hundred thou from old man Deutsch's bank account. He won't miss it." He paused. "I'll give you half of it."

Florence didn't speak.

"Talk," he said.

"Why talk?"

The tone of her voice made him twist around. She was standing by the bureau, naked, smiling at him. "Take off *your* clothes now," she said.

Fischer stood up quickly. "Fight it."

"Fight what?" she asked. "My love of cock?"

"Florence—"

"Strip. I want to wallow. Like a pig." She started toward him angrily. "Strip, you bastard. You've wanted to fuck my ass all week; now *do* it!"

She seemed to think his sudden movement toward her indicated interest, and she ran to him. Fischer grabbed her wrists and jerked her to a halt. "Fight it, Florence."

"Fight what? My—?"

"*Fight* it."

"Let me go, goddamnit!"

"*Fight* it!" Fischer gouged his fingers into her wrists until she gasped in pain and rage.

"I want to fuck!" she screamed.

"*Fight* it, Florence!"

"I want to *fuck*, I want to *fuck!*"

Releasing her left wrist, Fischer slapped her face as hard as possible. Her head snapped to the right, her expression one of shocked amazement.

When her head turned back, he saw that she'd been given back her mind. For several moments she stood trembling, gaping at him. Then she glanced down at her body, shamed. "Don't look," she begged.

Fischer released her other wrist and turned away. "Dress," he said. "Forget your bags; I'll bring them later. Let's get out of here."

"All right."

God, I hope it *is* all right, he thought. He shuddered. *What if he was not allowed to take her from the house?*

7:48 A.M.

"More coffee?"

Lionel twitched, and Edith realized that he'd been half asleep, despite his open eyes. "I'm sorry; did I startle you?"

"No, no." He shifted on the chair, grimacing; started reaching for the cup with his right hand, then did it with his left instead.

"You've got to have that thumb looked at, first thing."

"I will."

The great hall was without a sound again. Edith felt unreal. The words they'd spoken had seemed artificial. Eggs? No, thank you. Bacon? No. Chilly? Yes. I'll be glad to leave this place. Yes, so will I. Like dialogue from some inferior domestic drama.

Or was it a carry-over from the tension between them last night?

She stared at Lionel. He was drifting off again, his eyes unseeing, almost blank. He'd been working on the Reversor for more than an hour before they'd eaten, laboring without cease while she dozed in a nearby easy chair. He'd said that it was almost ready now. She turned and looked across the hall at it. Despite its imposing size, it was impossible to believe that it could conquer Hell House.

She looked back at the table. Everything about this morning had conspired to make her feel unreal, a character manipulated through some inexplicable role. Coming down the stairs, they'd seen the cat go running down the corridor toward the chapel—soundlessly, a fleeting, orange-mottled form. Then, while Lionel had been working on the Reversor, she'd heard a sound, and starting awake, had seen an old couple crossing the hall, carrying a coffeepot and covered trays. Half asleep, she'd stared at them in silence, thinking them ghosts. Even when they'd set the trays on the table and begun collecting the supper dishes, she hadn't realized who they were. Then, in a rush, it had come to her, and smiling at her own deluding mind, she'd said, "Good morning."

The old man grunted, and the woman nodded, mumbling something indistinct. In moments they were gone. Still groggy from sleep, Edith had begun to wonder if she'd really seen them. She'd drifted back into a shallow sleep, jolting awake with a gasp when Lionel had touched her shoulder.

She cleared her throat, and Lionel twitched again. "What time will we be out of here?" she asked.

Barrett tugged at his fob and pulled the watch from its pocket. Opening the cover, he gazed at its face. "I'd say early afternoon," he answered.

"How do you feel?"

"Stiff." His smile was tired. "But I'll mend."

They looked around as Fischer and Florence entered the hall, dressed for outdoors. Barrett eyed them questioningly as they approached the table. Edith looked at Florence. She was pale, her gaze avoiding theirs.

"You have the car keys?" Fischer asked.

Barrett repressed a look of surprise. "Upstairs."

"Would you get them, please?"

Barrett winced. "Could *you?* I really can't face those stairs again."

"Where are they?"

"In my overcoat pocket."

Fischer glanced aside. "You'd better go with me," he said to Florence.

"I'll be all right."

"Why don't you join us, Miss Tanner; have some coffee?" Barrett invited.

She was about to speak, then changed her mind, and nodding once, sat down. Edith poured a cup of coffee and passed it across the table. Florence took it from her, murmuring, "Thank you."

Fischer looked uneasy. "Don't you think you'd better come along?"

"We'll keep an eye on her," said Barrett.

Fischer still hesitated.

"What Ben doesn't want to tell you," Florence said, "is that I was possessed by Daniel Belasco last night and could lose control of myself at any moment."

Barrett and Edith stared at her. Fischer could tell that Barrett didn't believe her, and the realization angered him. *"She's telling the truth,"* he said. "I'd rather not leave her alone with you."

Barrett regarded Fischer in silence. Finally he turned to Florence. "You'd best go with him, then," he said.

Florence looked up pleadingly. "Couldn't I have a cup of coffee first?"

Fischer's eyes narrowed with suspicion.

"If anything happens, just take me outside."

"I'll buy you coffee in town."

"It's such a long way, Ben."

"Florence—"

"Please." She closed her eyes. "I'll be all right. I promise you." She sounded as though she were about to cry.

He stared at her, not knowing what to do.

Barrett spoke to break the painful silence. "There's really no need to stay," he said to Florence. "The house will be cleared by afternoon."

She looked up quickly. "How?"

Barrett's smile was awkward. "I'd intended to explain it to you—but, under the circumstances . . ."

"Please. I have to know before I leave."

"There isn't time," said Fischer.

"Ben, I have to know." Her look was desperate. "I can't go until I do."

"Damn it—"

"If I start to lose control, just take me out," she said. She turned to Barrett pleadingly.

"Well . . ." His tone was dubious. "It's somewhat complicated."

"I have to know," was all she said. Fischer sat down gingerly near Florence. Why am I doing this? he wondered. He didn't believe that Barrett's machine would have the least effect on Hell House. Why wasn't he dragging her out of here? It was her only hope.

"To begin with fundamentals," Barrett said, "all phenomena occur as events in nature—a nature the order of which is larger than that presented by current science, but nature, nonetheless. This is true of so-called psychic events as well, parapsychology being, in fact, no more than an extension of biology."

Fischer kept his eyes on Florence. She had slipped in and out of possession so frequently before.

"Paranormal biology, then," Barrett said, "setting forth the premise that man overflows and is greater than the organism which he inhabits, as Doctor Carrel put it. In simplest terms, the human body emits a form of energy—a psychic fluid, if you will. This energy surrounds the body with an unseen sheath; what has been called the 'aura.' It can be extruded beyond the borders of this aura, where it can create mechanical, chemical, and physical effects: percussions, odors, movement of external objects, and the like—as we have seen repeatedly these past few days. I believe that when Belasco spoke of 'influences,' he may have been referring to this energy."

Fischer looked at Barrett, ambivalent emotion rising in him. The older man sounded so confident. Was it possible that all the beliefs of his life could be reduced to something one could probe at in a laboratory?

"All through the ages," Barrett continued, "evidence in proof of this premise has been forthcoming, each new level of human development bringing about its own particular proof. In the Middle Ages, for example, much superstitious thought was directed toward what were called demons and witches. Accordingly, these things were manifested, created by this psychic energy, this unseen fluid, these 'influences.'

"Mediums have always produced phenomena indigenous to their beliefs." Fischer glanced at Florence, seeing that she'd tightened at these words. "This is certainly the case with Spiritualism. Mediums adhering to this faith create its own particular phenomenon—so-called spirit communication."

"Not *so-called*, Doctor." Florence's voice was strained.

"Let me continue, Miss Tanner," he said. "You may refute me later if you wish. By record, the only time religious exorcisms have an effect on haunted houses or possessions is when the medium who causes the phenomena is highly religious, thus profoundly moved by the exorcism. In far more cases—including this house—gallons of holy water and hours of exorcism fail to alter anything, either because the medium involved is not religious or because more than one medium has contributed to the effect."

Fischer glanced at Florence. Her face was pale, lips pressed together.

"Another example of this biological mechanism," Barrett was saying, "was that of animal magnetism, which produced psychic phenomena equally as impressive as those of Spiritualism, but entirely devoid of any religious characteristics.

"How does this mechanism function, though? What is its genesis? Reichenbach, the Austrian chemist, in the years between 1845 and 1868 established the existence of such a physiological radiation. His experiments consisted, first, of having sensitives observe magnets. What they saw were gleams of light at the poles, like flames of unequal length, the shorter at the positive pole. Observation of electromagnets brought about the same results as did observation of crystals. Finally, the same phenomenon was observed on the human body.

"Colonel De Rochas continued Reichenbach's experiments, discovering that these emanations are blue at the positive pole, red at the negative. In 1912 Dr. Kilner, a member of the London Royal College of Physicians, published the results of four years of experimentation during which, by use of the 'dycyanine' screen, the so-called human aura was made visible to anyone. When the pole of a magnet was brought into proximity with this aura, a ray appeared, joining the pole to the nearest point of the body. Further, when the subject was exposed to an electrostatic charge, the aura gradually disappeared, returning when the charge was dissipated.

"I oversimplify the progression of discovered facts, of course," he said, "but the end result is irrefutable; *the psychic emanation which all living beings discharge is a field of electromagnetic radiation.*"

He looked around the table, disappointed at the flatness of their expressions. Didn't they realize what he was saying?

He had to smile then. There was no way they could realize the import of his words until he'd proved them.

"Electromagnetic radiation—EMR—is the answer, then," he said. "All living organisms emit this energy, its dynamo the mind. The electromagnetic field around the human body behaves precisely as do all such fields—spiraling around its center of force, the electric and magnetic impulses acting at right angles to each other, and so on. Such a field *must* impinge itself on its surroundings. In extremes of emotion, the field grows stronger, impressing itself on its environment with more force—a force which, if contained, *persists* in that environment, undischarged, saturating it, disturbing organisms sensitive to it: psychics, dogs, cats—in brief, establishing a 'haunted' atmosphere.

"Is it any wonder, then, that Hell House is the way it is? Consider the years of violently emotional, destructive—*evil,* if you will—radiations which have impregnated its interior. Consider the veritable *storehouse* of noxious power this house became. Hell House is, in essence, a giant battery, the toxic power of which must, inevitably, be tapped by those who enter it, either intentionally or involuntarily. By you, Miss Tanner. By you, Mr. Fischer. By my wife. By myself. All of us have been victimized by these poisonous accumulations—you most of all, Miss Tanner, because you actively sought them out, unconsciously seeking to utilize them to prove your personal interpretation of the haunting force."

"That isn't true."

"It *is* true," Barrett countered. "It was true of those who entered here in 1931 and 1940. It is true of you."

"What about *you?*" demanded Fischer. "How do you know *your* interpretation isn't wrong?"

"Simply answered," Barrett said. "Shortly, my Reversor will permeate the house with a massive countercharge of electromagnetic radiation. This countercharge will oppose the polarity of the atmosphere, reverse and dissipate it. Just as the radiation of light negates mediumistic phenomena, so the radiation of my Reversor will negate the phenomena of Hell House."

Barrett leaned back in his chair; he had not been aware, until now, of leaning forward. Florence sat in stricken silence. Edith felt a rush of pity for her. After what Lionel had said, how could anyone doubt that he was right?

"One question," Fischer said.

Barrett looked at him.

"If the aura can restore itself after an electromagnetic charge is turned off, why can't the power in this house?"

"Because human radiation has a living source. The radiation in this house is only *residue*. Once it's been dissipated, it cannot return."

"Doctor," Florence said.

"Yes?"

She seemed to brace herself. "Nothing you've said contradicts what I believe."

Barrett looked astounded. "You can't be serious."

"I am. Of course there's radiation—and, of course, it persists. Because its possessor survives after death. *Your radiation is the body it survives with.*"

"Here we part company, Miss Tanner," Barrett said. "The residue I speak of has nothing whatever to do with the survival of personality. The spirit of Emeric Belasco does not prowl this house. Neither does that of his son or any of the so-called entities you have believed yourself in contact with. There is one thing in this house, and one thing only—*mindless, directionless power*."

"Oh," she said. Her voice was calm. "There's nothing else to do, then, is there?"

Her movement caught them by surprise. With a fluid, twisting stand, she was on her feet and running toward the Reversor. The three sat frozen for a moment. Then, simultaneously, Barrett gasped and Fischer lurched up from his chair, knocking it over in his haste to rise. He charged from the table, dashing after Florence.

Before he'd gone halfway, she had the crowbar in her hands and was swinging it with all her might at the face of the Reversor. Barrett cried out, jarring to his feet, his face gone ashen. He jolted at the ringing sound of steel on steel, flinching as though the blow were striking him instead. "No!" he shouted.

Florence swung again, battering at the front of the machine. The glass face of a dial exploded underneath her blow. Barrett started from the table with a look of horror on his face. His right leg buckled under him, and with a startled gasp, he fell. Edith jumped up. "Lionel!"

Fischer had reached Florence by then. Clutching at her shoulder, he yanked her back from the Reversor. She whirled and swung the crowbar at his face, her expression one of manic rage. Fischer dodged, the crowbar missing his head by inches. Lunging in, he grabbed her right arm, wrestling for possession of the bar. Florence lurched back, snarling like a maddened animal. A bolt of shock numbed Fischer as she flung her arms up, breaking his grasp. *She was too strong!*

Blind to everything except the threat to his Reversor, Barrett didn't even glance at Edith as she helped him to his feet. Pulling free of her, he started hobbling rapidly across the floor without his cane. "Stop her!" he cried.

Fischer had grabbed at Florence's arms again. She heaved back, and the two of them crashed against the front of the Reversor. Fischer felt her hot breath on his cheek, bubbly spittle dribbling from her mouth. She jerked her right arm free and swung at him. Fischer ducked, the crowbar smashing against the metal face. He started reaching for her arm again, but she swung too fast for him. He threw his arms up, crying out as the crowbar struck him on the right wrist. Ragged, burning pain shot up his arm. He saw the next blow coming but could not avoid it. The crowbar smashed against his skull, and blinding pain exploded in his head. Eyes staring, he crumpled to his knees. Florence raised the bar to strike again.

Barrett was on her then, the strength of frenzy in his arms; with a single wrenching motion he had jerked the crowbar from her grasp. Florence spun around. Barrett's face had gone abruptly blank. Gasping, he was stumbling back from her, right hand clutching at his lower back. Edith screamed and started forward as the crowbar slipped from Barrett's grasp and thumped on the rug. He started falling.

Florence's sudden lunging movement made Edith freeze in her tracks. Florence snatched the crowbar up. Instead of turning back to the Reversor, though, she turned toward Edith and began advancing on her. "Now you," she said, "you lesbian bitch."

Edith gaped at her, as much unnerved by the words as by the sight of Florence stalking her, crowbar raised. "I'm going to smash your fucking skull in," Florence said. "I'm going to beat it into jelly."

Edith shook her head, retreating. She glanced at Lionel desperately. He was writhing on the floor in pain. She started toward him, then jumped back, looking at Florence again, as, with a savage howl, the medium broke into a run at her, brandishing the crowbar. Edith's breath cut off. She whirled and bolted toward the entry hall, her mind washed blank by panic. She heard the driving thud of shoes behind her, glanced across her shoulder. Florence was almost on her! She sprang forward with a gasp, darting across the entry hall and up the stairs.

She knew the moment she'd reached the landing that she couldn't make their room; side vision showed her Florence only several yards behind. Impulsively she raced across the corridor to Florence's room and plunged inside, whirling to slam the door and lock it. A groan of horror tore her lips back as she saw the broken lock. Too late. The door was surging in at her. She stumbled back and, losing balance, fell.

Florence stood across the room from her, panting, smiling. "What are you afraid of?" she asked. She tossed aside the crowbar carelessly. "I'm not going to hurt you."

Edith crouched on the floor, staring at her.

"I'm not going to hurt you, baby." Edith felt a spasm in her stomach muscles. The medium's voice was honeyed, almost purring.

Florence started to remove her coat. Edith tensed as she dropped it on the floor. Florence started to unbutton her sweater. Edith began to shake her head.

"Don't shake your head," said Florence. "You and I are going to have a lovely time."

"No." Edith started edging backward.

"Yes." Florence removed the sweater, dropped it. Starting across the room, she reached back to unhook her bra.

Oh, God, please don't! Edith kept shaking her head as Florence moved in on her. The bra was off now. Florence began unzipping her skirt, the smile fixed to her lips. Edith bumped against a bed and caught her breath convulsively. She could retreat no farther. Cold and weak, she watched Florence drop her skirt, bend over to remove her panties. She stopped shaking her head. "Oh, no," she pleaded.

Florence dropped to her knees, straddling Edith's legs. Sliding both hands underneath her breasts, she held them up in front of Edith's face; Edith winced at the purplish teeth marks on them. "Aren't they nice?" said Florence. "Aren't they delicious-looking? Don't you want them?" Her words drove a spear of terror into Edith's heart. She stared up frozenly as Florence fondled her breasts in front of her. "Here, feel them," Florence said. She released her left breast, reached down, lifted Edith's hand.

The feel of the warm, yielding flesh against her fingers

broke a dam in Edith's chest. A sob of anguish shook her. *No, I'm not that way!* screamed her mind.

"Of course you are," said Florence, as though Edith had spoken. "We're both that way; we've always been that way. Men are ugly, men are cruel. Only women can be trusted. Only women can be loved. Your own father tried to rape you, didn't he?"

She couldn't know! thought Edith, horrified. She jerked both hands against her chest and pressed them tightly to her body, jammed her eyes shut.

With an animal-like sound, Florence fell across her. Edith tried to push her off, but Florence was too heavy. Edith felt the medium's hands clamping on the back of her head, forcing up her face. Abruptly Florence's lips were crushed on hers, mouth open, tongue trying to force its way inside her mouth. Edith tried to fight, but Florence was too strong. The room began to spin around her, burgeoning with heat. A heavy mantle fell across her body. She felt numb, detached. She couldn't keep her lips together, and Florence's tongue plunged deep inside her mouth, licking at the tender roof. Curls of sensation flickered through her body. She felt one of Florence's hands wrap her fingers around the breast again. She couldn't pull the hand away. There was a pounding in her ears. Heat poured across her.

The sound of Lionel's voice cut through the pounding. Edith jerked her head to one side, trying to see past Florence. The heated mantle vanished. Coldness rushed across her. She glanced up, saw the twisted face of Florence looming overhead. Lionel called her name again. "In here!" she cried. Florence pulled away from her, looking at herself with sickened realization; she lunged to her feet and ran into the bathroom. Edith struggled up and moved across the room unevenly. She fell against Lionel as he ran in, clinging to him, eyes shut, face against his chest. She started crying helplessly.

9:01 A.M.

"You'll be all right." Barrett patted Fischer's shoulder. "Just stay in bed awhile; don't move."

"How is she?" Fischer mumbled.

"Asleep. I gave her pills."

Fischer tried to sit up, fell back, gasping.

"*Don't move,*" Barrett told him. "That was quite a blow you took."

"Have to get her out of here."

"I'll get her out."

Fischer looked at him suspiciously.

"I promise," Barrett said. "Now rest."

Edith was standing by the door. Barrett took her arm and led her into the corridor. "How is he?" she asked.

"Unless he has a more serious concussion than I think, he should come around."

"What about you?"

"Just a few more hours," Lionel said. Edith saw that he was holding his right arm against his chest as though it were broken. There was a stain of fresh blood on the thumb bandage. When he'd wrenched the crowbar out of Florence's hands, he must have torn apart the edges of the cut. She was about to mention it, then gave it up, a sense of utter hopelessness oppressing her.

Lionel opened the door to Florence's room, and they crossed to her bed. She was lying motionless beneath the covers. After Lionel had spoken to her for a long time, she'd emerged from the bathroom, a towel wrapped around her. She hadn't spoken, hadn't met their gaze. Eyes downcast like those of a repentant child, she had accepted the three pills, slipped beneath the bedclothes, and in moments closed her eyes and gone to sleep.

Barrett raised her left eyelid and looked at her staring eye.

Edith averted her face. Then Lionel was taking her arm again; they crossed the room and went into the corridor. Moving to their room, they went inside.

"Would you get me some water?" he asked.

Edith went into the bathroom and ran cold water into the glass. When she returned, Lionel was on his bed, propped against the headboard. "Thank you," he murmured as she handed him the glass. He had two codeines in his palm. He washed them down his throat. "I'm going to telephone Deutsch's man for an ambulance," he said. Edith felt a momentary burst of hope. "Have Fischer and Miss Tanner taken to the nearest hospital."

The hope was gone. Edith looked at him without expression.

"I'd like you to go with them," Lionel said.

"Not until you go."

"It would make me feel much better."

Edith shook her head. "Not without you."

He sighed. "Very well. It'll all be over by this afternoon, at any rate."

"Will it?"

"Edith"—Barrett looked surprised—"have you lost your faith in me?"

"What about—?"

"—what happened just before?" He drew in a hitching breath. "Don't you see? It proves my point precisely."

"How?"

"Her attack on my Reversor was the ultimate tribute. She *knows* I'm right. There was nothing else to do—her very words, if you recall—except to destroy my beliefs before they could destroy hers."

Barrett reached out his left hand and drew her onto the bed. "She's not possessed by Daniel Belasco," he told her.

"She's not possessed by anyone—unless it's by her inner self, her true self, her *repressed* self."

Like I was yesterday, she thought. She stared at Lionel hopelessly. She wanted to believe him, but it wasn't in her anymore.

"The medium is a most unstable personality," he said. "Any psychic worthy of the name invariably turns out to be a hysteric and/or somnambulist, a victim of divided consciousness. The parallel between the mediumistic trance and the somnambulistic fit is absolute. Personalities come and go, methods of expression are identical, as are psychological structures, the amnesia upon awakening, the artificial quality of the alternate personalities.

"What we've witnessed this morning is that part of Miss Tanner's personality she's always kept hidden, even from herself—her patience turning into anger, her withdrawal into furious expression." He paused. "Her chasteness into wanton sexuality."

Edith declined her head. She couldn't look at him. Like me, she thought.

"It's all right," Barrett said.

"No." She shook her head.

"If there are . . . things to be discussed, we'll discuss them at home."

At home, she thought. Never had a phrase implied such impossibility to her.

"All right," she said. But it was someone else's voice.

"Good," said Barrett. "In addition to my work, then, some extra value has come of this week, some personal enlightenment." He smiled at her. "Have heart, my dear. Everything will work out."

9:42 A.M.

Barrett opened his eyes, to find himself looking at Edith's sleeping face. He felt a twinge of worry. He hadn't meant to sleep.

Taking hold of his cane, he slipped his legs across the edge of the mattress and stood, wincing as he put his weight down. He winced again as he slipped his feet into shoes. Sitting on the other bed, he crossed his left leg over his right, and worked the lace out of the shoe, using the fingers of his left hand.

He set the foot down. That was some improvement. He did the same to his right shoe, then drew out his watch. It was getting close to ten. His expression grew alarmed. That couldn't be P.M., could it? In this damned, windowless hulk, there was no way to be certain.

He hated to wake Edith. She'd had so little sleep this week. Did he dare leave her, though? He stood irresolutely, staring at her. Had anything happened to them in their sleep? It was an aspect of the EMR he had not investigated, but it did seem that one had to be conscious in order to be affected by it. No, that wasn't true; she'd walked in her sleep.

He decided to leave the door open, go downstairs as rapidly as possible, make the call, and come right back. If anything happened, surely he'd be aware of it.

He limped across the room and into the corridor, setting his teeth against the pain in his thumb. Despite his having taken codeine, it still throbbed unrelentingly. God knew what it looked like by now; he had no intention of checking. It would undoubtedly require minor surgery when this was over; he might even lose partial use of it. Never mind, he thought. The price was acceptable.

He opened Fischer's door and looked inside the bedroom. Fischer hadn't stirred. Barrett hoped he'd remain asleep when they carried him out of here on a stretcher. He didn't belong here; never had. At least he was surviving once more.

Turning clumsily, he hobbled to Florence Tanner's room and looked inside. She was also immobile. Barrett gazed at her sympathetically. The poor woman had a lot to confront after she was out of here. What would it be like to face the lie of her past existence? Was she up to it? Most likely, she would slip back into pretension; it would be less difficult.

He turned from Florence's door and limped to the staircase. Well, it's been quite a week, all in all, he thought. He smiled involuntarily. That was, without a doubt, the understatement of his life. Still, all was well. Thank God Miss Tanner had been blinded by her rage. A few well-placed blows, and he would have been confronted by days, perhaps weeks, of work to put the Reversor into working condition. Everything would have been ruined. He shivered at the thought.

What would they all do after they had left the house? he wondered as he descended the staircase haltingly, his left hand on the banister rail. It was an interesting speculation. Would Miss Tanner return to her church? *Could* she return to it after this appalling insight into herself? What about Fischer? What would he do? With a hundred thousand dollars, he could do a great deal. As for Edith and himself, the future was relatively clear. He avoided thinking of their personal problems yet to solve. That was for later.

At least they would all be out of Hell House. As the unofficial leader of the group, he felt some pride in that, although it was, perhaps, absurd for him to feel it. Still, the 1931 and 1940 groups had been virtually decimated. This time, four of them had entered Hell House, four would be safely out by tonight.

He wondered what to do with the Reversor after today. Should he have it delivered to his laboratory at the college?

That seemed most likely. What a delivery that would be; tantamount, he thought, to displaying the capsule that had taken the first astronaut into space. Perhaps, someday, the Reversor would occupy a place of honor in the Smithsonian Institution. He smiled sardonically. And perhaps not. He was hardly deluding himself into thinking that the world of science would topple in submission before his accomplishment. No, there were still a good many years ahead before parapsychology was conceded its rightful place beside the other natural sciences.

He moved to the front doors and opened one. Daylight. He shut the door and hobbled to the telephone, picked up the receiver.

There was no answer. Barrett jiggled the cradle arm. A fine time for communication to be broken off. He waited, jiggled the cradle arm again. Come on, he thought. He couldn't possibly get Fischer and Miss Tanner out of here without help.

He was about to hang up when the receiver was lifted on the other end of the line. "Yes?" said Deutsch's man.

Barrett exhaled loudly with relief. "You had me worried there. This is Barrett. We need an ambulance."

Silence.

"Did you hear me?"

"Yes."

"Will you have it sent out right away, then? Mr. Fischer and Miss Tanner require immediate hospitalization."

There was no reply.

"Do you understand?"

"Yes."

The line was silent.

"Is something wrong?" Barrett asked.

The man drew in a sudden breath. "Oh, hell, this isn't fair to you," he said angrily.

"What isn't?"

The man hesitated.

"*What* isn't?"

Another hesitation. Then the man said quickly, "Old man Deutsch died this morning."

"*Died?*"

"He had terminal cancer. Took too many pills to dull the pain. Accidentally killed himself."

Barrett felt a numbing pressure on his skull. What difference does it make? he heard his mind inquiring; but he knew. "Why didn't you tell us?" he asked.

"I was ordered not to."

By the son, thought Barrett. "Well . . ." His voice was faint. "What about—?"

"I was ordered to just—leave you stranded out there."

"And the money?" Barrett had to ask, even though he knew the answer.

"I don't know about that, but under the circumstances—" The man sighed. "Is there anything in writing?"

Barrett closed his eyes. "No."

"I see." The man's tone was flat. "Then that bastard son of his will doubtless—" He broke off. "Look, I apologize for not having called you, but my hands are tied. I have to go back to New York City right away. You have the car there. I suggest you all leave. There's a hospital here in Caribou Falls you can go to. I'll do what I can to . . ." His voice faded, and he made a sound of disgust. "Hell," he said. "I'll probably be out of a job myself. I can't stand that man. The father was bad enough, but—"

Barrett hung up as a wave of dark despair broke over him. No money, no provision for Edith, no retirement, no chance to rest. He leaned his forehead against the wall. "Oh, no," he murmured.

The tarn.

Barrett whirled with a gasp and looked around the entry

hall. The words had leaped into his mind, unbidden. No, he thought. He clenched his teeth together tightly. No, he told the house. He shook his head deliberately.

He started toward the great hall. "You don't win," he said. "I may not get that money, but you're not going to beat me; not you. I know your secret, and I'm going to destroy you." He had never felt such hatred in his life. He reached the archway and pointed at the Reversor with a look of triumph. "There!" he shouted. "There it stands! Your conqueror!" He had to lean against the archway wall. He felt exhausted, racked by pain. It doesn't matter, he told himself. Whatever pain he felt was secondary now. He'd worry later about Fischer and Miss Tanner, worry afterward about Edith and himself. There was only one thing that mattered at this moment: his defeat of Hell House and the victory of his work.

10:33 A.M.

She felt herself begin to rise from darkness. Daniel's voice cajoled her. *You don't have to sleep*, he said. She seemed to feel her veins and arteries compressing, tissues drawing in, her body forcing out the darkness. There was burning pressure in her kidneys. She tried to hold it back but was unable to. The pressure kept building. *Go on*, Daniel told her; *let it go*. Florence groaned. She couldn't stop herself. She felt the gushing from her loins, and cried aloud in shame.

Suddenly she was awake. She pushed aside the bedclothes and stood, looking groggily at the patch of wetness on the sheet. He was so rooted in her, he controlled the very workings of her body now.

"Florence."

She jerked her head around and saw his face projected on the hanging silver lamp. "Please," he said.

She stared at him. He started smiling. "Please." His tone was mocking.

"Stop it."

"Please," he said.

"*Stop* it."

"Please." He bared his teeth in a derisive grin. "*Please*."

"Stop it, Daniel!"

"Please, please, please, please, please, please, please!"

Florence spun around and lurched for the bathroom. A cold hand grasped her ankle, and she toppled to the floor. Daniel's icy presence flooded over her, his voice, demoniac, howling in her ears: "Please, please, please, please!" She couldn't make a sound; his presence seemed to suck away her breath. "Please, please, please!" He began to laugh with wild sadistic pleasure. Help me, God! she thought in agony. "Help me, God!" railed his voice. *Deliver me!* she pleaded. "Deliver me, deliver me!" his voice impersonated. Florence pressed both hands across her ears. "*Help me, God!*" she cried.

His presence vanished. Florence gasped in air convulsively. She struggled to her feet and started for the bathroom. "Leaving?" said his voice. She set her mind against its blandishment. Stumbling into the bathroom, she ran cold water and splashed it on her face.

She straightened up and stared at her reflection. Her face was pallid, marked by dark scabbed scratches and discolored bruises. What she could see of her neck and upper chest was scored by jagged lacerations. Leaning forward, she saw that her breasts looked inflamed, the teeth marks almost black now.

She stiffened as the door swung shut, then saw the full reflection of her body in the mirror fastened to the door. She started to resist, but something cold snaked up her spine. She gasped; eyes opening wide.

In a moment she began to smile. She leaned back, eyes

half-closing. Daniel was behind her. She could feel his hardened organ sliding deep into her rectum. His hands were clutched around her breasts, kneading them. Florence leaned back as Edith slipped into the bathroom, falling to her knees in front of Florence, darting her extended tongue to Florence's vagina. Florence's tongue lolled out. She bucked against Daniel eagerly. This was what she wanted, what she was.

She twitched as though electric current surged through her. Suddenly she saw herself, half-crouched before the mirror, face slack with vacuous abandonment, the fingers of her right hand thrust into her body. With a sickened noise she jerked the fingers free. A harsh laugh rasped behind her, and she whirled. The bathroom was empty. I was watching, his voice spoke in her mind.

She flung open the door and ran into the bedroom, Daniel's laughter following. She bent to pick her robe up. Something jerked it from her grasp and flung it away. She moved after it. The robe kept flapping from her. Florence stopped. No use, she thought, despairing. "No use," parodied his voice. The robe flew up and fell across her head. She jerked it off and pulled it on her body, buttoning it hastily. He's *playing* with me, she thought; making me do everything that's most abhorrent to me.

"—most abhorrent to me," his voice parroted, mockingly falsetto. He giggled like a girl. "Most abhorrent to me, most abhorrent to me."

Florence fell on her knees beside the bed and, resting both arms on the mattress edge, pressed her forehead to her tightly clasping hands. "Dear God, please help me; Red Cloud, help me; spirit doctors, help me; I have been possessed. Let the fire of the Holy Spirit burn this sickness from my mind and body. Let the strength of God rush through me, let his might instill me with the power to resist.

"Let his God cock sink into my mouth," she said. "Let me drink his holy, burning jism. Let me—"

A wail of torment jerked back her lips. She drove the knuckle of a fisted hand into her mouth and bit until the pain had filled her mind. Daniel vanished. After several moments she withdrew the still-clenched fist and looked at it. Her teeth had broken the skin; blood was trickling on the back of her hand.

She looked around uncertainly. It seemed as though the flare of pain had cleared her mind, driving him away. She pushed down on the mattress, standing. Now, she thought, the chapel. That was where the answer lay.

She ran across the room and jerked open the door. Hurrying into the hall, he turned toward the staircase. I'll reach it, she thought. He can't possess me every moment. If I keep on going, no matter what happens, I can get there.

She stopped, her heartbeat jolting. A figure blocked her way: a gaunt man dressed in ragged, filthy clothes; bones showing through his skin; long hair shaggy; face malformed by sickness; tiny, glowing eyes buried in dark-rimmed sockets; mouth distended, filled with thick, discolored teeth. Florence stared at him. It was one of Belasco's victims, she knew. He'd looked like this before he died.

The figure disappeared. Florence began descending the stairs. The acid coldness started up her spine again. She felt the gray defilement in her blood and fought it off, biting on her hand until the pain had driven it away. Pain was the answer! Whenever Daniel tried to take control, she'd drive him off with pain, because it filled her mind and left no room for him!

She stopped, hitched back. Two figures sprawled across the steps below, a man and woman. The man was plunging a knife into the woman's throat. He started sawing at the jagged wound, blood spouting, splashing on his twisted, gleeful face. He was cutting off the woman's head. Florence jammed her fist into her mouth and bit down, stiffening at the burst of pain. The man and woman vanished. She descended farther, wondering where the others were: Fischer, Edith, Barrett. It didn't matter; they couldn't help.

As she crossed the entry hall, she caught sight of Barrett in the great hall, working on his machine. Fool, she thought. It wasn't going to work. He was full of shit, the stupid—

No! She ground her teeth into her hand again, eyes wide and staring. Let her bite her fingers to the bone before succumbing to Daniel's sway again. She wished she had a knife. She'd thrust it far enough into her flesh to keep the pain there constantly. It was the answer: agony that blocked his contaminated soul from hers.

She started down the corridor. A wild-eyed man was hunched across a naked woman's back. She was dead, a sash cord pulled around her neck, her face purplish, eyes bulging from their sockets. Florence sank her teeth into her hand. Blood was running down her lips now, dripping onto her throat. The figures vanished as she reached the chapel door. A man was crouched in front of it. His face was white, his expression drugged. He held a severed human hand to his lips, sucking on one of the fingers. She bit into her hand. The figure vanished. Florence fell against the door and pushed it in.

She stood wavering at the head of the center aisle. A maelstrom of power filled the air. This was the nucleus, the core. She started down the aisle, then jerked back with a gasp as she saw the cat lying in the puddle of blood. It had been cut in two.

She shook her head. She mustn't stop now. She was almost to the answer. She had beaten Daniel; she would beat the house now. She stepped across the cat, advancing on the altar. Dear God, the power was incredible! It radiated through her, pulsing, driving. Darkness flickered in her mind. She thrust her aching hand into her mouth again and bit. The darkness cleared a little, and she moved against the power. It was like a living wall before her. She was almost to the altar now. Her eyes were staring, fixed. She'd win her battle yet. With God's help, she would—

Sudden weakness turned her limbs to stone. She fell against the altar heavily. The power was too strong! She looked up dumbly at the crucifix. It seemed to move. She stared at it in horror. It was moving toward her. No, she thought. She tried to back off, but she couldn't budge, rooted to the spot as though by some gigantic magnet. *No!* The crucifix was falling. It was going to hit her!

Florence cried out as it struck her head and chest and knocked her backward violently. She crashed to the floor, the massive cross and figure crushing down on her, knocking out her breath. The serpentine chill went lashing up her spine. She tried to scream but couldn't. Darkness flooded through her.

The possession ended instantly.

Florence's eyes bulged, her face distorted by a look of agony. She couldn't breathe, the pain was so intense. She tried to push the crucifix away, but it wouldn't move. The pain of trying made her gag. She lay immobile, groaning at the endless waves of agony that filled her. Once again she tried to push the crucifix. It moved a little, but the movement nearly made her faint. Her face was gray, dewed with cold sweat.

It took fifteen minutes to do. She almost fainted seven times before she'd finished, holding on to consciousness only with the most intense exertion of will. Finally she pushed aside the heavy crucifix and tried to sit up, gasping at the agony of the attempt. Slowly, ashen lips pressed together, she struggled to her knees. Blood started running down her thighs.

The sight of the phallus made her vomit. Hunching over, she expelled the contents of her stomach on the floor, eyes glazed with pain. *He'd tricked her.* There was no answer here. He'd only wanted to commit this final profanation on her mind and body. Florence rubbed a palsied hand across her lips. No more, she thought. She looked around and saw the huge nail sticking from the crucifix's back; it had been pulled out from the wall. She dragged herself across the floor until she'd reached the nail. Hovering above it, she began to saw the insides of her wrists across its point, hissing at the pain. She began to sob. "No more," she said. "*No more.*"

She slumped back. Blood was flowing from her wrists like water. She closed her eyes. He can't do anything more to me, she thought. Even if my soul is held in bondage in this house forever, I won't be his living puppet anymore.

She felt life draining from her. She was escaping. Daniel couldn't hurt her now. Feeling had begun to leave; pain was fading. God would forgive her self-destruction. It was what she had to do. Her lips drew back in a surrendering smile.

He would understand.

Her eyes fluttered open. Were those footsteps? She tried to turn her head but couldn't. The floor seemed to tremble. She tried to see. Was that a figure standing by her, looking down? She couldn't focus her eyes.

Suddenly it struck her. Horrified, she tried to push up, but was too weak. She had to let them know! Florence struggled fitfully to rise. Clouds of darkness were enveloping her. Everything felt numb. She turned her head and saw her blood running on the floorboards. Help me, God! she pleaded. *She had to let them know!*

Slowly, agonizingly, she reached out to shape the moving scarlet ribbons.

11:08 A.M.

Fischer jarred up, heartbeat pounding, and looked around in dread. His head was throbbing violently. He wanted to fall back on the pillow, but something kept him from it.

He dropped his legs across the mattress edge and stood. He began to reel, and pressed both hands against his head, eyes closed, body rocking back and forth. He groaned, remembering that Barrett had given him pills. Damn fool! he thought. How long had he been unconscious?

He started for the door, moving like a drunken man, trying to maintain his balance. He moved unevenly into the corridor and started toward Florence's room. He entered and stopped. She wasn't in bed. His gaze jumped to the bathroom. Its door was open; there was no one there. He turned and stumbled back into the corridor. What the hell was wrong with Barrett, anyway? He tried to move faster, but the impact inside his head was too painful. He stopped and leaned against the wall, a billowing of nausea in his stomach. He blinked and shook his head. The pain grew worse. To hell with it! he thought. He staggered forward willfully. He had to find her, get her out of here.

He glanced into the Barretts' room in passing, jarred to a halt. He moved inside and looked around incredulously. Barrett wasn't there; he'd left his wife alone! Fischer clenched his teeth in fury. *What the hell was going on?* He moved across the room as quickly as he could and dropped his hand on Edith's shoulder.

She jerked back from his touch, eyes open suddenly, gaping at him.

"Where's your husband?" Fischer asked.

She looked around in shock. "He isn't here?"

He watched dazedly as she stood. From the look on her face, he saw that she was taken aback by his appearance.

"Never mind," he mumbled, heading for the corridor. Edith didn't speak. She brushed past him, calling, "Lionel!"

She was halfway down the stairs before he'd reached the landing. "Don't go alone!" he cried. She paid no attention. Fischer tried to hurry down the steps but had to stagger to a halt, clinging to the rail as pain drove spikes into his skull. He leaned against the banister, trembling. "Lionel!" he heard her calling as she ran across the entry hall. He heard an answering call below and opened his eyes. Where else? he thought bitterly. Barrett was so anxious to prove his point, he was leaving his wife alone now, ignoring Florence. Stupid bastard!

Fischer hobbled down the stairs and walked across the entry hall, teeth set against the jolting pain. Entering the great hall, he saw Barrett and Edith standing by the Reversor. "Where is she?" he demanded.

Barrett looked at him blankly.

"Well?"

"She's not in her room?"

"Would I ask if she was?" snarled Fischer.

Barrett started limping toward him, joined by Edith. From the look on her face, Fischer could tell she was upset with Barrett too. "But I listened," Barrett said; "I checked you awhile ago. And the pills I gave her—"

"To hell with your pills!" Fischer cut him off. "You think possession can be stopped with pills?"

"I don't believe—"

"Screw what you believe!" Fischer's head was pounding so hard now that he could barely see. "She's gone, that's all that matters!"

"We'll find her," Barrett said; but there was no assurance in his voice. He looked around uneasily. "We'll try the cellar first. She might—"

He stopped as Fischer clutched his head, his face distended by a look of agony. "You'd better sit," he said.

"Shut up!" Fischer shouted hoarsely. He hunched over, making retching noises.

"Fischer—" Barrett started forward.

Fischer stumbled to a chair and dropped down heavily. Barrett approached as fast as he could, followed by Edith. They stopped as Fischer jerked down his hands and looked at them in shock.

"What?" asked Barrett.

Fischer began to shiver.

"What is it?" Barrett's voice rose involuntarily. Fischer's look unnerved him.

"The chapel."

Edith's scream of horror pierced the air. She spun away and stumbled to the wall.

"Oh, my dear God," Barrett murmured.

Fischer walked unsteadily to the body and stared at it. Her eyes were open, looking upward, her face the hue of pale wax. His gaze shifted to her genitals. They were caked with blood, the outer tissues shredded.

He twitched as Barrett stopped beside him. "What *happened* to her?" the older man whispered.

"She was killed," said Fischer venomously. "Murdered by this house." He tensed, expecting Barrett's contradiction, but there was none. "I don't see how she could have gotten up with all that sedative inside her," was all Barrett said, his tone one of guilt.

He saw that Fischer had turned to look at the crucifix lying nearby and did the same. Seeing the blood on its wooden phallus, he felt his stomach walls contract. "My God," he said.

"Not here," Fischer muttered. He shouted suddenly, as if he'd gone berserk: *"There's no God in this fucking house!"*

Across the chapel, Edith jerked around to look at Fischer

startledly. Barrett started to speak, then held it back. He drew in a trembling breath. The chapel smelled of gore. "We'd better get her out of here."

"I'll do it," Fischer said.

"You'll need some help."

"I'll do it."

Barrett shivered at the look on Fischer's face. "Very well."

Fischer crouched beside the body. Darkness pulsed before him, and he had to put down both hands to support himself; he felt them pressing into her blood. After a while his vision cleared, and he looked at her face. *She tried so hard,* he thought. Reaching out, he closed her eyes as gently as he could.

"What's that?" Barrett asked.

Fischer glanced up, wincing at the pain the movement caused. Barrett was staring at the floor near Florence. He looked down. It was too gloomy to see. He heard Barrett fumble in his pockets, then the scratching of a match end on a striking surface. The flare of light made his eyes contract painfully.

She'd drawn a symbol on the floor, using a finger dipped in her blood. It was a crude circle with something scrawled inside it. Fischer looked at it intently, trying to decipher it. Abruptly he saw what it was. Barrett spoke at the same moment.

"It looks like the letter 'B.' "

11:47 A.M.

They stood in the doorway, watching Fischer's slowly moving form until it vanished in the mist. Then Barrett turned.

"All right," he said.

She followed him into the great hall. Barrett hobbled quickly to the Reversor, and she stopped to watch him, trying not to think of Florence. Barrett made a final check on the Reversor, then turned to look at her.

"It's ready," he said.

She wished, for his sake, she could experience the emotion he obviously felt. "I know this moment is important to you," she said.

"Important to science." He turned to the Reversor, set its timer, turned several knobs, then, after hesitating for a moment, threw the switch.

For several seconds Edith thought that nothing was happening. Then she heard a resonant hum rise to audibility inside the giant structure and began to feel a throbbing in the floor.

She stared at the Reversor. The hum was rising in pitch and volume, the vibration in the floor increasing; she could feel it running up her legs, into her body. *Power,* she thought—the only thing that could oppose the house. She didn't understand it, but feeling its heavy throb in her body, its reverberation starting to hurt her ears, she almost believed.

She started as, behind the Reversor's grillwork, tubes began to glow with an intense phosphorescence. Barrett backed off slowly. His fingers trembled as he drew out his pocket watch. Exactly noon. Fittingly precise, he thought. He pushed the watch into his pocket and turned to Edith. "We have to go."

Their coats were on the table by the front door; Barrett had brought them down earlier. Hastily he helped her on with hers. As she assisted him, she glanced toward the great hall. The noise of the Reversor was painful even here now. She could feel its pulsing in the floor beneath her, hear the rattling of a vase nearby. "Quickly," Barrett said.

A moment later they had left the house and were hurrying

along the gravel path, around the tarn, the sound of the Reversor fading behind them. As they crossed the bridge, Edith saw the Cadillac standing in the mist, and tightened at the thought of Florence being in it.

Barrett pulled open the back door, flinching as he saw that Fischer had the blanket-covered body on the seat with him, cradling its head and upper torso in his arms. "Couldn't we—" he started, breaking off as Fischer glared at him. He hesitated, then reshut the door. No point in setting Fischer off. He was close enough to the edge as it was.

"She's in there *with* him?" Edith whispered.

"Yes."

Edith looked ill. "I can't sit in there with—" She couldn't finish.

"We'll sit in front."

"Can't we go back in the house?" she asked, fleetingly aware of the grotesqueness of her requesting to go back inside Hell House.

"Absolutely not. The radiation would kill us."

She stared at him. "All right," she finally said.

As they got into the front and closed the door, Barrett glanced into the rearview mirror. Fischer was bent over Florence's body, his chin resting on what must have been the top of her head. How badly had her death affected him? he wondered.

Remembering then, he turned to Edith. "Deutsch is dead," he told her.

Edith didn't respond. At last she nodded. "It doesn't matter."

Unexpectedly, Barrett felt a flare of anger. *Doesn't* it? he thought. He turned away. Why brood about it, then? He'd done his best to provide for her. If she didn't care . . .

He willed away the anger. What else could she say? He

straightened up, grimacing at the pain in his thumb. "Fischer?"

There was no reply. Barrett looked around. "Deutsch is dead," he said. "His son refuses to pay us."

"What's the difference?" Fischer mumbled. Barrett saw his fingers tightening on Florence Tanner's shoulder. He turned back to the front and, reaching into his overcoat pocket, withdrew the ring of keys. Fingering through them, he found the ignition key and pushed it into its slot. He turned the key enough to activate the dial needles without starting the engine. There wasn't enough fuel to run the engine for forty minutes so they could keep the interior warm. Damn, he thought. He should have remembered to bring more blankets from the house, some brandy.

He leaned his head back, closed his eyes. Well, they'd have to endure it, that was all. Personally, he didn't care— This moment was too engulfing for anything else in the world to overshadow it.

Behind those windowless walls some several hundred yards distant, Hell House was dying.

12:45 P.M.

Barrett snapped his watch cover shut. "It's done."

Edith's face was without expression. Barrett started feeling disappointment at her lack of response, then realized that she could not conceive of what had taken place inside the house. Reaching across the seat, he patted her hand, then turned. "Fischer?"

Fischer was still slumped over Florence, holding her body against himself. He looked up slowly.

"Will you go back in with us?"

Fischer didn't speak.

"The house is clear."

"Is it?"

Barrett wanted to smile. He couldn't blame the man, of course. His claim *did* sound preposterous after what had taken place this week. "I need you with me," he said.

"Why?"

"To verify that the house is clear."

"What if it isn't?"

"I guarantee it is." Barrett waited for Fischer's decision. When nothing happened, he said, "It will take only a few minutes."

Fischer stared at him in silence for a while before he edged away from Florence's body and, shifting carefully to a kneeling position on the floor, lowered her to the seat. He looked at her for several moments, then withdrew his arms and turned to the door.

They came together in front of the car. *Déjà vu*, thought Edith. It was as though time had been reversed and they were about to enter Hell House for the first time. Only the absence of Florence prevented the illusion from being complete. She shivered, drawing up the collar of her coat. She felt numb with cold. Lionel had run the engine and heater for brief periods of time during their wait, but minutes after he switched off the engine each time, the cold had returned.

The walk to the house was eerily reminiscent of Monday's arrival: their shoes ringing on the concrete bridge; her glancing back to see the limousine being swallowed by the mist; the circling trudge around the tarn, its hideous odor in her nostrils; the crunch of gravel underneath their shoes; the cold penetrating flesh; her feelings as the massive house loomed up in front of them. It was no use. She couldn't believe that Lionel was right. Which meant that they were walking back into a trap. They'd gotten out somehow; three of them, anyway.

Now, incredibly, they were returning. Even realizing that Lionel had to know the effect of his Reversor, it was impossible to comprehend the suicidal folly of their move.

The final yards along the gravel path. The approach up the wide porch steps; the click of shoes on concrete again. The double doors ahead of them. Edith shuddered. *No,* she thought, I won't go back inside.

Then Barrett had opened the door for her, and without a word she'd entered Hell House again.

They stopped, and Barrett shut the door. Edith saw that the vase had fallen to the floor and shattered.

Barrett looked at Fischer questioningly.

"I don't know," Fischer said.

Barrett tensed. "You have to open up." Was it possible that Fischer had no extrasensory perception left? The thought that he might have to bring another psychic all the way to Maine before finding out was appalling to him.

Fischer moved away from them. He looked around uneasily. It did feel different. That could be a trick, though. He'd been fooled before. He didn't dare expose himself like that again.

Barrett watched him restively. Edith glanced at her husband and saw how impatient he was. "Try, Mr. Fischer," he said abruptly. "I guarantee there'll be no trouble."

Fischer didn't look around. He walked across the entry hall. Amazingly, the atmosphere *had* changed. Even without opening up, he could sense that. Still, how *much* had it changed? How much faith could he really have in Barrett? His theory had sounded good. But Barrett wasn't just asking him to believe a theory. He was asking him to put his life at stake again.

He kept on walking. He was passing through the archway into the great hall now; he heard the Barretts' footsteps following. Entering the hall, he stopped and looked around. The floor was littered with broken objects. Across from him, a tapestry hung askew on its wall. What had the Reversor *done?* He wanted very much to know but was afraid to try to find out.

"Well?" asked Barrett. Fischer waved him off. I'll do it when I'm ready, he thought angrily.

He stood immobile, listening, waiting.

On impulse then, he dropped the barriers. Closing his eyes, he spread his arms, his hands, his fingers, drawing in whatever might be hovering in the atmosphere.

His eyes jerked open, and he looked around in bafflement.

There was nothing.

Distrust returned. He whirled and darted past them. Edith looked alarmed, but Barrett grabbed her arm, preventing her from panic. "He's startled because there's nothing to pick up," he told her.

Fischer ran into the entry hall. Nothing. He raced down the corridor to the chapel, shoved the door in violently. Nothing. He turned and ran to the steps, descending them with avid leaps, ignoring the pain in his head. Straight-arming through the pool doors, he raced to the steam room, pulled open its door, braced himself.

Nothing.

He turned in awe. "I don't believe it."

He sprinted back along the pool and out into the corridor. He ran into the wine cellar. Nothing. He dashed back up the stairs, gasping for breath. The theater. Nothing. The ballroom. Nothing. The billiard room. Nothing. He raced along the corridor with frenzied strides. The kitchen. Nothing. The dining hall. Nothing. He charged across the great hall, back into the entry hall. Barrett and Edith were still there. Fischer rocked to a panting halt in front of them. He started to speak, then broke into a run for the stairs. Barrett felt a rush of exultation.

"Done," he said. "It's *done*, Edith. *Done!*" He threw his arms around her, pulled her close. Her heart was pounding. She still couldn't believe it. Yet Fischer was beside himself. She watched him leaping up the staircase, two steps at a time.

Fischer ran across the corridor to the Barretts' room. He plunged inside. Nothing! Spinning with a dazzled cry, he ran into the corridor again, to Florence's room. Nothing! Along the corridor to his room. Nothing! Over to Belasco's quarters. Nothing! God Almighty! *Nothing!* His head was pounding, but he didn't care. He raced along the corridor, flinging open doors to all the unused bedrooms. Nothing! Everywhere he went, nothing, absolutely nothing! Jubilation burst inside him. Barrett had done it!

Hell House was clear!

He had to sit. Staggering to the nearest chair, he dropped down limply. Hell House cleared. It was incredible. He thrust aside the knowledge that he'd have to alter everything he'd ever believed. It didn't matter. *Hell House had been cleared,* exorcised by that fantastic—*what?*—down there. His laugh broke hoarsely. And he had called it a pile of junk. Jesus God, a pile of *junk!* Why hadn't Barrett kicked him in the teeth?

He slumped against the chair, eyes closed, regaining breath.

Reaction came abruptly. If she'd lasted one more hour. Just another *hour!* He felt a sudden, anguished rage at Barrett for having left her alone.

It wouldn't last. It was overpowered by the awe he felt for the physicist. Patiently, doggedly, Barrett had done his work, knowing that they'd thought him wrong. Yet he'd been right all the time. Fischer shook his head in wonderment. It was a miracle. He inhaled deeply, had to smile. The air still stank.

But not with the reek of the dead.

2:01 P.M.

Fischer braked a little as the Cadillac moved into another pocket of impenetrable mist. He'd decided to keep the car and sell it if he could, splitting the take with Barrett. Failing that, he'd drive the damn thing into a lake; but Deutsch would never see it again. He hoped that Barrett had some way of getting the Reversor out of Hell House before Deutsch could get his hands on it. It had to be worth a small fortune.

Reaching forward, he turned on the windshield wipers, his eyes fixed on the road as he drove through the dark woods, trying to dovetail the pieces in his mind.

First of all, Barrett had been right. The power in the house had been a massive residue of electromagnetic radiation. Barrett had negated it, and it had vanished. Where did that leave Florence's beliefs? Were they totally invalidated now? Had she, as Barrett had claimed, created her own haunting, unconsciously manipulating the energy in the house to prove her points? It seemed to fit. It shook his own beliefs as well, but it fitted.

Still, why had her unconscious will chosen to effect a type of phenomena she'd never effected in her life? To convince Barrett, to whom physical phenomena were the only meaningful kind, the answer came immediately.

All right, there really had been a Daniel Belasco, he thought. He'd been bricked inside that wall alive by someone, probably his father. That much Florence had picked up psychically, reading the house's energy like the memory bank of a computer. That Daniel Belasco was, therefore, the haunting force had been her mistaken interpretation of those facts.

Why had she carried it to such suicidal extremes, though? The question baffled him. After a lifetime of intelligent mediumship, why had she literally killed herself to prove that she was right? Was that the kind of person she'd really been? Had her outward behavior been entirely a deception? It seemed impossible. She'd functioned as a psychic for many years without incurring harm; or inflicting it, as she apparently had on Barrett. Had the power of Hell House been so overwhelming that she simply hadn't been able to cope with it? Barrett would undoubtedly say yes; and it was true that, facing it that single time yesterday, he had almost been destroyed by its enormity. Still . . .

Fischer lit a cigarette and blew out smoke. He had to force himself back to the unassailable fact that the house was clear. Barrett had been right; there was no denying it. His theory made sense: shapeless power in the house requiring the focus of invading winds in order to function. What had the house been like between 1940 and last Monday? he wondered. Silent? Dormant? Waiting for some new intelligence to enter? Undoubtedly—since Barrett was correct.

Correct.

He tried to fight away encroaching doubts. Damn it, he'd been in the house! He'd run from room to room, completely opened. There'd been nothing. Hell House had been clear. Why were these stupid qualms assailing him, then?

Because it was all too simple, he realized abruptly.

What about the debacles of 1931 and 1940? He'd been in one of them and knew how incredibly complex the events had been. He thought about the list Barrett had. There must have been more than a hundred different phenomena itemized on it. This week's occurrences had been staggeringly varied. It simply didn't make sense that it had all been radiation to be turned off like a lamp. True, there was no logic to back up his misgiving, but he could not dispel it. There had been so many "final answers" in the past, people swearing that they knew the secret of Hell House. Florence had believed it of herself and had been lured, by that belief, to her destruction.

Now Barrett felt *he* had the final answer. Granted that he had what seemed to be complete verification of his certainty. What if he was wrong, though? If there'd been any recurrent method at all to the house, it had been that at the moment when a person thought the final answer had been found, the house's final attack was launched.

Fischer shook his head. He didn't want to believe that. Logically, he *couldn't* believe it. Barrett had been right. The house was clear.

Abruptly he recalled the bloody circle on the chapel floor, the "B" inside it. Belasco, obviously. Why had Florence done that? Had her thoughts been blinded by the imminence of death? Or crystallized?

No. It couldn't be Belasco. The house was clear. He'd felt it himself, for Christ's sake! Barrett had been absolutely right. Electromagnetic radiation was the answer.

Why, then, was his foot pressing down harder and harder on the accelerator? Why was his heart beginning to pound? Why was there an icy prickling on the back of his neck? *Why did he have this constantly increasing dread that he had to get back to the house before it was too late?*

2:17 P.M.

Barrett came out of the bathroom, wearing robe and slippers. He limped to Edith's bed and sat on the edge of it. She was lying down, the comforter pulled over her. "Feeling better?" she asked.

"Marvelous."

"How's the thumb?"

"I'll have it checked as soon as we get home." He wouldn't tell her that he'd tried to unwind the bandage in the shower but had been forced to stop because he'd almost fainted from the pain.

"Home." Edith's smile was bemused. "I guess I still can't believe we're really going to see it again."

"We'll be there by tomorrow." Barrett made a face. "We'd be there by tonight if Deutsch Junior wasn't such a—"

"—son of a bitch," she provided.

Barrett smiled. "To put it mildly." The smile disappeared. "I'm afraid our security is gone, my dear."

"You're my security," she said. "Leaving this house with you by my side will be worth a million dollars to me." She took hold of his left hand. "Is it really over, Lionel? All of it?"

He nodded. "All of it."

"It's so hard to believe."

"I know." He squeezed her hand. "You don't mind if I say I told you so, do you?"

"I don't mind anything as long as I know it's over."

"It is."

"What a pity she had to die when the answer was so close."

"It *is* a pity. I should have made her leave."

She put her other hand on his and pressed it reassuringly. "You did everything you could."

"I shouldn't have left her alone before."

"How could you have known she'd wake up?"

"I couldn't. It was incredible. Her subconscious was so intent on validating her delusion that her system actually rejected the sedation."

"The poor woman," Edith said.

"The poor, self-defrauded woman. Even to the final touch—scrawling, in her own blood, that circle with the 'B' inside it. She had to believe, even as she died, that she was right; that it was Belasco destroying her—the father or the son, I don't know which. She couldn't allow herself to believe it was her own mind doing it." He winced. "How pitiful an end it must have been; pain-racked, terrified—"

Seeing the look on Edith's face, he stopped. "I'm sorry."

"It's all right."

He forced a smile. "Well, Fischer should be back in an hour or so, and we can leave." He frowned. "Assuming he isn't detained when he brings in her body."

"Can't say I'll miss the old place," she said after a few moments.

Barrett laughed softly. "Nor can I. Although"—he thought about it for a moment—"it is my scene of—how shall I term it?—triumph?"

"Yes." She nodded. "It *is* a triumph. I can't really comprehend what you've done, but I sense how terribly important it is."

"Well, if I do say so myself, it's going to give parapsychology rather a leg up into polite society."

Edith smiled.

"Because it's science," he said. "No mumbo-jumbo. Nothing the critics can pick at—though I'm sure they'll try. Not that I argue with them when they cavil at the usual approach to psychic phenomena. Their resentment of the aura of trivial humbug which hovers over most of the phenomena and its advocates is justifiable. By and large, *psi* doesn't have an air of respectability. Therefore the critics ridicule it rather than risk being ridiculed themselves for examining it seriously. This is *a priori* evaluation, unfortunately—one hundred percent unscientific. They'll continue to overlook the import of parapsychology, I'm afraid, until they're able—as Huxley put it—'to sit down before fact as a little child—be prepared to give up every preconceived notion, follow humbly wherever and to whatsoever abysses nature leads.' "

He chuckled self-consciously. "End of discourse." Leaning

over, he kissed her gently on the cheek. "The speechifier loves you," he said.

"Oh, Lionel." She slipped her arms around his back. "I love you, too. And I'm so proud of you."

She was asleep now. Barrett carefully disengaged his fingers from hers and stood. He smiled down at her. She deserved this sleep. She hadn't had a decent night's rest since they'd entered Hell House.

His smile broadened as he turned from the bed. Hell House was a misnomer now. From this day forth, it would be merely the Belasco house.

As he dressed with slow, contented movements, he wondered what would happen to the house. It ought to be a shrine to science. Deutsch would doubtless sell it to the highest bidder, though. He grunted with amusement. Not that he could imagine anyone wanting to own it.

He combed his hair, looking at his reflection in the wall mirror. His eye was caught by the rocking chair across the room, and he smiled again. All of that was over now, the endless little outputs of meaningless kinetics. No more winds or odors, no percussions; nothing.

He crossed the room and went into the corridor, heading for the stairs. He was glad that Fischer had insisted on taking Florence Tanner's body into town immediately. He knew the other man would not have placed the body in the trunk, and it would have been terribly painful for Edith to ride all the way to Caribou Falls with the body in the back seat. He hoped that Fischer didn't take too long in returning. He was working up quite an appetite; his first of the week. A celebration meal, he thought. Poor old Deutsch, it suddenly occurred to him; he'd never know now. Perhaps it was kinder that way. Not that Deutsch had wanted—or deserved—kindness.

He descended the staircase slowly, eying the enormous entry hall. A museum, he thought. Really, something should be done with the house now that the terror had been exorcised.

He hobbled across the entry hall. He'd examined his body in the full-length bathroom mirror after taking his shower, imagining it was how a prizefighter's body looked after a particularly grueling bout—the purple-black contusions everywhere. The burned skin on his calf was still contracting, too; he could feel the tautness of the scalded area pulling at the skin around it. The abrasion on his shin still hurt as well; and, as for his leg and thumb—Barrett had to smile. The Olympics I'm not ready for, he thought.

He crossed the great hall, walking to the Reversor. Once again, he stared at the main dial in awe: 14,780. He'd never dreamed the reading could be so high. No wonder this place had been the Everest of haunted houses. He shook his head almost admiringly. The house had been aptly named.

He turned and limped to the table, frowning as he visualized the necessary packing. He looked at the array of equipment. Maybe he wouldn't have to pack it, after all. If they put blankets in the limousine trunk for padding, the equipment could probably be wrapped in towels or something. Maybe they should take a few *objets d'art* as well, he thought, repressing a smile. Deutsch would never miss them. He ran a finger over the top of the EMR recorder.

Its needle stirred.

Barrett twitched. He stared at the needle. It was motionless again. Odd, he thought. Touching the recorder must have activated the needle by static electricity. It wouldn't happen again.

The needle jumped across the dial, then fluttered back to zero.

Barrett felt a tic in his right cheek. What was happening?

The recorder couldn't function on its own. EMR was convertible to measurable energy only in the presence of a psychic. He forced a dry laugh. Grotesque if I discover I'm a medium after all these years, he thought. He made a scoffing noise. That was absurd. Besides, there was no radiation left in the house. He'd eliminated it.

The needle started moving. It did not jump or flutter. It inched across the dial as though recording a build-up of radiation. "No," Barrett said. His tone was irritated. This was ludicrous.

The needle continued moving. Barrett stared at it as it passed the 100 mark, the 150 mark. He shook his head. This was absurd. It couldn't record by itself. Moreover, there was nothing left in the house to record. "No," he said again. There was more anger than dismay in his voice. This simply could not be.

His head jerked up so suddenly that it hurt his neck. He watched the needle of the dynamometer begin to arc across its dial. This was *impossible*. His gaze leaped to the face of the thermometer. It was starting to record a drop in temperature. "*No*," he said. His face was pale with malice. This was nonsense, totally illogical.

He caught his breath as the camera clicked. He gaped at it and heard the film inside it being wound, heard the lens click shut again, He gasped again, muscles spasmed as the rack of colored lights went on, turned off, went on again. *"No."* He shook his head unyieldingly. This was not acceptable. It was a trick of some kind; it was fraudulent.

He started violently as one of the test tubes broke in half, falling from its rack to clatter on the tabletop. *This cannot be!* he heard a voice protesting in his mind. Abruptly he remembered Fischer's single question. "No!" he snapped. He backed off from the table. It was utterly impossible. Once dispelled, the radiation had no restorative power whatever.

He cried out as the rack of lights began to flicker rapidly. "No!" he raged. He would not believe it! The needles of his instruments were not all quivering across their dials. The thermometer was not recording a constant drop in temperature. The electric stove had not begun to glow. The galvanometers were not recording on their own. The camera wasn't taking photographs. The tubes and vessels weren't breaking one by one. The EMR recorder needle hadn't passed the 700 mark. It was all delusion. He was suffering some aberration of the senses. *This-could-not-be-happening.* "Wrong!" he shouted, face distorted by fury. "Wrong, wrong, *wrong!*"

His mouth fell open as the EMR recorder started to expand. He stared at it in horror as it swelled as though its sides and top were made of rubber. *No.* He shook his head in disavowal. He was going mad. This was impossible. He would not accept it He would not—

He screamed as the recorder suddenly exploded, screamed again as metal splinters drove into his face and eyes. He dropped his cane and threw his hands across his face. Something shot across the table, and he jolted backward as the camera struck him on the legs. He lost his balance, fell, heard equipment crashing to the floor as though someone were flinging it. He tried to see but couldn't, staggered blindly to his feet.

It struck him then, a crushing, arctic force that jerked him from his feet as though he were a toy. A cry of shocked bewilderment flooded from him as the glacial force propelled him through the air and flung him violently against the front of the Reversor. Barrett felt his left arm snap. He shrieked in pain, dropping to the floor.

Again the unseen force grabbed hold of him and started dragging him across the hall. He couldn't break away from it. Trying in vain to scream for help, he bumped and slithered along the floor. A massive table blocked his way. Sensing it, he flung his right arm up, crashed against its edge, his bandaged thumb driven back against its wrist. His mouth jerked open in a strangling cry of agony. Blood began to spout from the hand. Yanked across the tabletop and somersaulted down onto the floor again, he caught an obscure glimpse of the thumb dangling from his hand by shards of bone and skin.

He tried to fight against the power which hauled him brutally across the entry hall, but he was helpless in its grip, a plaything in the jaws of some invisible creature. Eyes staring sightlessly, face a blood-streaked mask of horror, he was dragged into the corridor feet first. His chest was filled with fiery pain as clutching hands crushed his heart. He couldn't breathe. His arms and legs were going numb. His face began to darken, turning red, then purple. Veins distended on his neck; his eyes began to bulge. His mouth hung open, sucking at the air in vain as the savage force bounced him down the stairs and drove his broken body through the swinging doors. The tile floor rushed beneath him. He was hurtled into space.

The water crashed around him icily. The clutching force dragged him toward the bottom. Water poured into his throat. He started choking, struggled fitfully. The force would not release him. Water gushed into his lungs. He doubled over, staring at the bottom as he strangled. Blood from his thumb was clouding everything. The power turned him slowly. He was staring upward, seeing through a reddish haze. There was someone standing on the pool edge, looking down at him.

The sound of his enfeebled thrashing faded. The figure blurred, began to disappear in shadows. Barrett settled to the bottom, eyes unseeing once again. Somewhere deep within the cavern of his mind a faint intelligence still flickered, crying out in anguish: *Edith!*

Then all was blackness, like a shroud enfolding him, as he descended into night.

2:46 P.M.

Edith's left hand jumped abruptly. Her wedding band had sheared in half and fallen to the bed. She snapped her eyelids back. The room was dark. "Lionel?"

The door was opened. The corridor was dark, too. Someone entered. "Lionel?" she said again.

"Yes."

She sat up groggily. "What happened?"

"Nothing to be concerned about. The generator just went out."

"Oh, no." She tried to see. It was too dark.

"It's not important," Lionel said. She heard his footsteps cross the room, felt his weight settle on the other side of the bed. She reached out nervously and felt his hand. "You're sure everything is all right?"

"Of course." The hand began to stroke her hair. "Don't be afraid. Let's take advantage of it."

"What?" She reached for him, but he was farther away than she'd thought.

"We haven't been together for a long time." Lionel's hand slid down her cheek. "And you're in need of it."

She made a questioning sound. His hand slid over to her left breast and began to squeeze it. "Lionel, don't," she said.

"Why not?" he asked. "Aren't I good enough for you?"

"What are you—?"

"Fischer's good enough," he interrupted. "Even Florence Tanner was good enough." His fingers tightened on her breast, hurting it. *"How about a little pussy for the old man now?"*

Edith tried to pull away his hand. She felt her heartbeat quicken. "No," she murmured.

"Yes," he said. The hand moved down abruptly, shoving up her skirt to clutch between her legs. *"Yes, you lesbian bitch."*

The lights went on.

Edith screamed. The hand released her, pulling back. It was bloodless, severed at the wrist, floating up above her chest now, gamboling in the air before her stricken face, vein ends dangling from it. Edith recoiled against the headboard. The hand dropped to her breast again, pinching her nipple between its thumb and index finger. She cried out shrilly, tried to knock it loose. The hand jumped forward like a leprous spider, clamping on her face, cold and smelling of the grave. A crazed shriek flooded from her, and the gray hand flew back. Edith jerked her legs up, kicking at it berserkly. The hand jumped up and started gesturing in the air, fingers wriggling wildly.

Suddenly it darted downward, vanishing into the bedclothes, and the comforter began to swell, ballooning quickly. Gasping, Edith flung herself across the mattress, springing to her feet. She lurched around the corner of the bed, fleeing for the door. The comforter flew upward. In an instant, she was covered by a cloud of moths. Flailing at the surge of insects, she stumbled blindly across the room. The moths enveloped her completely, gray wings beating at her face, bodies fluttering in her hair. She tried to scream, but moths flew in her mouth; she spit them out in horrified revulsion, pressed her lips together. Moths flew in her ears. Their dusty wings whipped frenziedly against her eyes. Both arms flung across her face, she crashed against the octagonal table and began to fall.

Before she hit the floor, the moths were gone. She landed hard and scrabbled to her knees. The table thudded down nearby, pages of Lionel's manuscript spilling across the rug in front of her. The pages leaped into the air. She swung at them in mindless panic as they tore in shreds before her eyes. The pieces shot into the air and fluttered downward like a rain of giant snowflakes. Edith backed away from them, pushing at the floor with hands and feet. A man began to laugh. She looked around in terror. "Lionel," she muttered. "Lionel." She heard her own voice played back like a tape recording. "No," she pleaded. "No," her voice repeated. Edith whined. She heard the whine again. She started crying, heard an echoed crying in the air. With a desperate lunge, she found her feet and dashed across the room. She jerked the door in, leaped back with a choking scream.

Florence stood in the doorway, naked, staring at her, dark blood running down her thighs and legs. Edith shrieked. Darkness swept across her. She began to fall.

She jerked erect as an electric current spasmed through her body. Darkness fled; she was acutely conscious, knowing even as she flung herself into the empty doorway that she hadn't been allowed to faint. She lunged into the corridor and headed for the stairs. The air was thick with mist. She smelled the odor of the tarn. A figure blocked her way. Edith jolted to a stop. The woman wore a white gown. She was soaking wet, her dark hair plastered down across her gray face. She was holding something in her arms. Edith stared at it in loathing; it was half-formed, monstrous. *Bastard Bog!* a voice screamed in her mind. She backed off, a demented moaning in her throat.

Something spun her, slammed against her back. To keep from falling, she was forced to run. She wasn't headed for the stairs! She tried to stop herself and turn but couldn't control her limbs. She screamed as Florence rushed at her. She felt the cold arms clamp around her, and her scream was cut off as the dead lips crushed on hers. She reached up, gagging, crazed with terror, tried to pull the head away.

Florence vanished. Edith's yanking motion made her fall. She landed on her knees. "Lionel!" she screamed. "Lionel!" roared a mocking voice. Cold wind rushed across her, whipping at her clothes and hair. She tried to stand. Something icy crashed against her neck. She screamed as teeth dug deep into her flesh. Her hands flew up, but there was nothing. Fetid spittle trickled down her skin. She felt the pitted indentations. "Lionel!" she screamed in anguish.

"Here!" he answered. Edith's head jerked up. He was running down the corridor toward her! She scrambled up and rushed toward him. She threw herself against him. Instantly she jerked back, staring at the man who held her. It was her father, with the slack expression of an imbecile on his face, his red-rimmed eyes regarding her with stupid glee, his mouth agape, his tongue protruding. He started pulling her against him, a sound of animal amusement rumbling in his chest. He was naked, bloated. Edith wrenched away from him. She tried to run, but something smashed against her side. She lost her balance and went floundering toward the banister that overlooked the entry hall. She crashed against it, crying out in pain. Her father advanced on her, holding his enormous penis with both hands. She started clambering across the rail, to die below, escape this horror.

Strong hands grabbed her. Edith whirled in horror. Lionel was holding her. She stared at him, refusing to believe. "Edith! It's me!" The sound of his familiar voice made her fall against him, sobbing. "Take me out of here," she begged.

"Right away," he answered. Left arm fixed around her back, he ran her to the stairs. She looked at him. He had no cane, he wasn't limping. "No," she moaned. "It's quite all right," he said. He rushed her down the staircase. Edith tried to pull away from him. "It's me," he said. She sobbed again. He wouldn't let her go. Hollow laughter rippled in the air. She looked around and saw the people grouped below, watching them elatedly. She turned to Lionel, but it wasn't Lionel anymore. It was a monstrous caricature of him, every feature gross, exaggerated, his voice a vicious mocking as he said, "It's me. It's me." "No!" she screamed. She wrestled with him helplessly. His grip was too strong. He wasn't even looking ahead. He was grinning at her as they ran. Edith closed her eyes. Let it be quick! she pleaded.

The entry hall, the corridor. She felt herself rushed along the floor. She couldn't make a sound. The theater door flew open; she was thrust inside. She opened her eyes and saw a crowd of naked people sitting in the velvet chairs, keening with amusement at her plight. She was half-dragged up the steps. The bloated parody of Lionel bound her to a post. She looked out at the audience. They howled with fierce anticipation. Edith cried out as her clothes were ripped away. The people cheered. It sounded muffled, from another world. Edith heard a coughing growl and turned her head. A crouching leopard stalked across the stage. She tried to scream, but nothing issued from her throat. The audience screamed. Edith closed her eyes. The leopard sprang. She felt its huge teeth sinking deep into her head, its heated, blood-sour breath flooding across her face. She felt its rear legs start to thrash berserkly, felt the talons ripping out her stomach. Black pain seared her, and she fell back, shrieking.

She was crumpled on the dusty stage. Heartbeat staggering, she sat up. The theater was empty. No. There was someone, sitting in the shadows of the last row, dressed in black. She seemed to hear a deep voice resonating in her mind. *Welcome to my house,* it said.

She tried to stand. Her legs began to buckle, and she fell against a wall. She pushed away and staggered to the steps. Lionel stood in front of her. "It's me," he said. She cried out, agonized. Laughter boomed inside the theater. Edith stumbled to the door and pushed it open. Lionel was standing in the corridor. "It's me," he said.

She tried to make the entry hall but couldn't; her body was turned to the side. Lionel was waiting on the landing of the cellar stairs. "It's me!" he cried. The stairwell yawned before her. Lionel was standing at the bottom, grinning up at her. "It's me!" he cried. Edith whimpered, clutching at the banister rail, half-pushed, half-descending on her own. Lionel was standing by the metal doors.

"It's me!" he cried. The swinging doors flew open, crashed against the wall inside. Lionel was standing by the pool. "It's me!" he cried. The force impelled her toward him. Edith staggered forward, stopped beside the pool. She stared into the bloody water.

Lionel was floating just below the surface, staring up at her.

Madness took her then. She backed off, screaming, stumbling out into the corridor. A figure came leaping down the stairs and grabbed her by the arms. She fought it with demented strength, shrieks of frenzy flooding from her throat. The figure shouted at her, but she heard only her own voice. Something struck her on the jaw, and suddenly she was falling, screaming endlessly, as she went plummeting into the depths.

3:31 P.M.

Edith stirred again. Her eyes fluttered open. For several moments she stared toward the front of the car. Then she turned in confusion, twitching as she saw him. She looked at him in questioning silence.

"I'm sorry I had to hit you," he said.

"That was you?"

He nodded.

Edith looked around abruptly "Lionel."

"His body's in the trunk."

She started for the door, but Fischer restrained her. "You don't want to look at him." She continued struggling against his grip. "Don't," he said.

Edith fell back, averting her face. Fischer sat in silence, listening to her cry.

She turned to him abruptly. "Let's get out of here," she said.

He didn't move.

"What is it?"

"I'm not leaving."

Edith didn't understand.

"I'm going back inside."

"Inside?" She looked appalled. "You don't know what it's like in there."

"I have to—"

"You don't know what it's like!" she cut him off. "It killed my husband! It killed Florence Tanner! It would have killed me if you hadn't gotten back! No one has a chance in there!"

Fischer didn't argue.

"Aren't two deaths enough? Do you have to die too?"

"I don't plan to die."

She clutched his hand. "Don't leave me, please."

"I have to."

"No."

"I have to."

"Please don't do it!"

"Edith, I *have* to."

"No! You don't! You *don't!* There isn't any reason to go back inside!"

"Edith." Fischer took her hand in both of his and waited for her crying to abate. "Listen now."

She shook her head, eyes closing.

"I have to. For Florence. For your husband."

"They wouldn't want you to—"

"*I* want it," Fischer interrupted. "I need it. If I leave Hell House now, I might as well crawl into my grave and die. I haven't done a thing all week. While Florence and your husband were doing everything they could to solve the haunting—"

"They couldn't solve it, though! There isn't any way of solving it!"

"Maybe not." He paused. "I'm going to try, though."

Edith glanced up quickly at him, then said nothing, silenced by his look. "I'm going to try," he said.

They were silent. Finally Fischer asked, "You drive, don't you?"

He saw a telltale flare of hope in her expression. "No," she said.

He smiled gently. "Yes, you do."

Edith's chin slumped forward on her chest. "You're going to die," she said. "Like Lionel. Like Florence."

Fischer drew in a slow breath.

"Then I will," he said.

Fischer crossed the bridge and trudged along the gravel path which ringed the tarn. He was alone now. For several moments the realization filled him with such dread that he almost turned and ran.

Edith had been crying when she left; she'd tried, in vain, to control it. Tears running down her cheeks, she'd turned the Cadillac and driven off into the mist. He had to go inside the house now anyway. He couldn't walk to Caribou Falls in this cold.

The bottoms of his tennis shoes made crunching noises on the gravel as he walked. What was he going to do? he wondered. He had no idea. Had Florence accomplished anything? Had Barrett? He had no way of knowing. He might be confronted with starting from the beginning all over again.

He began to shake, stiffening his back to fight it off. It didn't matter what he had to do. He was here; he'd do it.

Edith would bring back food and leave it on the porch for him. How long it lasted didn't matter either. Only one thing counted at the moment.

As he continued walking, he became conscious of the medallion Florence had given him pressed against his chest. He'd told Edith he was doing this for Barrett too, but really it was all for Florence. She was the one he could have helped, the one he should have helped.

The house again, a mist-obscured escarpment up ahead. Fischer stopped and looked at it. It might have stood there for a thousand years. Was there an answer to its haunting? He didn't know. But if he couldn't discover it, then no one could: of that much he was certain.

He padded silently across the porch steps to the door. It was still ajar, the way he'd left it when he'd carried Barrett's body to the car. He hesitated for a long time, sensing that to walk inside would decide, finally and irrevocably, his fate.

"Hell." What fate did he have, anyway? He went inside and shut the door. Moving to the telephone, he picked up the receiver. The line was dead. What did you expect? he asked himself. He dumped the receiver on the table. He was cut off absolutely now. He turned and looked around.

As he crossed the entry hall, he had the feeling that the house was swallowing him alive.

6:29 P.M.

Fischer sat at the huge round table in the great hall, eating a sandwich and drinking a cup of coffee; Edith had brought two sacks of food and left again without a word. It's insane, Fischer was thinking. He'd thought it endlessly for the past hour.

The atmosphere of Hell House was completely flat.

He hadn't even had to open up to realize it. The awareness had developed quickly as he'd toured the house, first upstairs, all the bedrooms, used and unused. If there'd been any presence in the air, he would have sensed it. There was nothing. It was grotesque. What had killed Barrett so violently, then? What had almost killed Edith? He'd felt that presence strongly as he'd rushed down the cellar steps to rescue her before. Now it was gone; the house felt as clear as it had after the Reversor had been used. It wasn't any kind of trick, either; he was sure of that. When he'd opened up the first time yesterday, he'd known that there was something lurking in the house. He'd miscalculated its power and its cunning, but he'd known it was there.

Now it wasn't.

Fischer stared at the floor. One of Barrett's galvanometers was lying near his feet, its side cracked open, springs and coils protruding from the gash like polished entrails. His gaze shifted to the other equipment lying broken on the rug, shifted to the Reversor, and held on the huge dent on its face. Something devastating had struck this room, struck this equipment, struck Barrett.

Where had it gone?

He sighed, and propping the soles of his tennis shoes against the table edge, leaned the chair back slightly. Now what? he thought. He'd come back imbued with fine dramatic resolution. For what? He was no further along than he'd ever been. There wasn't even anything to work with now.

He'd walked through every room on the first floor, stood for almost twenty minutes in the dining hall, looking at its wreckage: the massive table wedged against the fireplace screen, the giant sanctuary lamp battered on the floor, the overturned chairs, the debris of broken crockery and glassware, the coffeepot and serving dish, the scattering of silverware, the dried food, the coffee stain, the sallow blots of sugar and cream. Staring at it all, he'd tried to calculate what had happened. Which one of the two had been correct? Had Florence caused the attack, as Barrett had claimed? Or had it been Daniel Belasco, as Florence had insisted?

No way of knowing. Fischer had walked through the kitchen, out through the west doorway and down the corridor to the ballroom. What had made the chandelier move? Electromagnetic radiation, or the dead?

The chapel. Had Daniel Belasco possessed Florence?—or suicidal madness?

He'd gone into the garage, the theater, the cellar, walked along the pool, into the steam room. What had attacked Barrett there? Mindless power, or Belasco?

The wine cellar. He'd stood there for minutes, staring at the open section of wall. Nothing there; a void.

Where was the power?

Fischer picked up the tape recorder and set it back on the table. Finding the extension cord, he plugged it in, surprised to discover that it still worked. He reversed the spool, then pressed the PLAY button.

"Hold it!" Barrett's voice said loudly. There were shuffling noises. He heard heavy breathing; was it his? Then Barrett said, "Miss Tanner coming out of trance. Premature retraction, causing brief systemic shock." After several moments of silence, the recorder was turned off.

Fischer reversed the tape farther, played it back. "Teleplasmic veil beginning to condense," said Barrett's voice. Silence. Fischer remembered the mistlike fabric which had covered Florence's head and shoulders like a wet shroud. Why had she manifested physical phenomena? The question still disturbed him. "Separate filament extending downward," Barrett's voice said. Fischer reversed the spool and switched the recorder to PLAY again. "Medium's respiration now two hundred and ten," Barrett's voice was saying. "Dynamometer fourteen hundred and sixty. Temperature—" He stopped as someone gasped; Edith, Fischer recalled. Momentary silence. Then Barrett's voice said, "Ozone present in the air."

Fischer stopped the spool, reversed it, let it run. What could he possibly hope to learn from reliving those moments? They hadn't added up to anything, except to confirm to Florence what she believed, and to Barrett what he believed. He stopped the spool, began to play the tape. "Sitters: Doctor and Mrs. Lionel Barrett, Mr. Benjamin—" Fischer switched it off and ran the tape back farther still.

He stopped and played it, starting as the hysterical voice—Florence's, yet so unlike hers—cried out, "—don't want to hurt you, but I must! I *must!*" A momentary silence. The voice near choking with venom as it said: "I warn you. *Get out of this house before I kill you all.*"

Sudden banging sounds. Edith's frightened voice asking, *"What's that?"* Fischer stopped the spool, reversed the tape, and listened to the threatening voice again. Had it been the voice of Daniel Belasco? He listened to it five times, gleaning nothing from it. Barrett could have been right. It might have been Florence's subconscious creating the voice, the character, the threat.

With a muffled curse, he reversed the tape again and played it back. "Leave house," said the imperious voice of Red Cloud. Had there ever been such an entity, or had it, too, been a segment of Florence's personality? Fischer shook his head. There was a grunting noise. "No good," said the voice, deep-pitched, but conceivably Florence's, forced to a lower register. "No good. Here too long. Not listen. Not understand. Too much sick inside." Fischer had to smile, although it pained him. It was such a poor excuse for the voice of an Indian. "Limits," it was saying. "Nations. Terms. Not know what that mean. Extremes and limits. Terminations and extremities." A pause. "Not know."

"Shit," said Fischer, jabbing in the button which stopped the spool. He reversed it farther, switched it on. Silence. "Now, if you'd—" Barrett began. "Red Cloud Tanner woman guide," Florence interrupted in the deep voice. "Guide second medium on this side."

He listened to the entire sitting: the rumbling voice of the Indian; the description of the caveman entity; the "arrival" of "the young man"; the hysterical voice, threatening them; the fierce percussions; Barrett's voice describing the unexpected onset of physical phenomena.

The second sitting: Florence's invocation and hymn; her sinking into trance—the low-pitched, wavering moans, the wheezing inhalations; Barrett's impersonal voice recording instrument readings; his description of the materialization; the rolling laugh; Edith's scream.

The tape moved soundlessly. Fischer reached out and switched off the recorder. *Zero,* he thought. Who had he been kidding, to come charging back in here like Don Quixote? What a laugh.

He stood. Well, he wasn't leaving. Not until something happened. Not until he started to pick up the threads. There had to be an answer somewhere. All right, he'd walk around the house again. He'd keep on ferreting in corners until he found that little mote of insight he was searching for. The house felt flat, but somewhere there was something still alive, something powerful enough to murder.

He was going to find it if it took a year.

As he moved across the great hall, he began to open up. There seemed no danger to it now. There seemed no point to it, either. Still, he had to do something.

He had scarcely let the last of his defenses down when something pushed him. He was moving into the entry hall, and the unexpected shove almost made him fall. Staggering to one side, he crossed his arms automatically, braced for resistance.

There was no more. Fischer scowled. He knew that he should open up again. Here was something tangible at last. Except that it had caught him by surprise. He didn't dare expose himself the way he had yesterday.

He stood hesitantly, sensing the presence hovering around him, wanting to confront it but afraid to.

Enraged at his weakness, he opened up.

Immediately something clutched his arm and flung him toward the south corridor. Fischer stumbled to a halt. He removed his crossed arms, which had, with instant self-protection, covered his solar plexus. He had to stop this opening and closing like a goddamned frightened clam!

He opened the door inside himself enough to feel the presence squeezing in. Again he was impelled toward the corridor. It was as though invisible hands were plucking at his clothes, holding his hand, clutching at his arm. He moved along with it, amazed by the blandness of the presence. This was no dark, destructive force. This was like some unseen maiden aunt hastening him to the kitchen for milk and cookies. Fischer almost felt inclined to smile at the feel of it—insistent, yes, demanding, but totally devoid of menace. He gasped at the sudden thought: Florence! She had sworn the answer lay in the chapel! A rush of joy burst through him. Florence helping him! He pushed in through the heavy door and went inside.

The chapel was oppressively still. Fischer looked around as though to see her. There was nothing.

The altar.

The words had flashed across his mind as clearly as though someone had spoken them aloud. He moved quickly down the aisle, wincing as he stepped across the cat, then the fallen crucifix. He reached the altar and looked at the open Bible. The page he saw was headed BIRTHS. "Daniel Myron Belasco was born at 2:00 A.M. on November 4, 1903." He felt a chilling disappointment. That wasn't it; it couldn't be.

He started as the pages of the Bible were flung over in a bunch. Now individual pages began to whirl by so fast he felt a breeze across his face. They stopped. He looked down, couldn't tell which paragraph he was meant to see. He felt his hand being lifted, let it move to the page. His index finger settled on a line. He bent across the book to read it.

"If thy right eye offend thee, pluck it out."

He stared at the words. It seemed as though Florence were standing beside him, anxious and impatient; but he didn't understand. The words made no sense to him.

"Florence—" he started.

He jerked his head up at the tearing sound behind the altar. A strip of wallpaper was hanging down, revealing the plaster wall behind it.

Fischer cried out as the medallion burned against his chest. Reaching frantically inside his shirt, he yanked it out and dropped it with a hiss of pain. It broke in pieces on the floor. Fischer stared at it in dazed confusion. A wedge like the head of an arrow had fallen from the other parts. It seemed to be pointing at—

It came with an appalling rush. Like some native paralyzed to mindless terror by the roar of an approaching tidal wave. Fischer looked up dumbly.

In the next moment, the power had smashed against him violently, driving him backward. He screamed in horror as it flung him to the floor and covered him with crushing blackness. There was no resisting it. Helplessly, he lay there as the cold force flooded through him, swelling every vein with dark contamination. *Now!* a voice howled in his mind, triumphantly. And suddenly he knew the answer, just as Florence

Tanner had, and Barrett had, and knew that he was being told because he was about to die.

He didn't move for a long time. His eyes did not blink. He looked like a dead man sprawled on the floor.

Then, very slowly, face without expression, he got up and drifted to the door. Pulling it open, he walked into the corridor and headed toward the entry hall. He walked to the front door, opened it, and went outside. Crossing the porch, he descended the broad steps, reached the gravel path, and started walking on it. He stared straight ahead as he walked to the edge of the tarn and stepped into the glutinous ooze. The water rose above his knees.

He seemed to hear a distant cry. He blinked, kept moving. Something crashed into the water with him, grabbed his sweater, jerked him back. There was an acid wrenching in his vitals and he gasped in pain. He tried to throw himself into the water. Someone tried to pull him back to shore. Fischer groaned and pulled away. The cold hands grabbed him by the neck. He snarled and tried to break away from them. His stomach muscles knotted, and he doubled over, falling to his knees. Icy water splashed across his face. He shook his head and tried to rise, to move into the tarn again. The hands kept pulling at him. Looking up, he saw, as through a veil of gelatin, a white, distorted face. Its lips were moving, but he couldn't hear a sound. He stared up dazedly. He had to die. He knew that clearly.

Belasco had told him so.

7:58 P.M.

For the past half-hour Fischer had been hunched in the corner of the seat, face as white as chalk, teeth chattering, arms crossed across his stomach, eyes unblinking for minutes at a time, staring sightlessly ahead. His shaking had kept dislodging the blanket from his shoulders; Edith had had to draw it around him repeatedly. Fischer had not responded to her attentions in any way. She might have been invisible to him.

It had taken her what seemed an endless amount of time to prevent him from walking into the tarn. Although his struggles had become progressively weaker, his obvious intention to drown himself had persisted. Like a somnambulist, he had tried stubbornly to wrest himself away from her. Nothing she'd said or done seemed to help. He hadn't spoken, was almost soundless in his single-minded attempt at suicide. Pulling at his clothes, clutching at his hands and arms and hair, slapping his face, Edith had thwarted his efforts again and again. By the time his struggles had finally ended, she'd been as soaked and shivering as he.

She looked around, trying to see the gasoline gauge. She'd been running the motor and heater since she'd gotten him into the car; the Cadillac was warm now. She saw that there was still more than half a tank, and turned back. The temperature did not appear to have the slightest effect on Fischer. His shivering continued unabated. Still, it was more than cold, she knew. She stared at his palsied features. Full circle; she could not avoid the thought.

The 1970 attempt on Hell House was one more item on the list of failures.

Fischer twitched convulsively and closed his eyes. His teeth stopped chattering; his body was immobile. As Edith watched in anxious silence, she saw faint streaks of color returning to his cheeks.

Several minutes later he opened his eyes and looked at her. She heard a dry, crackling sound in his throat as he swallowed. He reached out slowly toward her, and she took his hand. It was as cold as ice.

"Thank you," he murmured.

She couldn't speak.

"What time is it?"

Edith looked at her watch and saw that it had stopped. She twisted around to look at the dashboard. "Just past eight."

Fischer sank back with a feeble groan. "How did you get me here?"

He listened as she told him. When she was through, he asked, "Why did you come back again?"

"I didn't think you should be alone."

"In spite of what happened to you before?"

"I was going to try."

His fingers tightened on hers.

"What happened?" she asked.

"I was trapped."

"By what?"

"By *whom*."

She waited.

"Florence told us," Fischer said. "She *told* us, but I didn't have the brains to see."

"What?"

"The 'B' inside the circle," Fischer answered. "Belasco. Alone."

"Alone?" She couldn't comprehend it.

"He created everything."

"How do you know?"

"He told me so," he said. "He let me know, because I was about to die.

"No wonder the secret was never found. There's never been anything like it in the history of haunted houses: a single personality so powerful that he could create what seemed to be a complex multiple haunting; one entity appearing to be dozens, imposing endless physical and mental effects on those who entered his house—utilizing his power like some soloist performing on a giant, hellish console."

The motor was off now; the car was getting cold. They should be getting into town, but sitting in the darkness, stunned, subdued, she couldn't stir herself as Fischer's voice droned on.

"I think he knew, from the second we entered, that Florence was the one to concentrate on. She was our weakest link; not because she had no strength, but because she was so willingly vulnerable to him.

"When she sat on Monday night, he must have fed her various impressions, looking for one that would create a response in her. It was the young man that 'took' in her mind—the one Florence came to identify as Daniel Belasco.

"At the same time, in order to use her against your husband, Belasco caused her to manifest physical phenomena. It served a multiple purpose. It verified your husband's beliefs. It was the first wedge in Florence's assurance; she knew she was a mental medium, and even though she tried to convince herself that it was God's will, it always distressed her. She knew it was wrong. We both did.

"And, as a third effect, it prevented your husband from bringing another psychic into the house after I refused to sit for him." His eyes flinted. "Belasco keeping the group to a workable number.

"Then," he continued, "he started to evolve a situation of hostility between Florence and your husband. He knew that they disagreed on their beliefs, knew that, subconsciously. Florence would resent your husband's insistence on the physical examination, the intimation—however politely phrased—that she was capable of fraud, even if it was involuntary. Belasco worked on that resentment, worked on their differences of belief, built them up, then caused the poltergeist attack in the dining hall, using some of Florence's strength but mostly his own. Again, a multiple purpose was served. First, it weakened Florence, made her doubt her motivations. Second, it increased the animosity between her and your husband. Third, it further verified your husband's convictions. Fourth, it injured him, frightened him a little."

"He wasn't frightened," Edith said; but there was no conviction in her voice.

"He kept on working on Florence," Fischer said, as though she hadn't spoken, "draining her physically and mentally: the bites, the cat's attack—undermining her strength on the one hand, elaborating her misconception about Daniel on the other. When her confidence was flagging most, because of what your husband said, Belasco let her find the body—even staging an apparent resistance to her finding it, to make it more convincing.

"So she became persuaded that Daniel Belasco haunted the house. To guarantee the conviction, Belasco led her to the tarn in her sleep, let 'Daniel' rescue her, even gave her a fleeting glimpse of himself rushing from the tarn. She was positive then. She came to me and told me what she thought—that Belasco controlled the haunting by manipulating every other entity in the house. She was so close. *My God!* Even fooled every step of the way, she almost had it. That was why she was so certain. Because, in everything she said, there was only the thinnest wall between her and the actual truth. If I'd helped her, she might have broken through, might have—"

Fischer stopped abruptly. For a long time he stared through the window. Finally he went on.

"It was a matter of timing," he said. "Belasco must have known that, sooner or later, Florence would come up with the right answer. So he concentrated on her even more, used her memory about her brother's death, and tied it in to her obsession about Daniel Belasco. Her brother's grief became Daniel's grief, her brother's need"—Fischer clenched his teeth—"became Daniel's."

His expression was one of hatred now. "He clinched it by finally letting her into the chapel. Admitting her to the very place she was positive possessed the secret of Hell House. It was his final stratagem, showing her the Bible entry made when his son was born. Belasco knew she'd believe it, because it was exactly what she was looking for—a final verification. There was no room left in her mind for doubt after that. There *had* been a Daniel Belasco, and his spirit needed her help. Combining the facts of his son's existence with her lasting sorrow for her brother's death, Belasco had convinced her."

Edith twitched as, unexpectedly, Fischer drove the edge of a fist against his palm. "And I sensed what that help was going to be. I knew it inside!" He turned his face away from her. "And I let it go. Let her do what she should never have done, let her destroy herself.

"From then on, she was lost," he went on bitterly. "There was no way I could have gotten her out of the house; I was a fool for thinking that I could. She was his . . . a puppet to be played with, tortured." Again, the sound of self-derision. "There I sat at the table while your husband explained his theory to us, knowing she was possessed, yet not even questioning why—suddenly, illogically—she was so quiet and attentive, on her best behavior. Because it wasn't her listening at all; it was Belasco.

"He wanted to hear the details."

"Was it him that tried to break the Reversor, then?"

"Why should he break it? He knew it wasn't any danger to him."

"But you said the house was clear after Lionel used it."

"Another of Belasco's tricks."

"I can't believe—"

"He's still in that house, Edith," Fischer interrupted, pointing. "He murdered your husband, murdered Florence, almost murdered you and me—"

His laugh was cold with defeat. "His final jest. Even though we actually know his secret now, there's not a damn thing we can do about it."

8:36 P.M.

Fischer held back as they reached the house. Edith turned to face him. He was staring at the doors. "What is it?" she asked.

"I don't know if I can go back in."

She hesitated, finally said, "I have to have his things, Ben."

Fischer didn't respond.

"You said if you were closed off, Belasco couldn't touch you."

"I said a lot of things this week. Most of them wrong."

"Shall I go in, then?"

He was silent.

"Shall I?"

Stepping to the doors, he pushed the right one open. He looked inside for several moments, then turned to her. "I'll be as fast as I can," he said.

Fischer stepped inside the house. For a few minutes he stood motionless, anticipating. When nothing happened, he started across the entry hall, heading for the stairs. Again the atmosphere was flat. It did not assuage his fears this time. As he ascended the steps quickly, he wondered if Belasco was still in the chapel or moving about the house. He hoped that being closed off was enough defense. He wasn't even sure of that now. Entering the Barretts' room, he threw their suitcases on the bed and opened them.

What had unnerved him as much as anything, he thought as he started packing, was the realization that Barrett had been wrong. The man had seemed so confident; everything he'd said had made so much sense. Still, what did that weigh against the fact that he'd failed?

Fischer moved quickly between bed, closet, and bureau, grabbing clothes and other personal belongings and tossing them into the two open suitcases. Belasco must have decided, from the start, never to show himself, he thought. If no one ever saw him, they could never think him that important a part of the haunting. If, instead, they observed a fantastic array of phenomena, all apparently disconnected, they would work on separate elements of those phenomena, never once realizing that he was the cause of all of them. Bastard, he thought. His features hardened, and with angry movements he began to cram things together in the suitcases so he could shut the lids.

The only thing he couldn't understand was why Belasco—so diabolically efficient when it came to plotting Florence's and Barrett's overthrow—had chosen such an inefficient way to finish him. Sending him away from the house could not have been fail-proof under any circumstances. If Belasco's power was unlimited, why had he chosen such an inept method?

Fischer stopped packing abruptly.

Unless that power was not unlimited any more.

Was it possible? He'd certainly been vulnerable to Belasco in the chapel. If there had ever been a time when Belasco should have been able to crush him, that had been the time. Yet, despite that, the most he'd been able to do was direct him to commit suicide in the tarn. *Why?* Had Florence been right about him, too? Was his own power really so vast? He shook his head. That didn't make sense. It was ego-flattering, but unconvincing. Maybe when he was a boy, but not now. More acceptable an idea was that Belasco hadn't been strong enough to destroy him after destroying Barrett and Florence.

Again, *why*? With such power at his disposal as he'd manifested all week, why should he be weakened now? It couldn't be that the Reversor had worked. If it had, Belasco would be gone.

What was it, then?

Edith stamped her feet on the porch, waiting for Fischer's return. The blanket she'd wrapped around herself was not keeping her warm; her clothes, still damp, were getting chilled again. She looked into the entry hall. Would it hurt to step a few feet inside and get out of the worst of the cold?

She had to do it finally. Entering the house, she closed the door and stood beside it, looking toward the staircase.

It seemed as if they'd come into this house in another life. Monday seemed as distant in her mind as the time of Christ. That had been one reason she'd come back. Now that Lionel was gone, nothing seemed important anymore.

She wondered how long it would take before the full impact of his death hit her. Maybe when she saw his body again.

She thrust aside the thought. Had it been only yesterday that she'd come down those stairs after Fischer? She shivered. She'd been such an easy prey for Belasco.

When she was examining Florence, it had been Belasco looking in at her, noting her embarrassment. Belasco had shown her the photos, made her drink the brandy, turned her fear of possessing lesbian tendencies into a thoughtless counterdesire for Fischer; she winced at the memory. How weak she was; how easily Belasco had manipulated her.

She thrust aside that thought as well. Every thought about

Belasco was an affront to Lionel's memory. She was almost sorry she'd come back, to discover that he'd been wrong in everything he'd said and done.

She grimaced with self-accusing guilt. How could his entire body of work have been for nothing? She felt herself tighten with anger against Fischer for destroying her faith in Lionel. What right had he to do that?

A rush of sudden anguish made her start across the entry hall. Ascending the stairs, she crossed the corridor. The two suitcases stood outside their room. She looked around, heard sounds in Fischer's room, and moved there rapidly.

He started as she came in. "I told you—"

"I know what you told me," she interrupted. She had to get it out before he spoke. "I want to know why you're so sure my husband was wrong."

"I'm not."

The impetus of her anger carried her past the point of reaction. She began to speak again, then had to catch herself and backtrack. "What?"

"I'm wondering if he might have been partially right."

"I don't—"

"You recall what Florence said?"

"What?"

"She said, 'Can't you see that *both* of us can be right?' "

"I don't understand."

"I'm wondering if Belasco's power is electromagnetic radiation, as she said," Fischer told her. "I'm wondering if he was weakened by the Reversor."

He scowled. "But why would he allow himself to be weakened? It doesn't make sense. Especially when he had a chance to wreck the Reversor."

Edith wouldn't listen to his objection. Eager to restore validity to Lionel's work, she said, "Maybe he *is* weakened, though. You said he trapped you in the chapel. If he was still powerful, why would he have to do that? Why not attack you anywhere you were?"

Fischer didn't look convinced. He started pacing. "It might explain why he lured me there," he said. "If, in coming out after the Reversor had weakened him, he used up most of his remaining energy to destroy your husband and attack you—" He broke off angrily. "No. It doesn't add up. If the Reversor worked at all, it would have dissipated all his power, not just part of it."

"Maybe it wasn't strong enough. Maybe his power was too great for even the Reversor to destroy it entirely."

"I doubt it," he said. "And that still wouldn't explain why he'd allow the Reversor to be used at all when he had a chance to destroy it *before* it could be used."

"But Lionel believed in the Reversor," she persisted. "If Belasco had destroyed it before it could be used, wouldn't that be as much as an admission, to Lionel, that he was right?"

Fischer studied her face. Something was needling up inside him, something that had the same exhilarating sense of rightness he'd felt when Florence had told him her theory about Belasco. Seeing his expression, Edith hurried on, desperate to convince him that Lionel had been right, even if only partially. "Wouldn't it be more satisfying to Belasco to let Lionel actually use the Reversor, *then* destroy him?" she asked. "Because Lionel must have believed that he was wrong when he died. Wouldn't that be what Belasco would want?"

The feeling was increasing steadily. Fischer's mind struggled to fit the pieces together. Could Belasco really have been so determined to destroy Barrett in just that way that he'd deliberately let himself be weakened? Only an egomaniac would—

It sounded like a groan that shuddered upward from his vitals.

"What?" she asked in alarm.

"Ego," he said.

He pointed at Edith without realizing it. "Ego," he repeated.

"What do you mean?"

"That's why he did it that way. You're right; it wouldn't have been satisfying to him any other way. But to let your husband actually use his Reversor, apparently dissipate the power—and when your husband was at the peak of his fulfillment, to get him then." He nodded. "Yes. Only that way could satisfy his ego.

"He had to let Florence know before she died that it was him alone. Ego. He must have told your husband, too. Ego. He let you know in the theater. Ego. He had to let me know. Ego. It wasn't enough to lure us to our destruction. He had to tell us, at the precise moment when he had us powerless, that it was him. Except that, by the time he got to me, most of his power was used up, and he couldn't destroy me. All he could do was direct me to destroy myself."

He looked suddenly excited. *"What if he can't leave the chapel now?"*

"But you said he made you go there."

"What if he didn't? What if it *was* her? What if she *knew* he was trapped in there?"

"But why would she lead you to destruction?"

Fischer looked distressed. "She wouldn't. Why *would* she lead me there, then? It had to be for a reason."

He caught his breath. "The Bible entry." There was a throbbing in his system he had not experienced since he was a boy, the pulsing of force inside him, crying for release. *"If thy right eye offend thee, pluck it out."* He paced restlessly, feeling himself near the edge of the precipice, the mist about to part in front of him, the truth about to appear. *"If thy right eye offend thee—"*

He couldn't get it; turned his mind away from it. What

else had happened in the chapel? The torn wallpaper. What had that meant? The medallion—broken, like a spearhead pointing at the altar. And, on the altar, the open Bible. "God." His voice was trembling, eager. He was so close—so close. *"If thy right eye offend thee, pluck it out."* Ego, the thought recurred. *"If thy right eye offend thee, pluck it out." Ego.* He stopped, his inner senses heightening with awareness. He was almost there. Something; *something. "If thy right eye—"*

"The tape!" he cried.

He whirled and rushed for the doorway. Edith ran after him as he plunged into the corridor and over to the staircase. He was halfway down before she'd reached the landing, springing down the steps with vaulting leaps. Edith descended as quickly as she could and ran across the entry hall.

He was at the great-hall table, listening to the tape recorder. She bit her lip involuntarily as she heard Lionel's voice. "—causing brief systemic shock." Fischer made a grumbling sound and shook his head as he pressed the REVERSE button and turned the spool back, pressed the PLAY button again. "Dynamometer fourteen hundred and sixty," Lionel's voice said. Fischer made an impatient sound and reversed the spool again, waited, pushed the button for PLAY position. Edith heard Florence's voice saying, *"Get out of this house before I kill you all."* Fischer snarled and punched the REVERSE button again. He switched to PLAY. "Here too long," Florence's voice said deeply, supposedly the voice of her Indian guide. "Not listen. Not understand. Too much sick inside." There was a pause. Fischer leaned across the table tensely, unaware that he was doing so. "Limits," said the voice. "Nations. Terms. Not know what that mean. Extremes and limits. Terminations and extremities."

Edith flinched as Fischer cried out with a savage glee. He reversed the tape and played it again. "Extremes and limits. Terminations and extremities." Fischer snatched up the tape recorder and held it high above his head in triumph. "She knew!" he shouted. "She knew! She knew!" He flung the tape recorder across the room. Before it had crashed to the floor, he was running for the entry hall. "Come on!" he shouted.

Fischer sprinted across the entry hall and down the corridor, followed by Edith. With a howl like that of an attacking Indian, he flung open the chapel door and leaped inside. "Belasco!" he roared. "I'm here again! Destroy me if you can!" Edith ran in beside him. "Come on!" he yelled. "Both of us are here now! Finish us! Don't leave the job half done!"

Massive silence fell, and Edith heard how strangely Fischer breathed. "Come on," he mumbled to himself.

He shouted suddenly, *"Come on, you lousy bastard!"*

Edith's gaze leaped toward the altar. For a moment she could not believe her hearing. Then the sounds grew louder, clearer, unmistakable.

Approaching footsteps.

She drew back automatically, eyes fixed on the altar. The footsteps were louder now. She was unconscious of Fischer's hand restraining her. She gaped at the altar. The sounds were getting louder every second. The floor began to shake. It was as though an unseen giant were approaching.

Edith whimpered, pulling constantly at Fischer's grip. The footsteps were almost deafening now. She tried to lift her hands to shield her ears but could lift only one. The chapel seemed to shudder with the thundering noises coming closer, closer. She jerked back hard, her cry of panic engulfed by the titanic, crashing footsteps. Closer; closer. We're going to die, she thought.

We're going to die!

She screamed as a violent explosion filled the chapel; closed her eyes involuntarily.

Deathly silence made her open them.

She lurched back, gasping. Fischer held her. "Don't be

afraid." His voice was taut with excitement. "This is a special moment, Edith. No one's ever seen his nibs before; not unless they were about to die, that is. Take a good look, Edith. Meet Emeric Belasco. *'The Roaring Giant.'* "

Edith gaped at the figure.

Belasco was enormous; dressed in black, his features broad and white, framed by a jet-black beard. His teeth, bared in a savage grin, were those of a carnivore. His green eyes glowed with inner light. Edith had never seen such a malignant face in her life. Deep within the frozen dread she felt, she wondered why they weren't being murdered at this very moment.

"Tell me something, Belasco," Fischer said. Edith didn't know whether to feel reassurance or terror at the brazen insult in his tone. "Why didn't you ever go outside? Why did you 'eschew the sunlight,' as you put it? Didn't care for it?

"Or was it better hiding in the shadows?"

The figure started toward them. Released, Edith drew back quickly, horrified to see Fischer move forward.

"You walk with a labored tread, Belasco," Fischer said. "You dominate your movements at a cost, don't you?"

He shouted abruptly, fiercely, "Don't you, Belasco?"

Edith's mouth fell open.

Belasco had stopped moving. His features were ablaze with fury, but it seemed, somehow, a fury of frustration.

"Look at your lips, Belasco," Fischer said, still advancing. "Spastic pressure holds them together. Look at your hands. Spastic tension holds them fisted at your sides. Why is that, Belasco? Is it because you're a fraud?"

His mocking cackle rang out in the chapel. "Roaring Giant!" he shouted. "You? My ass! You bullshit artist! You sawed-off little freak!"

Edith caught her breath. Belasco was retreating! She rubbed a shaking hand across her eyes. And it was true.

He *did* look smaller.

"Evil?" Fischer said. He moved at Belasco steadily, a look of ruthless animosity on his face. "You, you funny little bastard?"

He stiffened as a cry of anguished rage burst from the lips of the dwindling figure in black. For a moment Fischer couldn't react. Then the grin returned. "Oh, no," he said. He started shaking his head. "Oh, no. You couldn't be *that* small."

He started forward again. "Bastard?" The figure drew back farther. *"Bastard? That* disturbed you? Oh, Belasco. What a funny little man you really were. What a funny little crawling bug of a ghost. You weren't a genius. You were a nut, a creep, a deviate, a slob, a loser. *And a sawed-off little bastard in the bargain!*

"BELASCO!" He howled. "Your mother was a whore, a slut, a bitch! You were a bastard, Emeric! A funny little dried-up bastard! Do you hear me, Evil Emeric? A bastard, *bastard,* BASTARD, *BASTARD!*"

Edith flung her hands across her ears to shut away the hideous wail that gorged the air. Fischer stumbled to a halt, his features washed of fury by the sound. He stared at the nebulous figure behind the altar—cowering, rat-faced, beaten—and it seemed as though he heard Florence's voice in his mind, whispering: *Perfect love casteth out fear*. And suddenly despite everything, he felt a sickened pity for the figure standing there before him.

"God help you, Belasco," he said.

The figure vanished. For a long time they could hear a screaming, as of someone falling down into a bottomless pit, the sound fading slowly, until the chapel was still.

Fischer moved behind the altar and looked at the section of wall revealed by the torn wallpaper.

He smiled. She'd shown him this too; if only he had known.

Leaning over, he pushed at the wall. It opened with a grating rumble.

A short staircase declined in front of him. He turned to Edith and extended his hand. She didn't speak. Moving across the chapel, she circled the altar and took his hand.

They descended the staircase. At the bottom was a heavy door. Fischer shouldered it open.

They stood in the doorway, looking at the mummified figure sitting upright on a large wooden armchair.

"They never found him because he was here," Fischer said.

They entered the small, dim-lit chamber and crossed to the chair. Despite the feeling Edith had that everything was over, she couldn't help cringing from the sight of Emeric Belasco's dark eyes glaring at them from death.

"Look." Fischer picked up a jug.

"What is it?"

"I'm not sure but—" Fischer ran his palms across the surface of the jug. The impressions came immediately. "Belasco set it down beside himself and made himself die of thirst," he told her. "It was his final achievement of will. In life, that is."

Edith averted her face from the eyes. She looked down, leaning forward suddenly. The chamber was so gloomy that she hadn't noticed before. "His legs," she said.

Fischer didn't speak. He set down the jug and knelt in front of Belasco's corpse. She saw his hands moving in the shadows; made a tiny sound of shock as he stood up with a leg in his hands.

" *'If thy right eye offend thee,'* " he said. " 'Extremities.' She was giving us the answer, you see." He ran a hand over the artificial leg. *"He so despised his shortness that he had his legs surgically removed and wore these instead, to give him height.*

That's why he chose to die in here—so no one would ever know. He had to be the Roaring Giant or nothing. There simply wasn't enough stature inside him to compensate for his shortness—*or* his bastardy."

He turned abruptly and looked around. Setting down the leg, he crossed the floor and put his hands against the wall. "My God," he said.

"What is it?"

"Maybe he was a genius, after all." He walked around the chamber, touching all the walls, examining the ceiling and the door. "The final mystery solved," he said. "It wasn't that his power was so great that he could resist the Reversor." His tone was almost awed. "He must have known, more than forty years ago, about the connection between electromagnetic radiation and survival after death.

"The walls, door, and ceiling are sheathed with lead."

9:12 P.M.

The two walked slowly down the steps, Edith carrying her suitcase, Fischer carrying Barrett's suitcase and his duffel bag.

"How does it feel?" she asked.

"What?"

"To be the one who conquered Hell House."

"I didn't conquer it," he said. "It took all of us."

Edith tried not to smile. She knew it was true, but wanted him to say it.

"Your husband's efforts weakened Belasco's power. Florence's efforts led us to the final answer. I just polished it off, that's all—and even that would have been impossible if you hadn't saved my life.

"It had to be that way, I guess," he said. "Your husband's

mentality helped, but wasn't enough by itself. Florence's spirituality helped, but wasn't enough by itself. It took one more element, which I provided—a willingness to face Belasco on his own terms, defeat him with his own weaknesses."

He made a scoffing noise. "Then again, Belasco may have beaten himself; I suspect that's part of it, too. After all, he'd been waiting thirty years for more guests. Maybe he was so eager to utilize his power again that he overextended himself, made the first mistakes of his existence in this house."

He stopped at the door, and both of them turned. For a long time they stood quietly. Edith thought about returning to Manhattan and to life without Lionel. She couldn't visualize it, but for now a kind of inexplicable peace had taken hold of her. She had the remnants of his manuscript with her. She'd see to its publication, see to it that people in his field learned what he'd accomplished. After that she'd worry about herself.

Fischer looked around, extending tendrils of unconscious thought. As he did, he wondered, consciously, what lay ahead for him. Not that it mattered. Whatever it was, he had a chance to face it now. It was bizarre that, in this house, where his horror had first begun, he should feel the returning stir of self-assurance.

He turned and smiled at Edith. "She isn't here," he said. "She just stayed long enough to help."

They took a final look around. Then, without another word, they went outside and moved into the mist. Fischer grunted, mumbled something.

"What?" she asked.

"Merry Christmas," he repeated softly.

About the Author

Beth Gwinn

RICHARD MATHESON (1926–2013) was the *New York Times* bestselling author of *I Am Legend*, *Hell House*, *Somewhere in Time*, *The Shrinking Man*, *Now You See It . . .*, and *What Dreams May Come*, among many others. He was named a Grand Master of Horror by the World Horror Society, and received the Bram Stoker Award for Lifetime Achievement. He has also won the Edgar, the Spur, and the Writers Guild Awards. In 2010, he was inducted into the Science Fiction Hall of Fame. In addition to his novels, Matheson wrote screenplays for movies and TV, including many *Twilight Zone* episodes.